THE FIGHTING EARPS

Also by Nicholas Osborn

Bullets Trilogy

A Day Late and a Bullet Short

Three Bullets to the Wind

Another Day, Another Bullet

THE FIGHTING EARPS

Bullets Legend

Book 2

NICHOLAS OSBORN

The Fighting Earps
Paperback Edition

Wolfpack Publishing
1707 E. Diana Street
Tampa, Florida 33610

www.wolfpackpublishing.com

Paperback ISBN 979-8-89567-423-9
Ebook ISBN 979-8-89567-422-2

THE FIGHTING EARPS

Chapter 1

Ordinary men have no place in any fight worth remembering.

More than a few have tried their hand at it in spite of this fact, and even more will follow in their unfortunate footsteps before the sun no longer sinks in the west, but it will always end the same. Sweat and grit and blood and bone have always amounted to a forgettable end. Death hangs over such men like the promise of each night, impossible to avoid and never in too much of a hurry, yet somehow always arriving before you're ready. For most, it was a shame they never saw it coming. For just a few, however, it was the only thing keeping them going.

Two of these very men stood apart from one another on a Friday night out in the middle of nowhere. Pines hugged them both from every direction as a Texas breeze whipped through their needles. It carried with it mostly pollen and thick humidity, but it was still cool against their cheeks. The earth was soft from the rain only hours before, and clouds blotted out the night sky overhead, waiting to see what may sprout in its wake.

The two were different in every way, polar opposites in everything except their desperation to be anything other than ordinary. One was overweight, the other in need of a meal. One was furious, the other eager. One was ready to kill, and the other was already having too much fun. Blood pooled in their fists. Against the advice of their friends and just about anyone who'd come to witness a car crash unfold up close and personal, the two men lifted their fists and took a step toward each other. Proof that if there was ever anything in this world worth remembering, it's the ironic truth that it's the ordinary men who end up doing most of the fighting.

The first strike brought with it a horrid cracking of bone and a swell of cheers from the audience hidden in the trees, blinded from view by spotlights and headlights. There was more red than there should ever be with a first punch. It splattered into the mud at their feet when they collided. The second strike came in retaliatory fear for what was sure to come. It landed as well as it could. It would be the man twice the size he should've been who'd spur a flurry of bets from those in attendance, setting the stage for what somehow spiraled into a bare-knuckle boxing match with tens of thousands of dollars and one man's life on the line.

On the losing end of those bets was a man known all throughout Walker County as T-Post, named as such for what most would assume to be rather obvious reasons. He was so small he could hide behind a t-post, which is what most would rattle off with a chuckle whenever he was mentioned. He wasn't all that bright, or that strong, and he lacked a certain sense of control to do much more than follow his worst instincts. This time, they'd gotten him in over his head.

The burly, hairy fist coming right toward poor T-Post's face belonged to a man named Clayton Collins. He'd spent the last thirty years of his life working at the local feed store as a trusted hand. Hidden beneath all those nights of too much beer and fast food were the kind of muscles that could put just about anyone in a world of hurt.

T-Post never saw the next hit coming. It struck his ribcage with more force than he'd ever felt before. It wasn't a matter of whether or not he'd broken a rib, it was just a question of how many. Breathing hurt a hell of a lot more, and standing still was a lot like being about ten shots of bourbon deep, but T-Post never faltered. He answered with a strike of his own, a wildly swung kick right up between Clayton's legs. The groan that followed echoed throughout the trees and silenced the crowd only seconds after they'd gotten started. Clayton was frozen. The pain paralyzed him for longer than it should have, and T-Post took every advantage he could find. With a handful of dirt and a few quick paces to close the distance, he hurled the mud at Clayton's eyes and wasted no time going for the throat. T-Post's thumb squeezed around his opponent's neck as his right fist came down over and over again.

After a while, the difference between the blood from Clayton's face and T-Post's knuckles had been lost in sprays of shadowy crimson and exasperated grunts. The crowd refused to let themselves be heard. T-Post cried out as he swung violently, but he was too careless. Clayton's hook found those broken ribs of his, and the impact sent him crumpling to the dirt. He writhed in pain and kicked his muddy boots like a toddler in a tantrum.

The fist that landed on T-Post from up above came like a freight train. It took his eyesight, his ability to breathe through his nose, and his will to crawl away in a split second. Any harder and it would've taken his own damn consciousness, too. He lay on his back, staring up into the darkness above, wishing for only a moment that he could see the stars. Instead of their thousand-year-old light dotting the skyline, he saw only another fist coming down before he could find the time to brace himself.

Clayton was ruthless. His boots dug into the mud as he forced all of his weight onto the man who'd dared to face him down. They sank down a little deeper as Clayton hurled his next punch. One second, T-Post looked too dazed to do so much as lift a finger, but in the next, he was up on his boots, scrambling away.

T-Post put just enough distance between the man hell-bent on beating him to death to think about what would happen if he ran away. It took only a few brief moments for him to consider the consequences and turn around to face Clayton once again. He squared his hips, widened his stance, lifted his fists, and clenched his jaw. He was back in the fight, even if he couldn't see straight.

There were a few cheers from faceless men in the distance, even an enthused whistle that pierced through the noise. All of that was lost in the dreadful distance shrinking between T-Post and Clayton. The only thing separating them from each other and the veil of life and death itself was their bloodied, bruised fists.

Clayton swung first. His hairy knuckle looked like it was moving in slow motion as it traveled in an arc just beyond his shoulder, right toward T-Post's face. With a quick step backward, Clayton missed entirely and was left reeling from the directionless power carelessly dumped into every punch. T-Post's only advantage was his speed, so he put it to use. One short sidestep and a blink of an eye later, T-Post landed his version of a haymaker right on Clayton's jaw with enough force to cause him to grunt in desperation.

Nothing happened, though.

Clayton was stoic. He stared a hole right through T-Post and took a single step closer.

"That all you got?" Clayton shouted. "That all you fuckin' got?"

T-Post swung again. This time, his left hand buried into Clayton's cheek, barely causing him to break eye contact.

"We're supposed to be fighting, you pussy," he told T-Post as a chorus of cheers began to swell from behind him.

Another jab from T-Post aimed right at Clayton's nose missed the mark. The only thing the man twice T-Post's size did was spit a loogie out into the dirt right in front of him. There wasn't even any blood in his mouth after three direct strikes. The look in T-Post's eyes said everything that needed to be said about how their fight was going.

"How are we supposed to give those people a show if you hit like a five-year-old girl in a wheelchair? You think I'm gonna make money on a fight like this? You might as well keep fightin' dirty, it's the only chance you got," said Clayton.

"What the hell is that?" T-Post broke his silence,

looking behind Clayton with a fear laced in his voice so sincere it made Clayton turn around for a fraction of a second.

It was all he needed.

T-Post was coiled around Clayton like a snake on a chicken before anyone knew what had happened. What was supposed to be a bare-knuckle boxing match devolved into an old-fashioned brawl—one where apparently anything was legal. He had his forearm wrapped around Clayton's neck and was using every bit of strength he could muster to crush his windpipe. That damn near did the trick until a hand with a grip like a cast-iron vise wrapped around the collar of T-Post's shirt and yanked him backward.

T-Post went tumbling to the ground while Clayton dropped down right where he stood.

A third man was standing between them, his arms outstretched, and a brimstone stare burned onto his face. He had a full mustache, torn from the 1800s—pulled up on either end, stretching across his entire face—plus a roughened demeanor and a temper to match. He wore a pristine white button-down shirt and starched pants cuffed over a worn pair of once-oiled brown leather boots. His hands were calloused with dirty nails, and his hair might have been slicked back long ago, but it draped down over his sweaty forehead now.

"Ain't gonna be none of that, you hear me?" the man said.

"You saw what he did," Clayton shot back immediately. "You gonna sit there and allow that?"

"What *I* did?" T-Post was already up on his feet. "If you think this is ever gonna be a fair fight, then you ain't no smarter than I was for signing up for this shit."

"We're past all that," said Clayton, this time finally spitting up some blood.

"I say we walk away from all this right now," T-Post said with his arms out. "Ain't no amount of money can convince me to die by the hands of a man who couldn't read a children's book."

"Go fu—"

"You two can decide that for yourselves," the man standing between them interjected. "You better do it now, though."

T-Post had the nerve to actually turn his back on the whole fight. Deep down, it was most likely an understanding that he had no chance of walking out alive any other way. It might've made him look like the weaker man, but he also might live to see the next sunrise if he made it away.

Clayton's thumping boots, picking up speed behind him, washed all those hopes right down the drain. The nearing-obese man swung his arms with every step and leaned forward, ready to bring T-Post down to the ground in one deadly swoop.

The man who had put himself between the two locked in a never-ending fight took a step backward and allowed the brawl to continue.

Heavy boots slammed into water and mud before skidding to a stop. It was another right hook that followed, and this time, Clayton knew he had no chance of missing this time. His teeth grit together as he put everything he had into that strike. One good hit on his glass jaw was all he needed, and this time, he knew he'd delivered it.

At the last second, T-Post ducked, fell out of sight, and tossed himself to the side in a tumbling roll before popping back up in a hurry. He had a smile on his face, but his eyes carried the look of a man facing his own demise. As Clayton closed the gap once more, he allowed himself what might be the final few seconds he had to spare to gaze around at what had become of his life.

Pickups circled the open patch of woods, parked alongside or behind the pines with headlights all pointed at the fight. Their drunken whoops and hollers cried out over a dozen different sad country songs blaring from speakers long past their prime. Steel guitars and fiddles and wailing old voices were a backdrop for spilled beer, giggles from women, and too much cash floating back and forth based on who was winning at that moment. The only decent thing around was something impossible to see. A cool breeze came rolling in right when T-Post looked around. It caressed his face and promised a future worth living for, then it was gone as quickly as it had come.

The fight ensued. Clayton swung first, connecting with a gut punch that sent the air pouring out of T-Post's lungs, and him struggling to stand upright. He followed suit, throwing a haymaker to Clayton's ribs without a second thought. They cracked beneath his knuckles, but Clayton barely even flinched.

The hits kept coming. T-Post went toe-to-toe with Clayton, exchanging blows and wincing in pain as the endless strikes kept coming. Blood poured from T-Post's mouth as he struggled not to choke on it. A gash on Clayton's cheek soon led to blood smeared across his face. It was a mixture of heavy breathing, grunts, and the breaking of bones that took place in the mud beneath their boots.

T-Post was the first to lose his balance, stumbling backward when a surprising left hook came out of nowhere. He tried to block with his forearm, but it did no good. The sheer power of the man who lifted feed sacks for a living made him almost lose consciousness more than once.

Clayton was deadly serious, but he'd never let slip that he was on the verge of blacking out himself. Exhaustion was setting in. Every punch T-Post landed chipped away at his steadfastness, revealing a man with too little left to give.

The punches slowed as each minute ticked by. Their strength dwindled, but their tenacity never wavered. It was a fight not just for money, but for something else. When it all came down to it, these were men who were fighting for survival. Black eyes and bloodied lips, labored breathing and burning muscles, all began to take their toll on each of the men.

"Fight, damn you!" the man standing beside them shouted through his mustache.

Clayton didn't hesitate.

He put everything he had into a single swing, starting from his right leg, up through his back and into his shoulder, transferring every bit of strength he had left into his fist, hurling right toward T-Post's jawline.

T-Post did exactly the same thing.

His arm lacked muscle definition, and his body lacked the weight needed to match the strength of Clayton's strike, but he had twice the heart and enough brain to know where to send his own attack.

Each fist connected at what seemed to be the exact same time. Each man crumpled to the ground in an instant, succumbing to blackness and collapsing into the mud they were just fighting in. T-Post and Clayton fell into slow, steady breathing, comfortable at last in their own unconsciousness, despite the blood still dripping from their faces.

The only man who walked away was the one who was refereeing the fight. He wiped his mustache with both hands and shook his head before turning his back on the men lying in the mud and walking away.

He kept walking, basked in the headlights, and was enveloped by the silence of the crowd, too stunned to come to terms with what they had just witnessed. He put one heavy boot down in front of the other until he'd put the drunks and harlots and cheats, their nauseating raucousness, and their need for blind violence, behind him.

He was a businessman at heart. Though not all industries were as bloody as this, they were all every bit as deadly. He'd prided himself on his uncanny ability to navigate them all. At the end of this venture, he had only to find a single face in the crowd, collect what was due, and keep on passing through.

"Fitzsimmons, is it?" he asked a stranger with a receding hairline and cauliflower ears.

"You're here about your money, I assume?"

"Right you are."

"Ain't none."

"The hell does that mean?"

"No winner means no money. Can't win a bet if no one wins the fight, right? Looks like we're all goin' home with empty pockets."

The blued end of a .45 Schofield revolver barrel was pressed against Fitzsimmons's neck before he could so much as blink his eyes. It jammed into his throat, almost making him cough, before the man who'd refereed the fight started talking.

"Not me," he said. "I'm goin' home with something." His thumb gently tugged back on the hammer of the revolver, causing a clicking sound of the cylinder rotating and locking into place, past the safety notch, all the way until it was fully cocked. A whiff of air on the trigger would send a pink mist that once was named Fitzsimmons, blowing haplessly in the night breeze.

"Okay, asshole," a quivering voice came from Fitzsimmons. "Here." In his fist was a wadded-up bundle of cash.

Just as the two were set to part ways, Fitzsimmons grabbed the man by the arm and stopped him from walking away.

"A guy named Virgil called for you, saying something about a bunch of gold needin' to be dug up at a place called the Holliday Ranch out in East Texas," he said. "I told him I'd send you his way after I was done with you."

"You're a real man of the people, Fitzsimmons."

"So are you, Wyatt. So are you."

Chapter 2

Dawn came with golden rays of what only hope could dare to bring.

Shadows filling the meadows stretching over the hills began to scatter back to the trees, where there would soon be nowhere left to hide. Oaks that survived every war to end all wars reached out with ancient intent, facing down another day as relentlessly as they have done so many times before. The sun was as eager as ever to begin its familiar climb in the east, casting its light down on the Holliday Ranch no different than it did back when frontier justice rode through the same hills. What started as dirt trails crossed by outlaws and makeshift barbed wire strands that changed the West, had turned to steel pipe fencing, pole barns, heavy equipment, and hundreds of registered Angus cattle roaming a thousand acres bearing the ranch brand. The place may have a few more cobwebs scattered around and a little less money flowing through it, but it was still an empire.

It wasn't just any other day for the Holliday Ranch,

though. This morning was a threat, a threat of everything that made the thousand acres worth living and dying for. The end was coming in hot for the Holliday Ranch, barreling forward like a steer being chased by a two-hundred-fifty-pound man on top of a horse.

There were only two people left willing to stand in the way of an inevitable, catastrophic end. Virgil McKey and his wife, Angeline, who was the heir of Holliday Ranch. She was the daughter of Mary Burroughs-Holliday, the next in line from the Holliday lineage tracing back to a single moment shared between Mary *Big Nose Kate* Katherine Horony Cummings and her gentlemanly outlaw man, John Henry *Doc* Holliday. What came from their love, or maybe lack thereof, would go on to become one of the final vestiges of a way of life born on the American frontier.

Virgil had moved Angeline back to her family home when her grandfather passed away. In the ten years that followed, her grandmother joined her husband in a plot at the family graveyard not too far from their home. They were buried side by side, just as they'd lived, and her death marked the thirteenth time someone was buried at the Holliday Ranch.

Life went on as it always does. Their children, Nathaniel and Nellie, went from baseball and softball games to chaperoned date nights to graduating, and both had found themselves in college chasing down their own lives. There wasn't much time to be mom and dad.

Virgil had only the woman he so fondly called his beloved Angel, and she had only the man who stood by her side.

Together, they'd faced down market pitfalls,

droughts, broken fences, thieves who hid their faces in the night, and others who walked right up to the front door in broad daylight, and even one escaped prison inmate with a grudge several generations old. It was almost more than they could bear—almost. Learning nature's laws of working the land wasn't something either of them took lightly.

Angel may have grown up in it, but she left it all behind, not too unlike what her own children did, to chase a life for herself. When she met Virgil, he was working his way up the ladder for a pipeline company, so returning to the ranch was never part of the plan. She was going to be an *oilfield* wife, for lack of a better term, and it was something she'd grown accustomed to.

Virgil, however, was new to everything their new world demanded. Long ago, he was just a kid trying to work his way out of poverty, the kind of kid people who came from luxury would call urban, but then he discovered that the oil and gas industry was his ticket to a better life. Through the years, he learned how to torque a wrench and say *yes sir* when he was told to head to a jobsite, but when it came to saddling horses and feeding cattle, he was about as green as they came. That didn't matter much in the end, because he'd already learned the hardest lessons, the ones that shape men out of boys, and he knew how to apply those to any line of work.

Their return to Holliday Ranch was spurred by a death in the family, but when it all fell into Angel's hands, neither of them could bring themselves to leave it all behind, only to be sold by a bank to some rich person from out of state. They couldn't let a legacy like that die for nothing. So, Virgil quit his job and traded his wrench for a fence stretcher. Instead of saying *yes sir* to some bossman with a beer gut, he started saying *yes ma'am* to his wife, as she took the lead on resurrecting the Holliday Ranch back to its former glory.

They'd found success, too. Training horses and riders alike, running weaned calves and pairs up to the sale barn, selling any beef they couldn't eat themselves, and even fixing up an old abandoned barn to become a venue for out-of-towners looking to take pretty pictures, all helped the Holliday Ranch finally start to turn a profit. Things ran smoothly for a few years, and they even made enough money to put some extra cash in their pockets, but nature's laws always hold true.

Every well eventually runs dry.

As Virgil and Angel sat out on the front porch in the same rocking chairs they'd found themselves in for much of the last decade, they watched the sun creep up over the horizon to shine its light on each and every one of their problems.

"Power company called yesterday," said Virgil. "I forgot to tell you."

"I appreciate that," said Angel, smirking without looking his way.

"We have until next week."

"Figured that."

"Water company was a little nicer," said Virgil. "They gave us two weeks."

"What about the feedstore?"

Virgil reached his calloused hand up to rub the back of his neck. "You know how ol' Tim is. He told us just to pay him when we could. He gets it."

"Always have loved that man."

"Our biggest problem is the bank."

"Ain't it always?"

"This one ain't a normal problem. We only made it the last couple of years because of the mortgage we took out on the few hundred acres of bottomland down by the highway. The bank is talking about collecting, one way or another."

"When?"

"Today."

The sigh that came from Angel was one that Virgil could feel all the way down to his bones. Despite knowing the last thing his wife wanted to do was talk business this early, he had no choice but to make his pitch anyway. "Look," he started, hesitating for a moment to choose his words carefully. "I know you said no business before breakfast, but there's somethin' I gotta tell you."

"You wanna go for a ride?"

Angel finally turned to face her husband and flashed him a smile. It was the kind that hid all the pain she was feeling deep down, the kind that masked her eyes welling up with tears, that begged Virgil to change the subject before it was too late. The only thing he could do was what he'd always done—give her exactly what she wanted.

"Sure," he obliged. "Let's go for a ride."

The heels of their cowboy boots clicked on the wooden porch as they walked single file down the steps and out into the yard. Since they couldn't yet talk about what was coming for them, there wasn't much more to be said. There were a million different ways for Virgil to come forward about what he'd done, but he couldn't seem to think of a single one that felt appropriate. It all felt wrong.

They walked without saying a word all the way down to the barn. It was a trail they'd normally reserved for the side by side, but the brisk morning air and the time to think things over were welcome for both of them. Morning dew wet their worn leather boots, and the air that filled their lungs was crisp. It should've been refreshing, and maybe it was for Angel. She sure hadn't lost the pep in her step that kept Virgil always coming back for more. But it wasn't for him. There could be nothing good on that kind of day, no matter how much he would've welcomed everything it had to offer on any other day.

The mare at the end of the barn, already in her stall, was waiting as if she'd been standing there all night, and growing more impatient by the second as Angel fidgeted with the saddle tossed over her back. The D-rings didn't work like they should, the blanket didn't sit just right, and the stirrup was set at a height that made her swear someone had messed with her rig. Angel and her mare, Coach, who had just turned twenty and stood a mere thirteen hands, tussled back and forth for the better part of five minutes.

Virgil just listened. He went about his business like he always had, sticking to the same routine that had eventually gotten him into the mess he was in. This part was simple, at least. His own horse was a spry ten-year-old Appaloosa gelding that had more *go* than *whoa*. He'd thought about naming him, but he was the kind of trainer who stuck to other habits. A gentle pat on the neck came after he'd cinched down his own rig. He grabbed the reins and turned to watch Angel continue to struggle.

"This stupid—" Angel grunted as she yanked down on the latigo harder than she ever should have.

"Here," said Virgil as he came up behind her, still holding the reins to his horse in his other hand. He put his hand over hers, and she allowed him to cinch down the saddle for her.

Angel hung her head as she fumbled the reins in her hand. Her husband finished adjusting her rig and getting it back to how she wanted, always the gentleman, even when she felt like she didn't deserve it. He could've said plenty, but he didn't. She held back her frustrated tears and focused on her clenched fists as hard as she could. Her mind was racing at a dizzying pace. She was sweating despite the breeze. Somewhere in the back of her head, she knew seeing the world from the back of a horse was exactly the perspective she needed.

Coming out of the barn on horseback was like finally taking a deep breath for both of them. The gentle, familiar sway, the trail walked a million times over, the reins with their grip worn into the leather like it was made for their hands alone. Humidity was already taking over the chill of the morning, and the tree line in the distance called to them with shade from the sun settling in overhead. They weaved their way through chained gates separating the steers from the bulls, the yearling heifers from the two-year-olds, and pairs. It was a chore to get on and off the horse to open and close all those gates, but it wasn't all like that. Just beyond one more fence were hundreds of acres to spare. They could ride all day and never make it back to face what was waiting for them back home.

"I used to ride out here with my grandma," said Angel. "She'd lecture me through the whole ride. They were never conversations. Hell, she never really gave me much time to speak for myself. It was like she planned it out. She'd begin right when we left the barn, and somehow, she'd end right when we walked the horses back to their stalls. I learned more about life during those rides than I did in any classroom, or from any book."

Virgil knew when it was time to talk, and more importantly, when it was time to listen.

"I miss those days," she said, knowing her husband could catch her cues. "I miss having her hold my hand and walk me through the biggest problems in my life before I even knew they were problems. I felt so prepared for whatever the world had to throw at me because of her. I ride out here all the time hoping to find just a sliver of that understanding, and that confidence, but I always come up short."

There were things Virgil had learned in their relationship through the years, things like when Angel needed flowers and chocolates, or when she needed a fifth of whiskey. He'd learned when she was smiling behind his back and when she was hiding her anger right in front of his face. He'd also learned when she was crying, as much as she tried to hide it. Her sunken shoulders, the quiver in her voice, and the soft tremble in her hands—they were all giveaways that urged him to hold her.

Unless he was planning on jumping horses, that wouldn't be happening this time. The best he could manage was an easy trot up beside her and a gentle pat on the shoulder. She wouldn't turn to look him in the eye, but she did keep talking.

"I know it's just a patch of dirt," she continued. "I know this place isn't any different than every other ranch that still exists across the country. I just don't think I'm ready to say goodbye to what my family built. What *we* built. I don't want to lose this place, Virgil."

"We ain't gonna lose nothing," he said, hesitating on whether or not he should keep talking.

Silence fell over the two once more as the horses slowed their pace to a crawl. Creaking leather and an occasional fly became their only blissful worries. Angel savored every second of the ride she feared may be her last at the Holliday Ranch. She gripped her reins a little tighter, pushed all those feelings down a little deeper, and lifted her chin up.

They stayed on horseback through pastures filled with wildflowers and bermuda, patches of woods filled with hickory, red oaks, and yaupon, across Butchers Creek, and over the bottom area they had mortgaged off in the hopes of a brighter future that would never come. They spent the better part of two hours riding along a winding path without saying much else worthwhile. A breeze came and went, wicking the sweat off their faces before more streamed down beneath their curled, dust-stained straw Resistols. Creaking leather and an off-key whistle from Virgil was all that filled the air, and for just a few minutes out of their trail ride, the couple was able to find a bit of peace.

As was so often the case, that peace was short-lived.

Their ride up the hill through the brush saw nothing but pens and more barbed wire first. The barn was the first building to rise up through the horizon. Covered in sheet metal that hadn't aged a day in thirty years, the barn was more of a home than the one that rose up in the distance behind it.

When they left, they were the only people home. No ranch hands or visitors, and no expected deliveries stopping by. When they were within eyesight of the porch again, both Virgil and Angel realized they weren't alone. It didn't take long for Angel to put the pieces together. Before they reached the front of the barn, she turned around to stare down Virgil, giving him the look he always dreaded most. It was pure hell-fire and brimstone, the kind of look that would make a pissed off rattlesnake back down in a hurry.

"I couldn't find the right time," was all Virgil could let out.

Angel widened her eyes in disbelief, still not saying anything.

"I'll explain."

"You better."

They hurried into the barn and shuffled their horses into stalls, tossing their saddles on the rack and grabbing the brushes once the blankets came off. It was the steady brushing sounds that spurred the conversation on.

"I called an old friend a couple weeks back," Virgil began. "It wasn't about anything in particular, but the ranch came up one way or another."

"Is that right?"

"Yes, ma'am. One thing led to another, and he passed along another guy's name for me to call."

"Do I know this old friend?"

"Does the name Davy ring a bell?"

"It sure doesn't."

"How about the Hunter family?"

"Nope."

"Then I'd say you don't know them."

"Must be really old, then."

"You could say that."

"And what did this old friend of yours have to say?"

"Well, he had a contact, said he might be able to help our situation. Said he could get us cash up front with the chance of a heck of a lot more where that came from."

"What did you do?"

"I didn't do—"

"Virgil, what in the hell did you do?"

"You want to sit down first?"

"I want you to tell me what the hell you did!"

"I sold a claim to mine the Holliday Ranch for gold."

When Angeline's jaw dropped, it fell right down to the damn dirt. She couldn't believe what her husband was telling her. It was so asinine, so silly, she didn't even know what to say. If she was being honest with herself, she didn't even know how she felt about it. By the time she collected her senses, Virgil had already started to explain why he did what he did.

"Remember when the kids were young and we came out here after your grandfather died?"

"When that guy escaped prison and tried to shoot up the place. Yeah, I remember," she said. "You almost died."

"As much as I try to forget about hearing your scream that day, I'll never be able to forget the look on Nathaniel and Nellie's faces when they saw those gold coins buried in the dirt in the driveway. What if there's more?"

"We know there isn't any, Virgil. The kids spent all summer, and almost every summer after that, digging holes in the yard looking for it."

"Well," Virgil sighed as he spoke, rubbing his neck and breaking eye contact. "Maybe we just leave that part out for now."

They walked together back toward their home holding hands, talking through their teeth in a way two people only can after being together for so many years. The path turned from dirt to gravel, and soon, the only thing separating them from the front porch was a single sixteen-foot cattle gate.

"What exactly is a claim?" Angel asked as they unlatched the gate.

"Well, Angel, it means that one man standing on the porch is gonna pay us a lot of money to mine the Holliday Ranch, as in dig for gold."

"How much do you call a lot of money?"

"How much did we owe the bank again?" A smile washed across Virgil's face as he winked at Angel.

"Honey, I gotta say, that is so stupid," she started before her own lips turned up into a smile. "I love you."

She leaned in, grasping his fingers in hers a little harder, and gave him a peck on the cheek. Her lips were dry, but somehow, her kiss was as warm as it ever was. All of Virgil's uncertainty and anxiousness washed away in an instant. It might not have been a permanent solution to their money problems, but it was an inexplicable relief to know the bank would be kept at bay for another day. Angel still had one question, though, and with the morning's honesty still swirling between them, she felt comfortable enough to ask without rushing to judgment.

"Who's the other guy, though?"

Chapter 3

Never have two men standing so closely been so far apart.

There are plenty of opposites in the world. Oil and water. Night and day. Right and wrong. It's always been that way. If you ask enough people just about any question, they'll start to align themselves one way or another, and the result will be the same. You'll end up with one man no different than the one standing on the left, and another no different than the one standing on the right. Morals and ethics and convictions may blow in the wind, but they can only go one way or another.

There wasn't much room to budge on the porch of the Holliday Ranch, but if there were, these two men would most likely still find themselves unable to yield any ground to the other. They repelled one another, but were stuck there all the same.

It didn't matter how anyone crossed paths with Wyatt—he treated them all the same every time, until they gave him a reason not to. He could've been the living ideal of stoicism if he wanted, but he was too much of a dreamer for such aspirations. He was cold enough to keep himself alive, eager enough to earn more cash than the rest, and hungry enough to be sure he never lost a bet. If there was one thing he carried with him in this world, however, it was the only thing in this world that would always be true. It was the pressing urgency and enduring righteousness of justice.

Wyatt couldn't say the same about the man standing next to him.

They exchanged a simple nod and nothing else. They could hear two people approaching from the pasture to the east of the home and knew it would just have to be an awkward wait until they were close enough to address properly. Wyatt didn't move. He didn't sway or fidget or smack his lips. He just stood there.

The one next to him took all of a few seconds to begin growing visibly impatient. He shifted his weight and sighed, then checked his wrist once before a device in his pocket a couple more times. His starched and pressed jacket looked like it alone was worth more than most men made in a year. That didn't count his boots made out of a leather Wyatt didn't even recognize, or the gold at his wrists, flickering in the Texas sun. His boot began to tap on the aging wooden floorboards as he rested his hands on his hips.

The couple they'd both come to see made their way up the steps and turned to face them. Their faces were pleasant, not at all so heavily troubled as Wyatt was told. They each carried themselves differently, for reasons difficult to explain than the fact that the husband's calluses on his hand were new, and those on his wife's had been there all along. Wyatt was in the middle of considering what kind of first impression the couple had on the already irritated man beside him when he turned to see that his entire demeanor had changed. A smile stretched from ear to ear, a warm right hand reached out to shake, and a trustworthy glint in his eye made him look like someone else entirely.

"Joe Clanton of Clanton Family Farms, Inc.," he said, like he'd done it a million times before. "I wanted to be the first to introduce myself to the local landowners in the county. You see, Clanton Family Farms, Inc. is the number one agriculture-based producer in the whole state and we are growing—quick. You might've heard Johnny's place was for sale a while back after a tragic death in the family. Well, we were the esteemed buyers, and we've got plans for the small plot. I want to tell you personally now, before you get some unannounced letter or faceless phone call, that we also have plans for you. We are looking to welcome the Holliday Ranch into our family so that we can stand together for the working class and not get run over by those suits down in Austin and all the way out in Washington."

"Wasn't Johnny's place a little over three thousand acres?" Virgil asked his wife without breaking eye contact with Joe Clanton. "Seems like more than a small plot."

"Did you just offer to buy the Holliday Ranch?" Angel blurted out, catching her husband up to speed in a hurry. "Wait. You did?"

"Yeah, ma'am," Joe Clanton said without hesitation. "I am offering to buy your fine ranch, it's true. But that ain't all of it. I'm also offering you a deal, a deal that says you can live and die in that mighty beautiful family home just like you always planned to do."

"What's the catch?"

"You run our cattle. You work our chicken houses. You grow our crops. You make this place what it always should've been, and you use *our* money to do it. That's it."

"You want us to sell out the one thing we're trying to save?" Virgil couldn't help but ask.

"If what I hear around town is right, I believe you've already started doing just that. I'm here to give you a better deal than the banks could ever offer. Because if your bank is anything like mine, they won't be all too thrilled if you try to live in a home they've already repossessed."

"Hold on," said Angel. "You're gonna show up unannounced, blow off this gentleman's appointment next to you to meet with us, brag about shutting down one of the few multigenerational family farms this state has left, and fuckin' *threaten* us to sell out. You might as well wipe that shit eaten' grin right off your face."

"In case you ain't following, sir," Virgil cut in. "She's taking the scenic route to tell you to go ahead and get the hell off of this property."

Joe took one last look at both Virgil and Angel, then turned to face the man standing patiently next to him, pretending not to have listened to everything that had just transpired right in front of him. Joe leaned in and scrunched his eyebrows real tight.

"Good luck with these two, they'll be dead in the water before the month is up."

"You have a good day now, you hear?" Virgil gave Joe a gentle nudge on the shoulder to tell him to keep it moving.

"We'll be seeing y'all soon, all right?" Joe tipped his barely worn hat with his finger and turned to leave. He was a man who'd gotten what he wanted in life, one way or another, and he never did take kindly to the word *no*. His eyes darted back as he strolled back to the SUV still running in the driveway, betraying his intention right then and there to anyone paying attention.

The only problem was that not a single person left on the porch cared enough to give that man a single second more of their time. Angel and Virgil had already greeted the second man waiting on their return with smiles and handshakes.

Virgil did his best to keep an eye on the SUV leaving their ranch while the next man started his own presentation. He should've paid more attention to the man he'd personally invited out to meet, but there was something about Joe Clanton that didn't sit right in his belly. A twisted smile and a crooked bargain always meant trouble in his book.

Angel never missed a beat. She had struck up a conversation like she hadn't just gotten so mad she could kill a man. It wasn't too unlike any other day for her. There were empty threats and accusations everywhere she looked these days. Every single one of them came from men just like Joe Clanton, with her family's ranch in their sights, practically drooling over the land.

When it came down to it, the man who'd introduced himself only as Wyatt wasn't all that different. He wanted the land for his own reasons, even if he couldn't quite come out and say it yet. Wyatt was a businessman, or as he so fondly described himself, a capitalist.

"Word came through about a bunch of gold needing to be dug up," said Wyatt rather calmly. "I'm an enterprising man, and despite the unfortunate timing of my arrival, I do come with a proposal for your family to consider. Lucky for me, I don't come empty-handed like that man before me."

Wyatt reached down to grab a bag that had gone unnoticed until now. It looked twice as old as him and reeked of a soured tobacco that made Virgil wince at the thought of what might be inside. Wyatt's hands were calloused and worn from years of labor and God only knows what else. Such a life made fumbling for a small metal zipper more awkward than it should have been, but after one quick motion to open the bag, everything troubling Virgil and Angel came to a sudden, gentle ease.

It was only green inside. It was the kind of green that men would kill for, that women would fall in love for. It was the only color capable of controlling everything in the world. It was cold, hard cash. Not just a few hundred dollars incapable of even keeping up with inflation, it was thousands, stacked nice and neat in perfect little piles, waiting to be spent without a trace of where it came from.

"Now this here ain't stolen or laundered, it's what old-fashioned men like me call saved money. I worked hard for this and I come here with an offer to invest it into the dirt of this fine home you got."

"You want to give us all of that cash so you can dig holes all over the Holliday Ranch looking for gold?"

"Yes, ma'am," Wyatt answered Angel bluntly. "That's exactly what I want to do. The plan is to turn that bag right there into about ten more just like it."

"How much gold do you think is actually out here?" Virgil asked.

"In my experience, if someone already found a

little, there's a lot more still hidden away. I aim to find it, pocket it, and be on my way."

Angel's thoughts drifted from the conversation. She looked out over the pastures stretching in the distance. She thought of her family that worked the land and then of the ones who wanted to take it all away. She'd spent every night for longer than she cared to admit trying to think of any solution that would solve their money problems, and not a single one of them ended with half the cash tucked away inside that bag. It wouldn't be enough to save them completely, but it would be enough to see them through another day.

Paying off the bank would put the entire ranch back in their name. It would give them a fresh start, a zeroed-out balance sheet, and it would give them a chance to finally look ahead instead of what was already past due. It would be freeing, but it would also set them down a path they have already walked before. The ranch still wasn't making any money. Even if their debts were paid in full two times over, it wouldn't be enough to keep the gates open and the lights on for more than six months. Those damn bills would just keep coming every month.

"It would sure be nice to wake up tomorrow without thinking about what time the bank is showing up," Virgil commented, nudging Angel's elbow with his own and sending her crashing back to the stark reality that this was the only option available.

"It sure would," she said, forcing a smile.

"I know all about money problems. It ain't my place to say one way or another, but if that bag helps you get a good night's sleep, and it helps me get back to work, well I don't see any reason why we don't have ourselves a deal."

Angel was the first to extend her right hand in search of a deal she didn't feel lucky enough to make. There wasn't much time to do things like ask questions about where the money came from or how Wyatt planned to dig up their whole ranch in search of a bunch of fool's gold. There wasn't even time to ask where Wyatt even came from. She needed the money to save her family's place, simple as that. Virgil was next to offer a handshake with a smile as long as a drive from Beaumont to El Paso

Wyatt seemed to have every intention of shaking both of their hands. His oversized, unwieldy mustache turned upward, almost resembling a smile of his own, and his hand was steady as ever as he started to reach out to Angel first.

It may have been the cries ringing out from the trees in the distance, but it was likely the gunshots blasting into the air that brought everything to a screeching stop. They came in bursts, arriving as terrible calls for violence where there had only been serenity in its place.

Bam. Bam. Bam.

"What in the fu—"

"They're stealing the cattle, Virgil!" Angel yelled, already running down the steps. "We got to go!"

To her surprise, it wasn't her husband who brushed past her, sprinting like the bullets were bouncing off his own heels as he ran. It was Wyatt. His boots seemed to never plant into the mud, no matter how many steps he took on the way to his horse. His ass was in the saddle, and his heels were pressed into the horse's flanks before either Angel or her husband, lumbering behind her, could even toss their rig over their horse's back.

"Hyah! Hyah!" Wyatt shouted as he pushed his horse faster and faster.

"Is that a gun?" Virgil stopped to ask his wife as they watched him ride away. "I'm pretty sure that's a gun."

Wyatt's arm was extended high into the air. In his grip was a blackened steel revolver with a six-inch barrel, with smoke pouring out of the end like a steam engine rushing down the tracks.

Bam. Bam. Bam.

It would be another dreadfully long few minutes before Virgil and Angel could meet Wyatt out on their own pastures. The men who trespassed on their property rode horses like wild outlaws with their faces covered by bandannas, but the firearms they carried never saw the days of frontier justice. These were modern weapons, the kind that real-life bringers of war and their weekend warrior wannabes carried on their hips. They were polymer pistols with twenty-round magazines and plenty more where that came from. Each one fired first into the air, then in the direction of the barn Virgil and Angel were riding from. Bullets slammed into the dirt around where they rode, sending plumes of dirt into the air.

"They're shooting at us!" Virgil hollered as they rode.

"No shit!"

"What the hell is happening?" Virgil whispered beneath his breath as he gripped the reins a little tighter.

They weren't too far away from Wyatt when he confronted the mysterious riders. They had pushed a few dozen head of heavy-bred cattle in front of them and were herding them haphazardly toward a downed barbed wire fence. There were five riders who kept firing one round after another, never finding much of a target, but there was only one gun firing back at them, and that one was held by Wyatt.

Wyatt's own shots echoed out across Holliday Ranch, but somehow, they were quieter than his booming voice that followed.

"You better run, you sons of bitches, 'cause when I find you, I'm bringin' hell with me!"

Bam. Bam.

Wyatt fired right at the masked riders, causing them to split off in separate directions, which forced the few dozen head of cattle to do the same. His gun only had six shots, and that meant he only had one left in the cylinder. As the cattle scattered every which way, he pushed his horse faster than he should have, holding the reins tight in one hand and aiming the revolver at the men less than thirty yards in front of him. They had given up their halfhearted attempt at stealing cattle and were now fleeing the ranch to save their own lives.

Virgil and Angel followed more closely behind Wyatt now, ignoring the cattle darting off into the pasture they called home. They rode up to flank the riders, pushing them into a group once again, forcing them to make a run for it, no different than the cattle they were just trying to steal. It was a torrent of hooves and dirt and screams. Everything moved too fast to think, hence they could only react. By the time they reached the downed barbed wire fence, everyone was out of ammo except for the man who'd just shown up on their doorstep not too long ago. Virgil glanced over at Angel, and they both matched their expressions of disbelief. Though not the wildest situation they'd found themselves in recently, it was certainly among the most dangerous.

Virgil and Angel were the first to stop at the boundary of their property. Wyatt and the rest of the riders barreled forward without much regard for anyone else, showing no signs of slowing down anytime soon. The couple watched as the man they'd just met single-handedly chase down a bunch of masked criminals with nothing but a six-shooter strapped to his hip like it was 1881 all over again. It would've been a chance to share a laugh if they weren't the victims of a bunch of rustlers trying to steal what little they had left in their name.

They forced their horses to hold still at the fence line and waited for a few minutes to see if Wyatt would make his way back to them. He came riding through the woods with a grin in no time. The revolver was still in his grip, like he couldn't afford to holster it once again, but he had a grin no one saw coming plastered across his face.

"You get 'em?" Virgil hollered as he approached.

"Good enough," Wyatt's reply came. "Y'all get these kinds of guys often out here?"

"Just lately," said Angel.

"She's right. Not too long ago, we had a pretty decent scare. They said a cartel cattleman was in the area, boosting just about any kind of cattle he could turn a profit on. Never did get hit, but damn near everyone around us lost more than a fair share of head."

"First time we've had to run them off like that, though," Angel commented. "Usually, they take one look at us holding a gun and hightail it the other direction.

"They usually don't hang around all that long when they see her totin' that .30-30."

"Well, I'll be sure to keep that in mind when me and my brother start diggin'," said Wyatt, rubbing the back of his neck and holstering his revolver. "We do have a deal, right?"

Without waiting for Virgil to answer, Angel took it upon herself. "We have a deal. Mr. . . ."

Wyatt reached out his right hand to shake on the agreement. "Earp," he said with a warm smile for Angel and a wink to Virgil before he answered. "The name's Wyatt Earp."

It should have been a time to bask in the rising sun climbing overhead on a new kind of day at the Holliday Ranch, a day where no one had to think about who was coming to claim the place for themselves next. It should have been a moment of reflection, hell, even reprieve, for the couple who'd spent so much time and money trying desperately to hold on to the family legacy. The cool wind wicking the sweat off their brow, the rustle of pines blowing in the distance, the knowledge that their home was safe for another day, none of it could pry Virgil and Angel's minds away from a single, glaring question: What in Sam Hill did they just get themselves into?

Chapter 4

Any enterprise of worth is built on three key principles—brains, grit, and decency.

If Wyatt was going to get anywhere, it was going to happen because of those three things. He knew this deep down to his core. He was a man of integrity, of morality. He was a man who had no qualms with doing what was right in the world. He was also a man, however, who was driven by a burning need for progress. It was undeniable, an inevitable pursuit of all men, but one that he had always taken upon his shoulders alone to accomplish. Whether that meant chasing it down on horseback with a gun in his hand, or putting calluses on his hands with a shovel while he dug it out of the ground. For Wyatt, on a fine Tuesday morning where the humidity had already swallowed the air, and where sunlight scorched the skin on his neck, he found himself doing the latter.

His fingers gripped the handle of the shovel until there were grooves indented into the wood. Rough hands had acted as sandpaper through the years, giving the shovel a smooth, worn finish that could only be built through countless hours of harder work than most men would be willing to take on. He'd split the earth open with that shovel a million times over, and he'd do it again if it meant he could buy his way through life without ever needing a shovel again. It wasn't the dirt on his hands or the dreams of gold in his heart that kept him going, it was something else, as if every strike of the shovel was guided by a hand that he had no control over.

Every man he'd ever worked with described such a feeling the same way. They'd say he was determined or had a strong work ethic. That wasn't what Wyatt would call it, though. What made him put his boot on the shovel simply had to be.

He was at least lucky enough to be standing beneath white clouds and blue sky as far as the eye could see. The Holliday Ranch was as pristine as any stretch of land that hadn't been covered in concrete. It was God's grace beneath his feet if he'd ever felt such a thing. It was more than pastures and ponds and patches of trees, it was an untouched holdover of a way of life long gone. Like a stone unturned for centuries, it protected the earth like nothing ever could. His eyes bore witness to the same sights of men more than a hundred years ago, preserved exactly as it should have been. For a moment, he basked beneath it, wondering if it wasn't luck at all, if some strange twist of fate had put him in such a place for a reason. The Holliday Ranch was a place he needed to be, even if he didn't know why.

The only thing he could do to bring himself out of his own drifting thoughts was the job he'd signed up to do. He had a bucket of dirty water and a pan, a wooden stool, and the shovel only he could hold. The owners, Virgil and Angel, had been kind enough to grant him a claim to the ranch, so long as he left them, and their cattle, to their own. It was one thing to make a good first impression at a job interview, but after what he'd done to chase off the gun-wielding rustlers, he just about had his pick of where he could start digging.

That brief exchange of gunfire had taken place only a couple of days ago, and he'd wasted no time getting his equipment, tent, wash box, and plenty of ammunition set up near his first site. As was so often the case, he wasn't alone in his endeavor, either. Any claim worth his time would always be worth the time of his dear old brother, Morgan, as well. He showed up just when he needed to, shovel in hand, eager to find gold beneath their boots. Wyatt never did need to call for help, as there was always a brother of his nearby to get him into something he shouldn't be in, or even out of something, if he needed it in a pinch.

Morgan was a man every bit as tall as Wyatt, but he lacked the mustache and deadly look in his eyes. He had slicked-over black hair and wore an unceremonious coat just about everywhere he went, no matter the weather. His demeanor was calm, but he knew how to lose his cool when he had to. For Morgan, there wasn't much more important in this world than a man's word. If that was ever gone, his respect was gone with it. Growing up closely with Wyatt, the two had forged a bond unlike their other brothers, and when push came to shove, it would be those two who'd always come out on top.

Together, they'd pushed pairs and sorted steers across countless valleys, roped Corrientes for rodeos in every state south of the Bible Belt, and even taken up arms policing fences for the biggest ranches in the state of Texas. It was the kind of brotherhood that was more than blood, it was born of gunpowder and sweat. They didn't need to catch up or ask how each other has been, they only needed the work at hand to tend to.

They stood side by side, dumbfounded by the beauty of Holliday Ranch as the sun continued its climb above their heads, stretching higher and hotter and brighter by the minute. It must've been noon before either of them had anything to say. Beads of sweat had already begun to stream down their forehead beneath stained cowboy hats. Their clothes were smeared with dirt, and the gallon jug of water at their feet had started to look more and more enticing.

"You know there's gold here, huh?" Morgan asked.

"That's what I was told."

"We been told a lot before."

Wyatt nodded his head with a smirk. "We sure have."

"Chased a lot of dead ends, too."

"Yes, sir," said Wyatt. "This was a good deal, though."

"You ain't never led me astray before, so I ain't got much of a reason to say otherwise this time. Would seem wise to get your hands on something more than a rumor and a promise before putting any holes in the ground."

"You know how many men have called me wise?"

"I'm guessing not many."

"And they've all been wrong so far."

Morgan let out a smile and then a sigh. "You ain't lying about that, brother."

The first shovel to strike the ground after their brief exchange was Wyatt's. His muscles were loose and eager to continue the work at hand, but his thoughts kept drifting back to the men who rode into the ranch uninvited. They were too organized, like it wasn't their first time breaking into someone's property and stealing their cattle. It was something unheard of in the world of surveillance and watchful eyes that everyone had grown to love so much. Things like that just didn't happen anymore. They were meant to be lost in the days of stagecoaches and stickups, where the only law was the six-shooter and a deadly stare, and where justice was delivered by gunpowder.

But there they were, plain as the day they worked in. The Holliday Ranch may be a place of untapped riches for the Earp brothers to dig up, but it also promised blood, one way or another.

"You still tote that pistol Dad gave you?" Wyatt asked, between shoveling lumps of dirt into a pile already half his height.

"Never stopped."

"When's the last time you used it?"

"I can still split a toothpick at twenty yards lookin' through a mirror, if that's what you're askin'."

"You got lucky one time, and you still bring it up every chance you get, but no, that ain't what I'm askin'. I mean, when's the last time you had no choice but to use it?"

Morgan rubbed the back of his neck. "Well, I guess I'm luckier than most when it comes to all that. The last bullet this thing fired off was in the air to scare off a bunch of coyotes one night a few months back." He patted the revolver peeking out of a worn leather holster on his hip. "They were scarin' my family."

"Yeah, I thought so," said Wyatt, allowing his voice to trail off as his eyes scanned the horizon. "There's something about this place. We're meant to be here. I can't explain why, but we are."

"If there's gold in the ground, then you're goddamn right we're supposed to be here," Morgan answered before spitting into the dirt at their feet. "We need to make some money if we plan on makin' that big move to Arizona."

"Arizona can wait." Wyatt grabbed his shovel and struck it into the earth one more time with a grunt. "I can feel it in my bones, brother. Whatever this place has to offer us, it's gonna be found right here."

Morgan shook his head a couple of times before they went back to digging. They were prospecting still, hoping to find a patch of dirt that showed even the slightest sign of gold flakes for them to pan. It was grueling, backbreaking work, but it had to be done. A shovel, a bucket of water, and a screen to filter out everything that didn't glitter in the sunlight were all they'd need to make their stay at the Holliday Ranch pay for itself a dozen times over. Just had to keep going.

Neither of them would ever go so far as to introduce themselves as miners by profession. They had their fair share of occupations, drifting where the wind blew, and finding only enough money to last until it picked up again. From gambling to toting a gun to investing, the Earp brothers did everything they could to earn a living. What they considered to be honest didn't always align with those around them, but they'd made their own way, and that wasn't something everyone could say for themselves.

Nothing ever came easy to anyone who shared Wyatt's last name, least of all him. It was a curse. He'd fought for every single thing he had in the world, and more often than not, in every sense of the word. His knuckles were worn and calloused. His fingers twisted and turned in every direction. His muscles ached from injuries he'd healed from long ago, but none of that would matter. The world demanded more from him, and he was doomed to wander until it had taken everything. The least he could do was scrape together enough money to eat steak instead of beans in the meantime.

His brother was no different. Together, Wyatt and Morgan had been in more brawls than they had fingers or toes to count on. They'd swung enough punches, chased enough injustice, and riled up enough evildoers to last a dozen lifetimes over. For reasons neither could fully explain, they always came out on top. Morgan was never one to ask who threw the first punch, as that didn't matter much to him. The only thing that ever mattered was who threw the last one.

The way of life for anyone who carried the Earp name was a brutal, relentless fight, but they'd never ask for it to be any other way. Wyatt knew this just as well as his brother and all those who came before them. They were born to wield fist and flame against the forces who'd stand in the way of what was rightfully theirs.

For today, the only thing standing in their way was more dirt than they could shovel. It was still a fight, every bit as exhausting as a half-hour scuffle with a drunk, but it was a fight they'd started, and that meant they'd rather die than finish it.

A rumble beneath their boots started soft at first. It was impossible to hear, coming to Wyatt only as slight vibrations working its way up the handle of the shovel as they dug. A dull roar in the distance began to grow. Wyatt kept digging. The screeching of metal followed soon after. Wyatt didn't even glance in its direction. He just kept shoveling dirt and hoping to see something worth seeing. It was his brother who stopped working first, spurring on a sigh from Wyatt, as Morgan dropped his shovel and put his hand over his eyes to shade his view.

Coming around the corner of a treeline was a green tractor bumping along a beaten path and Virgil's smiling face perched on top. The 1050 model diesel motor hummed like it had just rolled off the manufacturing floor, even though that particular model first came to the Holliday Ranch in 1980. The bucket was rusted and dented, but it was coming straight toward Wyatt and Morgan at less than ten miles an hour. It would be an awkward few seconds waiting on the tractor to reach them, and Virgil never did lose his smile. He just kept bouncing alone through the pasture, keeping the tractor's RPMs higher than they should have been because he never was able to find the right gear when he needed it. It was the kind of appearance that no man should have ever been proud of, but from what Wyatt could see, Virgil was practically beaming with pride.

"I'm coming to help!" Virgil shouted over the engine churning along. "I'm bringin' in the big guns!"

"What is going on?" Virgil was trying to get Wyatt to look, but he never would.

When the tractor rolled to a stop in front of the several dozen prospective holes Wyatt and Virgil had already dug, Virgil climbed out of the torn leather seat and planted his boots into the mud below.

Finally, as if he was bored of waiting, Wyatt turned his head and looked away from his work. When he saw Virgil, his voice changed, his shoulders fell back, and he found a way to put a smile across his face. "Howdy," was all that came out.

"I know this ain't part of the deal," Virgil said. "And I ain't sayin' I think you need any help. I just need something to do that might actually help Angel with everything she's goin' through. Just doesn't feel right to sit around even after all the work is done."

"Grab a shovel," said Morgan without waiting. "You don't get a cut though, that's the deal."

"I'm gonna do more than grab a shovel. Why do you think I brought out ol' mean green here? You just tell me where to bury that bucket."

"As long as we don't have to drive that damned thing," said Wyatt.

It was an infernal, insufferable racket. The tractor moved right alongside them, clanking and spewing fumes as if it were moving the entire earth and not just a patch of dirt. Its bucket tore through roots and all, hauling away more soil with one scoop than Wyatt could shovel in an hour. That didn't mean progress, though. They still had no idea if what they were digging up had any gold. Haul after haul, Wyatt watched as Virgil hauled away any notion of the entire reason he'd come to the Holliday Ranch. Grinding gears and worn hydraulic lines of the tractor mixed with mindless curses from its driver, fumbling through its mechanics to do something he'd never done before.

The hours dragged on slower than they ever had, working next to the diesel-sucking contraption. Wyatt did his best to pay no attention to the tractor, or the never-ending conversation between his brother and Virgil. Sunlight scorched everything it touched, dirt swirling into the air softened its touch with a suffocating presence, splinters dug their way into calloused hands, threatening to draw blood, and the roar of the motor became the only sound buzzing in Wyatt's head. It was doing nothing but driving him closer to the brink of insanity. No matter how many times he jammed his own shovel into the earth, he couldn't collect a single thought. It was a useless endeavor. When he'd finally just about had enough, he jammed his shovel into the ground, let his frustration turn his face beet-red, and turned to face both Morgan and Virgil, still yacking away.

"Would you shut that son of a bitch up for just five gaddam seconds?"

The engine died immediately, and Wyatt was met with blank stares. A sweet silence overtook them. Mockingbirds sang in the distance. A breeze whipped across the pasture if only to kiss Wyatt on the cheek. He basked in it.

"Did you need something, brother?"

Wyatt's moment of peace was interrupted by the question. He opened his eyes and glared at Morgan long enough to make his point known.

"If you didn't want me to help..." Virgil started before trailing off. "I just need somethin' to do while my wife does all the worryin'."

"Virgil, you're a good man," Wyatt admitted. "And my brother and I sure do thank you for grantin' us the claim to mine the Holliday Ranch."

"We really do," said Morgan.

"All that bein' said, I'm gonna try my best to be real nice when I tell you that I never—under any circumstances, even when there is a gun to my head—want to work next to that machine ever again in my life."

Wyatt's face was as cold and lifeless as any man's whose own spirit had been crushed to nothing. He didn't even blink. In his eyes was the same fire that waited to spew from the end of his revolver at the first sign of injustice.

"All you had to do was—"

Bam. Bam. Bam.

All three men collapsed to the ground, scrambling for cover. Wyatt was the only one who couldn't get to the tractor. He crawled until more shots rang out.

Bam. Bam.

They were farther away this time. Their echoes reverberate into Wyatt's bones as they reach out across the pastures. The shots were familiar.

Wyatt's boots were already pounding the dirt on his way back to his horse. As he sprinted away, he hollered at his brother, his voice trailing off into the distance, right toward where the bullets were being fired, "Get the guns!"

Chapter 5

The Holliday Ranch was home to the largest owner-operated ranch east of the capital, born of the bloodline of the gunfighter Doc Holliday—and that meant cattle and gunpowder were as true to the brand as sweat and tears.

Wyatt never did know all that much about running cattle. He'd come from a different kind of world, one where ranching and cowboying and living off the land didn't come as second nature. He could swing a rope, but he couldn't heel a steer if swung a hundred times. He could plant his ass in the saddle for hours every day, but he'd never taken a herd from pasture to pasture, much less into town.

Cattle had somehow always found a way to escape him, but not gunpowder.

The burn that came after a bullet scarred his hands at a young age. He could field strip any six-shooter, put any bullet through a silver dollar from fifty yards away, and feel the weight of a loaded handgun well enough to keep count by his grip alone.

What he lacked in familiarity with the ways of running fences, rounding calves, and haying fields, he more than made up with the trigger finger on his right hand.

Any man as good with a gun as Wyatt was even better in the saddle, though. He was taught by his family. Riding wasn't something they did because it was fun, it was a way of life. It was necessary to live. Wyatt and his brothers were given private lessons as soon as they could put on a pair of boots to shove into a stirrup. Those private lessons were led by one man from the time he couldn't saddle his own horse to when he owned a string all for himself—his dad.

Putting the two together wasn't an easy task. Most people struggled to hit a can from fifteen yards standing still, much less galloping on horseback at twenty-five miles an hour through uneven terrain. Wyatt could still reach out and touch a jackrabbit at fifty yards with his .45 long colt, though. It wasn't anything he hadn't done already. In fact, as he rode with a fury only to be found in the deadly pursuit of justice in the Wild West itself, he planned to take the life of a lot more than just an old rabbit.

Oaks and pines and hickory and sweetgum all became a blur. Wind whipped his face and threatened his balance, but he held firm. He could hear the hooves pounding the dirt, the branches slapping his arms and shoulders, and his own slow and steady breathing. He gripped the reins a little tighter, squeezing the leather, pinching it between his thumb and the top of his fist harder enough to leave indentations in his skin. Wyatt was barreling ahead, faster than he ever should've been.

He couldn't explain why. It was an innate, burning

disposition that he simply couldn't shake. There was no other way. It had to be done.

Morgan and Virgil were somewhere behind him, still doing their best to catch up. Wyatt knew he had to time it just right. If he reached those damned rustlers before Morgan was able to get his repeater to him, he'd be outmanned and outgunned. If he waited too long for his brother to catch up, he'd never catch a glimpse of their face, much less be able to run them down. It wouldn't be his first time to gamble, so he rolled the dice and doubled down, spurring his horse to find another gear and speed up.

Bam.

A bullet whistled by him, thrashing through the brush and limbs as it just barely missed where he was riding. It wasn't a stray shot. He was lucky it didn't hit him in the gut or worse, but he refused to stop.

The chase was on. He could hear half a dozen horses weaving through the trees in the distance. Frantic men hollered and fired off rounds that they weren't even aiming, most likely trying to scare off anyone following them. Bullet after bullet came whizzing by Wyatt. He pushed on. Once he could get close enough to make out silhouettes of the men riding away from him, he bit down on the reins, clenching his jaw to hold them tight, and yanked his revolver from the leather holster at his hip.

"Wyatt! Wyatt!"

Right when he turned to find his brother, a lever-action repeater rifle came flying through the air right toward him. It smacked against his palm, and a moment later, the fight was on. His trusty lever-action was chambered in his .45 long colt, no different than his revolver, but it gave him the distance he needed and the kind of accuracy that would put a stop to this whole chase in an instant.

With Morgan riding just behind him and Virgil still desperately trying to keep up, Wyatt shouldered the rifle and went to work. There were ten rounds ready to go, and only six riders he could spot through the trees in the distance. His first shot sent the leader ducking for cover, almost falling from his saddle. Wyatt slammed the lever down and chambered a new round before he shot again. This time, a spurt of red and a high-pitched yelp came from the rider just behind the leader, aiming a pistol in Wyatt's direction. That man dropped his gun into the dirt and clutched his right hand, crying out to his buddies as he came to terms with the fact that he only had nine fingers left. Wyatt didn't stop. He jerked the lever on the old Burgess and squeezed the trigger again. A third rider slumped over and dropped his reins, rode a few more paces, rag-dolling in the saddle, then collapsed off the horse face-first into the leaves and sticks, never to move again.

Wyatt was closing the distance, still biting the reins to his own horse with the lever-action resting against his shoulder. He watched the gap between him and the rustlers shrink as they scrambled to collect the body of the man he'd just gunned down. The bravest among them, two burly, bearded men, leaped from their horses and tossed the corpse over one of their horses just behind the saddle and were off again in a matter of seconds. It was exactly the delay he was waiting on.

A familiar *click-click* sent another .45 long Colt into the chamber, ready to fire. Three hundred and twenty-five grains of bullet were waiting patiently for just the right moment before it could be unleashed at more than thirteen hundred feet per second. Whether or not anyone would believe it wasn't of importance, but Wyatt wasn't actually aiming to gun down each of the men, he needed something else. The riders did their best to push their horses to an improbable escape. They could feel the crosshairs on their back, and it made them careless. They were scared, even though they outnumbered him, and they fired just about every bullet they could, trying to get Wyatt off their trail.

Bam. Bam. Bam.

Boom.

Bam. Bam.

"Wyatt, get down!" Morgan shouted.

Boom. Boom.

"Cut it out, Morgan!" Wyatt hollered back. "You're doin' more harm than good with that dadgum cannon!"

His brother was just behind him, spraying scattergun blasts at the riders. He peppered them with pellets and sent them spurring their horses in just about every direction you could imagine—except for where they had just come from. Wyatt followed closely, keeping the lever-action pushed to his shoulder, waiting for the right moment. With the riders separating and a choice to be made about which one to follow, Wyatt watched closely, desperate to find any indication of who deserved his attention the most. Most of the riders stared in his direction, firing aimless shots to scare him away. Only one never looked back. This one rode hard, right up a hill, dodging trees and screaming at his horse, desperately trying to get away. His guns were holstered, and his ass was sunk deep in the saddle. He was the one who had to escape, no matter what.

That man was, without a shred of doubt, the one

Wyatt was after. He kept his rifle aimed right at his back, but wouldn't squeeze the trigger. Wyatt pushed harder, digging his spurs into the horse's flank until he met the speed of the rustler's leader. There were two leather saddlebags on either hip of the man's horse, and Wyatt couldn't seem to take his eyes off them. They stumbled and twisted their way through the woods, losing Morgan and Virgil in the distance. Wyatt stayed close, but he held his fire. When he was no more than twenty yards away and separated by only a few saplings and yaupon, he leaned into his saddle and rested his cheek against the stock of his rifle. His breathing steadied, and his eyes focused. His finger eased back gently on the weight of the trigger, compressing it until the resistance that would unleash an explosion of gunpowder and lead made him hesitate. As the man whipped the reins around to urge his horse onto a sudden, sharp turn, the gelding rocked backward and gave Wyatt the opportunity he was waiting on.

With a gentle exhale and a slight squeeze of the trigger, the bullet set in motion a series of events that only a man such as Wyatt could ever command.

The gunshot cracked out through the trees just as the rider slid back into the saddle, giving it everything he had to hold on to the horse rearing up between his legs. The bullet ripped through both the front and rear rigging rings, sending the cinches free and the saddle flying from the back of the horse with the rider still holding on tight.

The horse bolted north right as the trespassing rustler landed on his ass in the dirt. He scrambled to find his composure and never looked back, sprinting after his horse, screaming every obscenity he was never allowed to say in front of his momma the whole way.

Wyatt could've taken one more shot. He could've put one between the shoulder blades of the rider and gone on with his day. While he stared down the barrel and lined the sights up on the fleeing man, he thought better of taking any more lives before he even understood what was going on. There was a question in the back of his mind he couldn't shake loose. It lingered in his thoughts, hanging over everything he knew he should've done, like pulling the trigger on the man he was watching run away from him.

He lowered the rifle from his shoulder and turned his attention to the saddle still half buried in the dirt. By the time he'd reached down to pluck it out of the ground, the rider and his horse were out of sight, and his brother was just starting to catch up. Wyatt kneeled down and ran his hands over the leather. It was branded with a letter *C* and tooled with floral patterns and baroque lines. It might've been the name of the rider, but Wyatt knew he was more than likely riding for a brand when he'd come onto the Holliday Ranch. He slung the saddle up onto his shoulder with a grunt. More than fifty pounds of dead weight hung on his back as he trudged back down the hill to where he'd left his horse.

It was humid, and the trees stifled any breeze trying to work its way in. Sweat dripped down his forehead and into his eyes. The leather band on the inside of his worn-down straw cowboy hat had become soaked in the chase, and the hat clung to his head as a result. Heaving the saddle around didn't help. He'd toted more than his fair share of saddles in his day, but this one was different. It was like each of the bags was filled with mud and gravel. By the time his brother Morgan had finally caught up, he was out of breath and every muscle in his arms burned, screaming for him to drop the saddle.

"Never seen you steal another man's rig," Morgan said as he walked up huffing and puffing for no reason.

"Shut up and help me with this dang thing."

"Did you shoot a saddle off a horse with a guy still on it?"

Wyatt shot a look at Morgan that was all the answer he needed.

"Ain't never seen that before either."

"Where the hell is Virgil at?" Wyatt ignored his brother, looking through the trees.

"He was right behind me."

"Well, he ain't now."

"He'll have to catch up. We got bigger problems on our hands. Did you notice something off about all those men we were chasing?"

"Hell, Wyatt, you were so far ahead I never even saw the back of their heads. All I got to see was the ass end of your horse leavin' me behind."

"The guys we ran off before rounded up a few dozen head and were trying to run them out of the property when we caught up. These guys weren't pushing any cattle. It was like they were goin' on a joyride through the pasture. Didn't make any sense."

"Still doesn't," said Morgan.

Wyatt tossed the saddle with the bags still attached back onto the ground and knelt in front of them. The first bag he opened was full of clumpy powder with fumes that reeked of rotten apples. He reached in and grabbed a handful to let it fall through his fingers, then he opened the second bag to find it full of the same substance.

"You know what I'm looking at, Wyatt?"

"I do," he said, still rubbing his fingers together and staring into the bags. "It's an additive. They were spreading it all through the pastures, that's why they weren't pushing any cattle."

"They were fertilizing? Well, that don't seem so bad at all. Maybe we shoulda just asked 'em what they were doing before opening fire."

"This ain't fertilizer, Morgan. It's a nitrate-rich additive. They were dumping it everywhere. Who knows how much of it actually got thrown out, or even *where* it got thrown out."

"You think they were trying to kill that family's cattle?"

"You know what nitrate does to their digestive tract? Cattle consume nitrate in damn near every plant they graze on, but if they eat too much, they can't convert it to ammonia, and all that shit builds up in their bloodstream. Makes it to where their blood won't carry oxygen. They're dead within a couple hours if you're lucky."

"It suffocates them..." Morgan whispered to himself as he joined Wyatt in thumbing through the powder.

"We need to find Virgil and Angel," said Wyatt, standing up and wiping his hands off on his jeans. "This ain't good at all."

"You really think we need to get involved in all this?"

"Morgan, we already are."

Morgan let out a sigh while Wyatt held his in. They both turned to grab their horses and backtrack through the woods. The new saddle was slung over the back of Wyatt's horse while they zigzagged through a patch of pines in desperate need of thinning. The towering trees rustled in the wind overhead, sending their needles falling to the ground like daggers. It was a serene experience, a moment of peaceful bliss as their horses walked gently through the woods despite the deadly scenario unfolding beneath their feet.

Wyatt expected to find Virgil doing his best to stay in the saddle, moving through the trees at a snail's pace on his Appaloosa gelding. He expected to smart off with an offhanded comment about how slow he was, then break the bad news.

He did not expect to find Virgil propped up against a tree, holding his blood-stained abdomen and struggling to breathe.

"Virgil! What the hell happened? Are you okay?"

"Never felt better," he told Morgan. Virgil looked up through bloodshot eyes and spoke through ragged breaths, staring at Wyatt. "Am I dyin'?" he asked.

Wyatt rode up next to him, nudging his horse forward with a tug on the reins and a click of his teeth. He slid down off the saddle and winced when he saw the hole Virgil was covering. A bullet had left his clothes and his flesh shredded. Wyatt gripped his shoulder and leaned him forward against his will. He was hoping to find blood on his back, and he wasn't disappointed. There was a hole there, just above his waist, from where the bullet had passed through him.

"You'll be fine," said Wyatt. "It came out the other side."

"Through and through," Morgan commented with a smile. "You're lucky."

"Could've fooled me," Virgil struggled to get out.

"I'm gonna help you up. You just get one leg over that horse, and we'll do the rest," explained Wyatt. "You think Angel can patch you up?"

"Well, I sure ain't gonna go to the hospital and try to explain myself if that's what you're askin'."

"Good man," said Wyatt as he pulled Virgil up to his feet and lined him up with the saddle on his horse.

After a few minutes of grunts and cussing, all three men had their asses in the saddle and were on their way back to the family homestead. It was more dreadful than awkward. Virgil was doing his best not to bleed out while whispering under his breath, rehearsing what he was going to tell his beloved wife when they did make it back. Morgan was more worried about getting back to work than he was about anything else. The gold beneath their feet was all he wanted, and anything else was either a distraction or an inconvenience.

Wyatt had other things on his mind, though. He knew deep down there'd be no gold to be found if they were killed in the process. He was drowning in ideals of justice and righteousness, searching for anything right in the world to conquer so much that was wrong. The fine people who owned the Holliday Ranch did not deserve what was happening to them. There was only one thing left to do. He could find no other answer to the problems that threatened his future—it was a cruel answer he'd learned a long time ago.

Some problems can only be solved by a bullet.

Chapter 6

Virgil had become one of the few unlucky enough to learn that a bullet wound hurts more the day after getting shot.

His memory of what happened was limited to a flash of light through the trees before he was clutched over, crawling away through the leaves and sticks on all fours. He didn't hear a gunshot or even see any blood. He just crawled. He ignored cuts and scrapes on the palms of his hands, the sweat dripping into his eyes, even the frantic surge of adrenaline that made his limbs shake and his teeth rattle. All he could think about was getting back home. He remembered thinking about Angel's face. The curve of her lips when she was about to smile, and the lines starting to form like delicate frames around her eyes. He thought of the way she turned to look at him when she was looking for his unspoken agreement about any of her opinions. He thought of the way she squeezed his neck when he hugged her, and how she always pushed her lips onto his a few seconds longer than he intended to kiss.

There was so much he should have thought about when he was out there bleeding into the dirt. His kids, Nathaniel and Nellie, and their lives without their father should have been the first thing he reflected on. The ranch, and how it would continue with only Angel working the land, should have been what he was worried most about.

All he could bring himself to think about was how grateful he was to have ever been able to call a woman like Angel his wife.

The last few hours of his life were mostly a blur of burning pain and completely unreasonable explanations. He was in and out of consciousness from the blood loss by the time he'd made it back home. Angel went through just about every emotion possible when she first saw what happened to him. There was little he could do to console her other than writhe around and groan in vain attempts to ease the torment raging in his belly.

Now that she was tending to him, Virgil knew everything was going to work out one way or another, even if he couldn't say it to her. They hadn't actually exchanged any words since he'd gotten home. She took him in her arms and went right to work. Sure, she had plenty of questions, but she directed each and every one of them to those Earp brothers who dragged him in. The only attention he received from her were warm touches with soothing hands and a promise that everything was going to be okay.

It would be almost seventy-two hours before they would actually be able to speak to one another. He woke up in a bed that wasn't their own. He was in the guest room, bandaged so tight he could barely move, and his mouth was drier than he ever knew it could be. He blinked a single time, still adjusting to consciousness, before a straw reaching out of an old plastic kitchen cup was pushed to his lips. He drank without question.

His eyes finally locked with Angel's, and everything he wanted to tell her when he was scared of death's cold hand reaching for him out in the woods was said right then and there. He did what he could to force a smile across his face before she finally spoke to him.

"You think you got somethin' to smile about, you son of a bitch?"

"I'm alive, and you're here next to me," said Virgil, still finding his voice. "For a little while, I thought I was about to die and never see you again."

"You almost left me all alone, asshole!"

"I'm sorry darlin', I really am. But I'm here now."

"Because I kept you alive, Virgil. I can't believe you went running after those men, trying to play hero. You were damn close to bleedin' out in our guest room, where your parents used to sleep when they came to visit. That how you always dreamed of dying? With me sobbing by your side, tryin' to play nurse?"

"I didn't go out there tryin' to die, Angel," Virgil explained, half-assed trying to sit up in the bed before realizing it was too painful to move by himself. "I went out there to protect our way of life. Seems like everyone these days has half a mind to tear down everything we built or just take it for themselves. We gotta let 'em know it ain't gonna work."

Angel let her head hang at her husband's words. She'd always pushed him to believe in the Holliday Ranch, and to take ownership of its legacy now that he'd worked the land so long. She never really considered that it might push him to die for the place, just like she would if the time ever came. There was something deep inside her that assumed Virgil would be by her side throughout her entire lifetime. Coming to terms with the fact that she almost lost him was rattling her to the core. The only thing she knew to do was to be angry at him for what he'd done, even if she would've done the exact same thing.

"I need you here, Virgil. I need you to fight by my side, not to run off and get killed tryin' to fight my battles for me. You hear me?"

"I hear you, babe, but you know damn well they ain't your battles anymore. They're ours."

"All the more reason to fight them together. No one will ever step foot on this land who ain't supposed to as long as we're side by side. So, no more goin' out there to play John Wayne, got it?"

"Got it," said Virgil with his eyes already closed and in the middle of an exhale that washed away every trouble he had.

Angel stood up and leaned over him, letting her hair fall down over her shoulders. If Virgil didn't know any better, he would've said his wife was going in for a kiss, but all that changed when she pushed against his wound and made him yelp.

"You ain't dyin' and leavin' all this mess to me. You hear me?" A sly smile stretched across her face as she spoke to him.

Virgil struggled to let out a chuckle between exasperated coughs. "Yes, ma'am, loud and clear."

Angel shook her head and went back to work checking his wound, cleaning the blood-stained wrappings, and sterilizing just about everything in the room for what had to be the tenth time. She grimaced when she saw the wound again. Smeared, dried blood gave way to bruising that had turned every color under the sun. Luckily, she'd been able to stop the bleeding and get a batch of antibiotics in him before any infections took hold, so the only thing either of them could do was wait and make sure nothing took a turn for the worse.

Angel could stitch up just about anything, but this was her first time closing up a bullet hole. If it had been on any other man, she could've handled it with even a modicum of tact, but seeing Virgil laid up in bed like that was destroying her a little more with every passing second. His wheeze that came with every breath, the random grunts of pain, the sheer amount of red on everything in the room, it was all putting her on the brink of losing what little composure she had left. All she wanted to do was scream.

Virgil wasn't a man to ignore what his wife was feeling, even if he was recovering from a bullet that almost took his own life. He watched Angel struggle with the nurse she had to be in the moment and the wife she desperately wanted to be. No words came to mind that could ease her suffering, but he had to try anyway.

"Those men out there rode for us, you know," he commented, as he turned over in bed to face her.

"We are not talking about them right now," she answered without looking.

"Something's going on, Angel. This place has had eyes on it from the other side of the fence ever since I got here. Plenty of people with plenty of big pocketbooks have tried to get their hands on the Holliday Ranch."

"You say this like I don't already know that."

"This time is different."

Angel stopped folding the towels just long enough to throw them down on the bed right at Virgil's feet. Her face was beet-red and her eyes swollen with tears. She was trying to find the words, but her mouth just hung open.

"I'm worried—"

"*You're* worried?" Angel finally screamed, forcing a vein to bulge out of her forehead. "I was just a few hours away from bein' a damn widow. If that bullet had hit you just a few inches higher, you'd be laid up in that bed, dead as a doornail. Do you care about that at all? Do you care that you almost left me alone to deal with all this shit by myself?"

"Angel—"

"Don't you dare, Virgil." She gave him the look she'd been waiting to give him since she saw him as a bloody mess riding up in the front yard.

"Hear me out. All I'm tryin' to say is there are wolves out there that need to be dealt with."

"And you think goin' out there to play cowboy is gonna do the trick? All it's gonna do is get you killed. You of all people should know that now."

"It wasn't just me out there. I would've died if it weren't for Wyatt and his brother. They came back for me after they ran off all those bastards. They found me bleedin' into the dirt, and they brought me back here."

"Good for them."

"They fought for us, Angel. Wyatt might've even killed a guy for us."

"Did we ask them to do that? I know I sure didn't."

"We didn't have to. That's what I'm tryin' to tell you. They stood up for us without hesitating. When shit hit the fan, those two were on their horses with their guns out like it was the damn Wild West."

Angel could see the worry in Virgil's eyes. She could feel the anxiety in his voice. But it wasn't concern for his own well-being laced into everything he was saying, it was for the land beneath their feet, the legacy of her family. He'd become no different than everyone else in her family. There was something about the Holliday Ranch that made people willing to die for it at a moment's notice. It was the same thing that forced her away so many years ago. She'd hoped to escape its pull, but here she was with the man who was supposed to be her ticket out, doing the exact same thing—fighting for the ranch.

She wanted to agree with him. Deep down, she knew he was looking toward the future they were still trying to create, but she couldn't stop thinking about everything she had almost just lost.

"We don't even know who is doing all this," she finally gave in.

Virgil propped himself up on his elbows, doing his best not to show just how much pain he was really in. "He already told us who he is. His name is Joe Clanton of Clanton Family Farms, Inc., the number one agriculture-based producer in the whole state," he said, mimicking the man who had already made an offer for the ranch. "He isn't even hiding. He may have smiled to our faces, but he threatens to kill us as soon as his back is turned. I'm tellin' you, that man is a problem. I know it."

Angel made her way to her husband's side before bending down to rest her head on his shoulder. She fought back the tears starting to burn her eyes, as Virgil patted her cheek and kissed her head.

"We need to invite Wyatt and Morgan up to the house and get all this out in the open," he explained to her. "If we're gonna fight back, we're gonna need all the help we can get."

"I'm scared," Angel admitted, without lifting her head from his shoulder. As the tears soaked her face, she asked the only question that made any sense. "Can we win this fight?"

"I'd bet my life on it," he said.

Chapter 7

Texas Hold 'Em is a game of skill where luck is the only real deciding factor between who wins and loses the final showdown.

Playing the hand you're dealt is often the difference between losing everything you're worth, or doubling it all. It all comes down to a single decision, whether to fold and try again, or throw the chips into the pile and see what comes of it. It's a decision that has broken more men than it has made. Pulling up a chair to ante up will lead everyone down the same path. One way or another, you must make the call to give up or push ahead.

To some, the flipping of cards or the clatter of old clay poker chips are the soundtrack to their life being flushed down the drain. To others, they are but a sweet serenade to wealth and riches gained without so much as breaking a sweat. It's a game with life and death consequences, where the stakes are as high, or as low, as what each man is willing to invest into it.

For Virgil and Angel, life at the Holliday Ranch

was no different than being dealt a new hand in a game of poker. They could either fold and give it all away, or they could push all their chips in and live to see another sunset. Every morning, the couple made the same decision. This had gone on for years and years, long enough for both to become numb to the sacrifice, the gumption, and the risk that it took to keep hold of such a place.

As they each took a look at the cards lying face down on the table, they barely registered the hand they'd been dealt in their own game. They were lost in the fight that had been thrust onto them just when they thought they'd found a moment of peace. They sat at a cheap folding table with a deck of cards that had been shuffled more times than the varnish that coated their faces could withstand. A cracked window did nothing to allow a breeze into the room, instead filling the air with enough humidity to cause sweat to drip from their brow. It smelled of cigarettes and whiskey that weren't their own, beer that had spilled against their wishes, and the musk of going too many days without a shower.

It had been four days since Virgil had felt the searing pain of a bullet that left him bleeding out in the woods behind their home. In that time, he'd managed to go from lying on his back in bed to sitting upright in a chair—a welcome change despite the soreness that came with every move he made. His bandages were no longer leaking through, and since the blood had finally stopped, he had enough composure to hold a conversation with minimal grunts and sighs. Most people feel like they received a gift when they survive being shot, like they were granted a second chance to do the things they never got around to doing. Virgil held no such regard. It was just another day to continue the same fight he and his wife had been entrenched in for so long.

"It was an attack, plain and simple," said Virgil as he tossed a couple of chips into the center of the table. "They are tryin' to scare us off. They cut fences, try to steal our cattle, try to kill what they couldn't get their hands on, and then use our fear to get what they want. The only problem is we're not scared of 'em."

Angel didn't hesitate to match his bet. "Don't matter if they hide their faces. We've seen their kind before."

"Our fights have always been in the courtroom, or some lawyer's office, where we are only allowed to use words backed up with money to have a chance at winning. This time is different," Virgil said.

"The Clanton family seems to think we can be bullied out of what my family built. That man thinks he can write a check for just about anything he wants."

"We might've even been the first people to tell him no to his face."

"Judging by the look he gave us before he left, I'd say you're right."

"Imagine what he'll think when we take the fight to his doorstep like he did ours."

Virgil watched as Morgan tossed a handful of chips of his own into the pile and kept his eyes focused on his cards. He let out a sigh that ruffled the hairs on his mustache and sent a wave of nauseating whiskey-filled breath across the table, and let his cards fall face down on the table again. "Y'all are good people. You work hard, you keep to yourself, you fight for what's right in the world. But my brother and I, we ain't here to get killed. We're here to get rich."

"You think that upstanding gentleman Mr. Clanton will let you keep diggin' up the place when he's gotten rid of us?"

"I don't think it needs to come to that."

Angel shot a look over to Morgan that would leave any lesser man dead right then and there, then she turned to her husband. "Looks like they ain't all gung-ho for the ranch after all."

"Now, wait just a second," said Virgil, lifting his palms up. "I watched you and your brother chase down those men without so much as a second thought. Hell, I've watched your brother do it *twice* now. The fight is already here."

The flop had hit the middle of the table without much notice from any of the players. There was a pair of aces to hit first, with a queen high third card. They sat lonely at the table, waiting for what would land next, but no one sitting at the table even bothered to check their hands. Virgil was the first to instinctively grab a couple more chips and up the bet rather than checking. Angel followed without missing a beat, and once again, Morgan was left deciding what to do.

"What if it's not Mr. Clanton? What if it's someone else you don't even know? Better yet, what if those people who busted in a few days ago aren't even associated with the ones before? You said it yourself, you've been fightin' for this place for a long damn time. You act like you got it all figured out, but you don't know shit, and you want my brother and I to risk our lives based on your hunch?"

"All I want is for you to do exactly what you've been doin'."

"You see, that's the whole thing." Morgan finally locked eyes with Virgil. "What we done so far had to happen. They rode up on us, and we protected what was ours. You forget it's your land that stands between them and what we came here for."

Morgan tossed his chips into the pile after he'd finished his explanation, matching the bet made by Virgil and his wife. He waited until after he'd thrown his chips in before checking his hand once again for good measure.

The game dragged on with the reveal of the turn card. It was another queen, putting two pairs on the table already before any hands had been shown. They each took a drink from their poison of choice, as if rehearsed in perfect synchronization, before returning their attention back to the conversation rather than the game.

"We sunk everything we had into this place years ago," Virgil started. "We've done that time and time again, too. There ain't nothin' we've made that hasn't gone right back into the ranch. Our money, our sweat, our blood—"

"Our tears," Angel finished his sentence for him before lingering on a pause longer than anyone expected. She cleared her throat and looked down at her cards before speaking again. "This place is more than just a patch of dirt and a name. It's worth fightin' for, every square inch of it."

"You think every family that owns more than twenty acres don't feel the same way?" Morgan shot back.

"I think those families aren't willin' to do what we are."

"Everyone dies," said Morgan. "And no one ever plans on it. That's just the way it is."

The river came without another word. No one

reacted or placed any more bets. The game came to a standstill, like each of the players had just run face-first into a brick wall. There were no drinks to be had or offhand comments to be made, even if only to break the tension. It was only silence. Rather than a drop of a pin, it was the dealer of the game himself who broke the unspoken reflection that had overcome the game, and he did it with a strict voice, a firm hand, and a single word.

"Showdown," Wyatt said.

Virgil was the first to reach for his cards, still lying face down on the table. He moved cautiously. His stomach was tied tight enough to keep him rigid, and the soreness kept him from hunching or slacking his shoulders. It was an awkward maneuver, but that was the last thing on his mind. His face was twisted, and his eyes were locked on Morgan. He picked up the cards and pushed them up in front of the Earp brothers' faces.

"The only people who are gonna die are the next sons of bitches who think they can step foot onto this ranch without starin' down the wrong end of a gun," he hollered. "You can get caught in the crossfire while you keep your head in the ground, or you can do what your brother has already done and stand up for what's right. You hear me?"

"Your damn neighbors would hear you if you had any," Morgan quipped.

"I mean every word of it. We have fought tooth and nail to keep this place in the family where it belongs. Every bill collector and bank this side of Texas has gotten every dime they ever asked for, too."

"You ever been shot at before today?"

"As a matter of fact, yes I fuckin' have." Virgil

struggled to sit up a little more in his seat. "I looked a man right in the eyes and shot him point blank when he was lookin' to do the same to me. I know what it's like to fight back when you don't have a choice to run away. We've been backed into more corners than you could ever understand, and we are still here."

Angel had fallen silent during her husband's tirade. Though she agreed with him, she couldn't find the will to fight the two strange men sitting at their table. They had wandered through life as drifters, and what Virgil was proposing went against just about everything she was sure they believed in. Don't get too involved. Don't get caught up in other people's problems. Don't do anything that might jeopardize the next paycheck. Angel allowed her eyes to glance back and forth between Wyatt and his brother. Their faces were cold. It was like everything they did was against their will, even the meaningless poker game where the chips were worth less than the air they breathed. She didn't expect to become so unsettled, but the way both of them stared a hole through Virgil as he continued yelling, the way they twitched their lips when he cursed at them, the way they never even asked for a drink of water—it all made her stomach knot up like she'd just watched someone get killed.

Virgil didn't pay any attention to his wife during his lecture. He spilled everything from their lonesome fears of maintaining the ranch to the expenses they've incurred trying to keep the doors open, down to the penny. It was a rant to end all rants, but it would do no good.

"You can either help us fight," he finally let out, almost out of breath. "Or you can stay the hell out of our way." He finally threw the cards down on the table, face up for the players to finally see what hand he'd been dealt.

The community held an ace of spades, an ace of hearts, a queen of hearts, and a queen of clubs before the river card revealed a king of hearts. Virgil slammed his cards down to reveal a pocket pair of aces, giving him four of a kind. Angel couldn't help but laugh and toss her cards haphazardly onto the table, letting them slide across the community to reveal her own pocket pair of queens, a four of a kind that couldn't match her husband's. It wasn't until Wyatt shot his eyes over to his brother that Morgan dropped his own hand onto the table without a word, revealing a ten of hearts and a jack of hearts—a royal flush.

"It was nice playin' with y'all," Morgan said, standing up from his chair. "But it's past our bedtime."

Wyatt pushed the metaphorically, and literally, enormous pile of chips toward where Morgan had been seated, then gathered the cards up and stacked them neatly in the center of the table. He pulled on either end of his mustache and kept his eyes down as he brushed off his shirt and pushed his chair back to join his brother. Before they each turned to leave the home, Wyatt paused to look Virgil right in the eyes. "Remember son, there's always a faster gun hand. The more you go out there shootin', the quicker you'll find him."

Chapter 8

The sun can be a treacherous deceiver, guiding us down paths, if only for the simple fact that we can see the way.

Wyatt was lost in a never-ending cycle of his shovel slamming into the dirt and his sleeve hastily wiping the sweat from his eyes. It went on for hours before he gave much of anything a thought other than the flicker of gold he hoped to see in the scorching sunlight. The heat, laced with humidity, and being surrounded by enough trees to stifle even the slightest breeze, proved to be his worst enemy. He'd been suffocated by a man twice his size and at least three times as drunk, and he'd even been damn near drowned to death by a woman with the worst intentions, but this was different. His lungs burned as bad as the skin on his neck. It was hell. His shovel just kept hitting the ground, though.

From the first light of day that touched the ground on the morning after their impromptu poker game, Wyatt knew what had to be done. That didn't mean he wanted to do it. It only meant there was an inevitable outcome to the situation he'd found himself in. He could keep his as-of-yet fruitless claim to dig until he could pan enough gold to pay his way up to Arizona with his brother, and he could even fool himself into hoping such luck would strike sooner rather than later. The end would be the same though. His muscles already ached, his bones were already weary, his breath already shallow, but if the only other option was to quit, there was no choice to be had. He just had to keep going.

For now, the only luck he could count on was the simple fact that he was alone in his business. The ranch owners had left early, before the sun, and his brother was not too far after them, saying he had to go out for supplies. Wyatt knew they had enough beans, and they could get all the water they needed from the ranch well, but he chose not to ask anyway. Instead, he just went to work.

He'd been at it for several days by now, and his eagerness had already begun to turn into frustration in the short time he'd been digging. The sun beating down all day was hard enough. Prospecting was already risky. His life was uncertain enough as it was. Whatever it was that brought him to the Holliday Ranch—the tug of fate's hand or the call of something else entirely—seemed desperate to make him long for the life he had before walking through those gates. Such thoughts would get him where he needed to be, but he was typically fool enough to have them anyway, and dwelling was something he'd unwillingly become more and more proficient at. He was a man who knew right from wrong, or at least he liked to think as much, but the world had found a way to disconcert even him.

For now, he was content with the fact that he wouldn't get involved any more than the situation demanded for him to get what he needed, mainly enough yellow ounces to keep him in search of something more. The pounding of his shovel carried him from one drifting thought to the next, each one less poignant than the last.

He kept his eyes down and his hands busy.

Noon came and went without a word spoken. When he found himself able to settle into the exhaustion, he was surprised to find that he had come to enjoy his most peaceful day yet at the ranch. There was no bickering with his brother about the lack of gold in the ground, no exchanging of bullets from the would-be enemies of the family, only the work at hand. Before he realized it had happened, a smile formed on his face. It stretched beneath his mustache from one end of his face to the other, forming creases on his face where there had been none for what felt like years.

It left as soon as it appeared, however. His good fortune that came by way of solace was cut short. A truck sped down the driveway, leaving rooster tails of dust in its wake. It was cleaner than any vehicle he'd ever laid eyes on before, bright and shiny and unable to ever venture off a path that wasn't paved.

It rolled up to a gentle stop in front of the house across the pasture from where Wyatt was and was swallowed completely by the dust it had thrown up during its entrance. The door swung open, and a bald, hulking man stepped out, though from the distance, there wasn't much else Wyatt could make out.

He sighed. The shovel fell to the ground, and his calloused right hand once more found its way to the revolver hanging at his waist. He pulled it slowly from the holster it had remained in for several days now and spun the cylinder. There was loaded brass in every hole when he slammed the cylinder back into place and stuffed the revolver back in its place.

The walk back was tiresome, but it was at least a moment to bask in what little contentment of silence he had left.

"Hello there, my boy!" said a booming voice that came through before Wyatt had gotten close enough to respond.

It would be another few minutes before the two were face-to-face. The first thing Wyatt noticed was a gold watch dangling from a vest beneath a tweed jacket. It was more gold than he'd seen in quite a while and it made him consider what kind of man he was talking to.

"The name's Newman," the man who stood at least six feet tall and pushing two hundred seventy-five pounds said as he pushed his right hand out.

Wyatt studied his hand first without saying anything. His nails were clean, his palms hadn't seen a rope in years, and his fingers bore no calluses. When Wyatt finally reached out to shake it, he knew right then and there what kind of man he was dealing with.

"Newman," said Wyatt, allowing his voice to trail off.

"Clanton. Newman Clanton, officer, analyst, and owner of the First Texas Credit Union in town, or as most like to call it, the bank."

"Wyatt Earp."

The laugh that followed could've been heard all the way back to the mess of concrete they called town, that Newman Clanton had driven from. It boomed louder than the birds or the breeze, and it was genuine in every sense of the word.

"Well, Mr. Earp, have you seen the homeowners today? Virgil and his dear wife Angel, I believe, is their names."

"Yep."

"You have? Are they home?"

"I mean, those are their names."

"Right."

"They ain't home, though."

"I am sorry to have missed them," said Newman, locking his eyes with Wyatt's. "Did they say when they'd be back?"

"No."

"Do you know where they went?"

"I don't."

"Well," the banker said and reached for the back of his head to hide his anxiety. "Maybe you can help me out with a slight problem we've run into down at the bank. You see, it has to do with the loan that was recently paid off by the homeowners. They were mistakenly told their debt was one number, you see, all the while it happened to be another number entirely. These things happen. I'm sure you can understand. I would just like to pass along a notice that there has been an issue—"

"Look, Clanton." Wyatt took a step forward to cut the man off mid-sentence. "I'm just gonna go ahead and stop you right there. What these fine people get up to in their spare time is none of my business. Your deciding of an impromptu and unannounced visit is also none of my business. But unless you have something to say to me, you might as well go ahead and get back in that pretty contraption you rode in on and come back another time."

"What was your name again, boy?"

"Wyatt."

"You might want to go ask some folks around town about me, they'd tell you the same words I'm about to impart on you so kindly—do not talk to me like that. I will ruin you and whatever life you hope to have in this world. You hear me?"

"There you are," said Wyatt. "I know a man who's all hat and no cattle when I see him. You ain't gettin' by me, Newman Clanton."

"Gettin' by you? I could do anything I want to you, boy, and you wouldn't even see it comin'. Now, we got some business with the owners, why don't you go ahead and give them a message for me? Because if there is one thing I am not gonna do, it's sit here and wait all day like my time ain't worth nothin'."

Wyatt stared ahead, clenching his jaw, trying his damndest not to move the wrong muscle and set something off he couldn't take back. He focused on the bead of sweat tracing down his temple, on his fingernail digging into his palm, hidden beneath a clenched fist. He watched the banker named Newman rattle on, his jowls jiggling with every word he spoke. For a few seconds, Wyatt didn't even pay attention to what he was saying. It was the sour look on his face and spit coming from his teeth that made him snap back to the conversation.

Newman was red in the face. He was sweating and tossing his hands around, squinting his eyes more and more against the sun, starting its descent in the west. The banker was about as patient as a pissed off rattlesnake. He had the money and last name to get just about whatever he wanted without waiting, and being told no wasn't something he took to with any kindness or rational sensibility.

"You understand anything I'm telling you, boy? Or is that dumbass look on your face all I'm gonna get outta you?"

"Sir, before you say somethin' you might regret and I do somethin' I might regret, let's just call it a day. I'll let Virgil and Angel know you were kind enough to stop by as soon as they get home. That all right?"

"I ain't never regretted a single thing in my life and I sure as shit ain't gonna start today. You might not be from around here, so let me let you in on a little secret. When the bank has a problem, it's everyone's problem. That means when I have a problem, so do you."

"Only problem I got is this conversation not endin'," Wyatt smarted off, as he turned to walk away and leave it at that. It was in his best interest, and even though Newman didn't quite understand it, it was in the banker's as well. He made not more than a few paces before another threat came his way.

"Don't you dare turn your back on me."

"Don't push your luck, Newman. Go on."

It was only boot steps hitting the dirt that came next. Before Wyatt could turn around, the banker was right on top of him. His hairy arm, ending in greasy fingers, reached out to clasp around his throat. All it took was a quick shove with both hands, hitting the center mass of the top-heavy banker with rolls on the back of his neck, to go toppling over backward.

By the time Newman was able to scramble to his feet in front of Wyatt, the fight was on.

Newman swung first. Wyatt ducked and countered all at once, landing a left hook to the false ribs, fracturing the lower two in the first strike and sending the banker crumpling to the ground once again. Adrenaline hit him like a freight train and he was back up on his feet in a few seconds. Despite the wheezing of his lungs and his clothes getting dirty for the first time, Newman went right back in.

Wyatt put his elbows up and started absorbing the frenzied blows against his forearms. He took small steps back, placing the heel of his boot into the dirt with each step, until he was back in the fighting position and able to find the right moment to hit back. He grunted against one more right hook and used his weight to hurl a haymaker at Newman's jaw.

For a man as large as the banker, he moved with unnatural speed. He sidestepped the crushing blow from Wyatt, and before another fist could be thrown, Newman speared Wyatt into the ground, throwing up a cloud of dirt that engulfed them entirely. It was a downright mess of wild kicking and blindly thrown punches that followed. They rolled around, grunting and cussing up a storm before things settled down long enough to see one another. Wyatt was on top, squeezing his knees into the banker's broken ribs, causing him to writhe and howl in pain.

Through it all, Wyatt never so much as worked up a sweat or lost his breath. He moved with deadly intent, slow and steady, calculated, as if it was a fight he'd trained for all his life. All this did was serve to piss Newman off even more, though.

"What the hell are you?" He screamed from the ground.

Wyatt answered only by raining down blows. His fists were hardened and calloused and able to withstand the kind of beatings that would make most men crack. He fought to stay on top of the overweight and frantic banker on his back in the dirt, using his knuckles as hammers to put an end to the fight that should've never broken out.

Everything was going Wyatt's way until a stray hit caught him off guard, hitting with enough power to dislocate a normal man's jaw, and sending him down to the ground at last. He still didn't bleed. He simply used the momentum—and anger—to push himself back up to his feet.

The two were staring at each other again, no more than six feet apart, one with a bloodied mouth and a black eye, the other not even breathing heavy. Wyatt took a step forward, and Newman took one back. Wyatt took another forward and Newman followed suit, keeping the distance between them.

"You wanted to fight, asshole," Wyatt spoke through his teeth laced with blood. "Don't run now."

"You must be some fuckin' freak! No wonder they got you diggin' holes. You don't know who you're fuckin' with, though, boy."

"Am I gonna have to break a few more ribs to shut you up?"

This time, it was Newman who closed the gap. He charged headfirst with gritted teeth and hands out, ready to strangle Wyatt to death. He made it no more than two paces before one of Wyatt's haymakers finally landed on the banker's left cheekbone. He may have been an entrepreneur of many trades, but his hands were no different than a man who broke his back for a living. His fist was wide, covering all the way from Newman's temple to his jawbone, and when he did land a hit, he hit harder than most men had ever felt, like getting kicked by a mule when you didn't see it coming.

Newman stumbled for a second. The adrenaline was draining from his body as the pain of what just happened was starting to settle in. His left eye had gone completely bloodshot, and a trickle of blood leaked from his ear. Then, he collapsed. Wyatt watched as the banker reached up to hold the side of his head. He watched the realization wash across the man's face as he pulled fingers dripping with blood away.

Wyatt took a few steps to stand over the top of him. Newman Clanton was almost bigger on his back than he was standing up, but he fell just like every other man who had raised a fist at him. The look in his eyes was pure, unfiltered fury. It was the kind of hate Wyatt had only seen in killers.

Right then, he understood who he was dealing with and took a step backward.

"Like I said, I'll let Virgil and Angel know you stopped by."

"You son of a bitch!" Newman coughed and sputtered. "You don't know what you've done here. You are gonna pay for this."

"Probably so. But if it's all the same to you, I'd rather get back to work."

Wyatt turned to leave again and was none too surprised to find that this time, there were no empty threats coming his way, but he changed his mind and turned around. Newman was struggling to pick himself up, but he managed. Wyatt put his hands on his hips and allowed his right hand to rest on the still-holstered revolver. It hung on his hip like a promise and a threat all his own, and even though he didn't have to use it this time, he wanted Newman to see what he'd be dealing with if they ever fought again.

"You go ahead and get outta here now," said Wyatt with a grumbling voice. "Boy."

Newman darted his eyes back for just a second before he climbed into the truck that brought him to the Holliday Ranch to find only an ass kicking. The truck spun its tires, turning around, spewing rocks and dirt back into the air as the motor hummed and the truck sped off.

"The hell was all that about?" Morgan's voice came from behind.

"Some guy wanted to talk to Virgil and Angel."

"You tell 'em they weren't home?"

"I tried."

"What's that supposed to mean?"

Wyatt finally turned to make eye contact with his brother who had arrived just in time to be late for everything. It didn't take long for Morgan to see the state he was in. His hair and mustache were a mess, and his clothes were covered in dirt. He looked like he'd just left a bar fight where no one could have possibly stood a chance against him. Even so, he did not bleed, or even huff for air. Wyatt was as calm and collected as he'd ever been. Morgan rolled his eyes and immediately turned to leave it all behind him.

"I know that look in your eye. One way or another, you're gonna pay for whatever just went down between you two," he said, walking away. "And that means we're *both* gonna pay."

"We'll see about that."

Chapter 9

It's downright cruel to have something so beloved torn from your grasp.

Wyatt was experiencing the kind of grief that only a man who once held all the answers in life—a job worth doing, a dream to chase, and peaceful means to do it all in—only to have them all taken away in the blink of an eye, never to return. It was the sort of loss that could put a man beside himself. The sun beating down, the burning in his muscles, the day dragging on without end, none of it compared to being interrupted at work when everything was going right.

He could've lost track of everything. Any gold worth finding at the Holliday Ranch was likely just beneath his boots right before that banker decided to show up and ruin a good thing he had going. He couldn't figure out what hole was what, and at this point, he wasn't even sure if he was in the right pasture. All he could remember was how good his morning had been going and the kind of luck that was surely about to come his way.

Instead, he was forced to fistfight a man he didn't even know, to protect a family that had been the source of at least three near-death experiences in a matter of days. If there was ever a time for him to be rightfully frustrated, it would be now.

The last thing he needed was another distraction.

A clatter from the pits of hell began to swell in the distance, coming from behind the

family home, a couple of pastures over on the horizon. It was a garish, mechanical nightmare of sputtering and banging, and it was almost enough to drive Wyatt over the edge for the day. He wanted nothing more than to return to some sense of peace to carry out his work. His brother, Morgan, had sensed as much no less than five minutes after arriving and decided to make himself busy, unloading and sorting the supplies he'd brought back. Virgil, however, had no such tact. He hauled the infernal tractor and its rattling, clinking, cumbersome bucket down through one pasture, crossed a sixteen-foot gate into the next, and pulled it to within inches of where Wyatt was digging.

It took a few seconds to endure the rage that was building up in Wyatt's belly. His day had soured. Even a sweet, cool breeze escaping through the pines lining the pasture on the west side of the Holliday Ranch couldn't lift his spirits. He stood there, leaned over on his shovel, staring at another empty hole as Virgil let the tractor idle aimlessly next to him.

"Figured I'd come to help for the rest of the day," shouted Virgil over the diesel humming without end.

"You're too kind, sir," was all Wyatt could let out.

"I'll never understand how you make any money diggin' with a shovel like that."

"Takes time."

"Too much, if you ask me."

"Sometimes."

Virgil tilted the bucket down on the tractor and tore through a patch of dirt next to Wyatt, creating a six-foot trench in the soil. Wyatt's own two-foot hole paled in comparison. He tried not to let his anger show in his gaze.

"I should tell you," he started to say, but his words were drowned by the tractor.

"I'm sorry?" Virgil continued to shout before realizing he was the cause of the problem. He snapped to, put the tractor in neutral, and killed the engine. "What was that?"

"…I should tell you, someone came by lookin' for you and your wife. Said his name was Newman Clanton. Said he was a banker."

"Shit."

"He wasn't too happy with y'all, and because I just so happened to be standin' out here when he showed up, he wasn't too happy with me either."

"Did he say why he came out?"

"Money problems."

"Shit."

"Said y'all had some business to tend to, and God as my witness, I told him I would pass the message along and to have a good day," Wyatt explained. "But he wasn't havin' that."

"What does that mean?" Virgil was climbing off the tractor as he asked the question. Fear about what the answer might be washed across his face as the words escaped his lips.

"He swung at me, sir, and I swung back."

"With your fist?"

"Well, yes. That's usually how men go about fightin'."

"You punched our banker? Are you out of your mind? You gotta be screwin' with me."

"I thought you should hear it from me. I did a lot more than punch that man. He had every bit of hurt he took comin', though. One second, he was tellin' me about all the problems he had with you and your wife, the next, he's charging' at me like a son of a bitchin' lunatic."

Virgil was speechless. He stared at Wyatt with a half-cocked smirk of disbelief still painted on. It was like the words had passed through him as another language, like they'd lost all meaning.

"Are you gonna assault or shoot every person who comes onto the ranch? I might as well hang my dang hat up for good. This keeps up, there won't even be a ranch."

"Those other guys had nothin' to do with me. I helped you, remember? I don't know this banker, but he came after me because of somethin' you did. Before you go barkin' orders and demandin' apologies, you might want to think about what I just did for you."

"What you just did for *me*? You did nothin' but make my life a whole lot harder. You're lucky you just got done savin' my life, because if you hadn't—"

"If I hadn't done what I just done, that banker would be kickin' both our asses off this property as we speak. At least now, he's gotta do it the right way."

"I can't believe what I'm hearin'. No wonder you ain't got no home or family of your own. You're batshit crazy, Mr. Earp. If that's actually your name."

Wyatt locked eyes with Virgil, and he stared a hole

right through him. He'd been insulted plenty in his life, but his integrity was something that would not be called into question. There were few things in life a man could stand by. His word and his handshake were among the most unshakable of promises, of truths that could never be tested—he'd spent a lifetime ensuring this was absolute in every way. Listening to Virgil call into question the very core of his morality was something he just couldn't stand by.

He took a step closer and pushed his face into Virgil's. He took a few breaths to try and cool his anger, but the second Virgil looked like he was going to pop off with something else, Wyatt let him have it.

"You listen here, you son of a—"

"Easy, easy, now!" Morgan's voice came from over the hill. "Let's put a stop to this before it's too late."

It took Morgan a couple of awkward seconds to make his way down to where Wyatt and Virgil were still inches away from each other, about to break out into Wyatt's second brawl of the day. It didn't matter that his bones already ached and his knuckles were still covered in someone else's blood. Wyatt was damned determined to never let another man question his word. Blood flowed through his veins and down into his fists, making his fingers tremble with anticipation of what was to come. Adrenaline surged in his chest and swelled in his throat, but he still didn't make a move. He fought the urge to swing, to land a blow to Virgil's orbital cavity and loosen his eyeball enough to make him think twice before spewing such revolting filth to him ever again.

Perhaps it was Morgan quickly approaching or the venom in Wyatt's glare, but Virgil backed down before

Wyatt took it any further. It was for the best. Drenched in sweat and fueled by pent-up rage, ready to unleash at the first glance gone wrong, Wyatt wasn't in the state of mind to do much of anything else.

"Now, why don't you just tell me what this was all about?"

"Are you slow in the head, Morgan? You know what this was about."

Virgil went to climb back on the tractor, then stopped halfway up to the seat, only to turn around and give his two cents. "You keep a tight leash on that hot-headed brother of yours, Morgan. He done went and beat the shit out of our banker, in case you weren't aware. So, dig while you still can, because if I can't talk my way out of this, it's both our asses that'll be gone."

"I told you, brother, that you'd pay for this, one way or another," said Morgan, turning to Wyatt.

"Not yet. He's just pissed off that I did what he couldn't, that's all."

"Maybe so."

"He'll get over it."

"I can still hear you," Virgil shouted over the tractor's roaring diesel engine and hissing hydraulics. "You put our family in harm's way with what you did. I ain't overreacting a single bit, either, before you go runnin' your mouth again."

Wyatt glanced over at Morgan, and even though he didn't say a word, his stare had gone from one inspired by the coming of death itself to the deadpan look of irony. Morgan fought back a laugh before it could escape.

Instead of the tractor returning to endless hauls of potential payloads being dumped in piles throughout the vacant pastures, Virgil maneuvered the old 1050 with more than fifteen hundred hours clocked in a tight circle and revved the engine to return it back where it came from. Wyatt knew he was furious, but the sound of that infernal motor getting prepared to leave him to even the slightest bit of solitude was almost enough to restore his day. The only thing left to do was turn around and get back to work. He gripped the shovel tight and turned his back on the tractor.

In his fit of anger, Virgil went to slam the tractor into gear and instead smacked the PTO. With nothing hooked up, the empty mechanism started spinning, and the engine whirred in response. Virgil started jerking back on another lever and let off the clutch as he turned from side to side in confusion, and when he did, the tractor, still in reverse, crept backward.

With his back turned, Wyatt never saw the tractor rolling in his direction. Morgan had returned to his work just the same, and in their combined negligence, the unthinkable occurred in an instant.

13.6-28 rear tires have a unique way of rolling over just about anything in their path. They are about as tall as a mailbox and made heavier by the sloshing water inside in an effort to maintain stability and traction, both of which were used to run right over both of Wyatt's legs from the ankle down, putting him to the ground in an instant.

The screams that came next could've been heard a town over, but they did not come from Wyatt. He was face down in the dirt, unable to move as the tractor rolled right over the backside of his work boots, pinning him down in the process. Instead, the screams came from Virgil, who had turned around to look where he was going just in time to see the tractor clip Wyatt, sending him collapsing down. What he thought he saw were the bones inside Wyatt's legs being crushed and ground to powder, the blood squeezed out of each leg like a tube to fill the earth's mud. Judging by the pitch of his scream, Virgil thought for sure he'd just killed the man he knew as Wyatt Earp.

When the tractor finally came to a stop, it wasn't a garish sight of blood and bone he found crumpled in the dirt, though. Wyatt popped back up with the same venom-laced look in his eye that he'd given him only minutes before. He was completely unharmed, even unbothered, by what Virgil had just done.

Wyatt didn't say a word. He lifted his shovel high into the air and slammed it down, striking it into the dirt hard enough to hold its own weight. He lifted his fist into the air, and his mustache twitched, then he hollered.

"Do it again, and you're dead. You hear me?"

Virgil went pale. He looked like he'd just seen a ghost. His jaw was slack, and his eyes were hollow. He'd lost all meaning to life and death in that moment, and his brain struggled to return to reality. He just sat there on the idling tractor, unable to force even a whisper out.

"I asked you a question, Virgil!"

"Yes," was all Virgil could let out, softer than a whisper, but his lips parted all the same.

Wyatt turned, grabbed his shovel, dragged it back to a hole a few feet away, and went back to work. The clanking and rattling of the diesel motor soon turned to a gentle hum as it retreated farther and farther into the distance behind him. His muscles burned from digging all morning, but that didn't stop him. He fought off a banker with a chip on his shoulder and was run over by a tractor that'd seen better days, but he didn't have a scratch on his body.

So, he just kept digging, searching for the elusive gold hidden at the Holliday Ranch—a promise of a better life that always managed to stay buried out of sight for those who needed it most.

Chapter 10

There are few problems in the world that cannot be solved by putting your ass in a saddle for a winding trail stretching out through the pristine wilderness of the Lone Star State.

Shod hooves had beaten this path through the Holliday Ranch for generations, each one marking a distinct curve or stretch or detour to accommodate, not disrupt, the natural forces at play. It was a single family that had passed through the dirt path year after year, tracing back all the way to the woman who left behind the infamous gunfighter and gambler extraordinaire known around the world as Doc Holliday. Her name was just Kate, though she had more nicknames than she had fingers and toes, and she was the first to carve a way through the brush and trees and fields to eventually guide the way for Angel to follow in her wake.

She and Virgil had been riding for the better part of two hours as the sun traced its familiar path across the westward sky, finding its resting place behind the sprawling oaks and towering pines. Conversation had been sparse. Both the husband and wife opted instead to listen for the gentle songs echoing from branches overhead and the rhythmic thumping of their horses beneath them. It was the only calm in life they might ever get, and they both understood just how important it was.

Virgil felt horrible for what he was about to say, but it had to be done. He sank down into the saddle a little deeper, gripped the old leather reins a little tighter, and cleared his throat. It was enough to give his wife plenty of pause, and judging by the look in her eye when she glared back at him, she seemed to already know it was bad news coming.

"Gotta talk to you about what Wyatt did this mornin'," Virgil started. "Newman Clanton showed up on our doorstep while we were out, and well, I am not too sure how to say this—"

"Just get it over with," her voice came, as calm and patient as ever.

"Words were exchanged, and ol' Wyatt proceeded to beat the shit out of Mr. Clanton, our banker, right in our front yard."

"My God."

"I already went and talked to him."

"What did he say?"

"Said he was doing us a favor by punchin' our banker in the face."

"No, he didn't."

"Swear on our soon-to-be grave."

"Don't do that."

"Well, I do," Virgil sighed afterward. "He said now if the bank wants to take the ranch from beneath our feet, he's gonna have to do it the right way instead of threatenin' us and makin' our life hell."

Angel didn't say anything this time. She gently prodded her heels into the flank of her horse and urged it to get out a little further ahead so she could think. She'd always been prone to dwelling even over the most mundane of problems in life. Money had become synonymous with trouble, with sleepless nights, with arguments and bitterness and insecurity. It was the thing hanging over her head when she got up every morning, and it was still there when she laid her head down on the pillow to stare at the ceiling each night.

Her husband didn't mean anything by it. She knew his intentions and just how pure they were. Virgil was a man of sincerity, even to a fault. He'd given up everything in his life to give her everything in hers, including his career in the oil and gas industry, where he was on track to make more money than they'd seen in the last half-decade. The Holliday Ranch asked for more than either of them could ever give, but they had tried nonetheless, over and over and over again. It had led them to believe this was the only way forward, and it had led Virgil to believe it was necessary to interrupt the beloved, fleeting moments of peace offered by their trail ride.

"We paid the bank," Virgil dragged the conversation forward. "We paid them in full, we don't owe them nothin'."

"They know we'll be back."

"We don't even know if we'll be back. We have a lot of irons in the fire. Our future ain't always gonna be up to that damn bank."

"We're spendin' more than we're makin'. The math is there, and I promise you they can see it too."

"We have the fall pairs we're taggin' tomorrow

mornin'. We have more we're bringin' down from the east pasture in just two weeks. Then the north pasture in two more weeks. We're rollin' right now."

"This place is feast or famine. You know that more than anyone. When this crop is gone, we won't have enough to make it to the next. That means we're gonna waltz our asses into that bank and tell 'em the same problem that's been plaguing us for years. One day, we won't be able to repay it, and that's when they'll step in."

"Newman seems to have other ideas."

"He's probably thinkin' to himself, why wait? Why not just go ahead and get the inevitable over with."

"It ain't inevitable. Not by a long shot."

Angel finally turned to look back at her husband. She wasn't in a contemplative daze or settling into doubt about their future. She was beaming. Her smile stretched further by the second, and when she saw her husband, she only felt more certain. "No, baby, it sure as shit isn't."

There were no answers or solutions discussed. There weren't any assurances to be had other than the simple fact that had always remained through it all. They always had each other. Tough times had molded them, hardships defined them, and this was no different. Insignificant to most, their marriage was ultimately the only thing that kept them going, and it was the only thing standing in the way of every single person who tried to get their hands on the ranch. As long as it held, so would their livelihood.

"We might have other, more immediate problems, that could need tendin' to," Virgil said.

"What could be worse than the bank trying to take our home, Virgil?"

"You're gonna think I'm crazy. Hell, I think I might be crazy."

"Well, we both know you already are crazy. So, go ahead and spit it out already."

"Somethin' ain't right with Wyatt and his brother, Morgan. Do they ever seem a little off to you?"

"Do the two guys using shovels to dig up our ranch lookin' for gold like their prospectin' California in the 1850s seem off to me? Yes. They seem off."

"I don't mean like that."

"I'm not following. What are you talkin' about?"

"I'm talkin' about the fact that I ran over him with the tractor earlier today, and he didn't even flinch. He just stood up and went back to work like it never even happened. He was more mad at me for even havin' the tractor out there to help than he was about it crushing his legs."

Angel burst out into a laughter that she hadn't felt in longer than she cared to remember. It came from the belly, a guttural explosion of cackles and smiles that did more to brighten her day than a steak dinner when it was all said and done. She laughed for longer than Virgil was comfortable with. When it came to enough of an end for Virgil to speak up again, he didn't waste the opportunity.

"I know what I saw, and there is somethin' weird about them two. That man should be in the hospital right now, but he ain't. He's out there diggin' holes."

"Leave 'em to it. A couple days on the tractor, when they're gone before the next calf crop starts droppin', and we'll be back to normal. I don't usually admit to you having many good ideas, but bringing those two in sure did help get us out of a bind. I'd rather you didn't try to kill them with heavy machinery, though."

"I didn't try to kill him."

"Did you even ask if he was all right?"

"I'll be honest with you, Angel. I got the hell outta Dodge as soon as I could. Pretended like it didn't even happen."

Angel pushed her palm to her face and sighed. "Lord knows I love you, Virgil. But I'll be damned if I don't understand you sometimes."

"Is what it is, darlin'. I just had to tell someone, and you're all I got. That man Wyatt Earp ain't who we think he is."

"I know it's been a hard few months, after a hard few years. And I know I probably haven't been as attentive as I should've been to you. I have been distant, and I know it. All I can do is ask you to hold on just a little longer, because when we get this problem fixed, it'll be fixed for good."

"Where is this comin' from?"

"When all our debts are paid and the collectors have long forgotten our number, when the cowboys we contract to help sort and haul are no longer bein' paid with money we don't have, when we can take rides like this without discussin' the possibility of losing everything we've worked our whole lives for, I know it'll be worth it. We just gotta make it there."

"Oh God. You think I've gone crazy, don't you?"

Angel turned to look at him again. This time there were tears lining her eyes, threatening to fall hard down her cheeks hard enough to break Virgil's heart. He knew they were both already stretched thin, that the breaking point was closer than ever, but this was something he couldn't shove under the rug. As much as it hurt, he stood firm, but that was still his wife, and he couldn't bear to cause more pain than was necessary.

"You're right. There are bigger problems for us to worry about. There is always a coyote in the distance, waiting for us to mess up. We don't have to keep talkin' about Wyatt and Morgan, but I know I'm not crazy. I know what I saw."

Angel chose not to respond. It wasn't out of frustration or annoyance, but of love. There were so few straws to grasp at this point, and she had made a nasty habit out of finding hope even when there had been none. For her husband, she'd do anything, even if that meant not telling him he could be mistaken for a mental hospital patient if he talked to the wrong person.

Virgil welcomed the silence that followed. He said what he needed to say, but he didn't feel any better about it. At this point, he was second-guessing himself. His wife was always the brains of their operation, and he tended to trust her more than himself when it came to matters of stark reality. It didn't really matter what he thought of Wyatt and his brother, because if the bank was coming after their ranch during the day, and the Clanton family was coming after it at night, they had no time to do anything but keep fighting. He knew that was where his attention should be, rather than worrying about something that couldn't even happen anyway, and he was grateful to his wife for keeping him on track.

But he couldn't forget the look on Wyatt's face after he ran him over.

That glare was burned into his brain, and it followed him everywhere he went. He was worried about what he'd brought into the ranch and what they would endure next, but he was terrified to think that it was already too late to stop the dominoes from falling on top of them.

Virgil and Angel kept riding through the woods and across the pastures of the Holliday Ranch. They rode until their thighs threatened to chafe and their arching backs argued with their hearts yearning for just one more hour. The sun was below the trees, and shadows were giving way to night before they decided to finally make their way home.

"You going to sort and brand with us in the mornin'?" Virgil asked, breaking yet another comfortable silence they had basked in for long enough. "Could use all the help we can get."

"When have I ever missed a branding day?"

"Jackson said he had a bunch of greenhands comin' this time, said we should be able to have a few laughs watchin' them get the hang of things."

"We could sure use that."

"I was thinkin' the same thing. I need to put more time in the saddle than starin' at all those bills you got scattered across the kitchen table. Honestly, we both do."

"You're right about that. If Jackson and all his cowboys will be out here in the mornin', we better get the barn ready. They'll be bringin' the pairs in at sunup."

"Bright and early."

They opened the gate for one another as they crossed through pastures and pens, leading back to their home with the barn out in the backyard. Their horses were more than ready to be rid of their saddles and to make their way to the alfalfa waiting for them in each of their stalls. Manure and hay wafted toward them like the welcome of a pie waiting in the windowsill, a comfort known only to those with enough calluses on their hands and years at the reins to appreciate what it really means.

Virgil was the first to slip his horse inside the barn. The Appaloosa gelding's hooves smacked against the worn pavement in four separate points as it slowed its walk down, navigating through the front gate and into its stall. Virgil patted its neck and brushed its hide all over after removing the saddle and the blanket resting beneath. He glanced over to see his wife doing the same thing with her mare, Coach.

"We never did celebrate her twentieth," Virgil said, nodding toward Angel's horse.

"Looks like we owe her one."

"I've got some cubes in the back of my truck. And we could run by the fruit stand down by the highway after brandin' in the mornin', put together a treat for her."

"Well, look at you bein' all thoughtful. Does that mean you're finally ready to name your gelding?"

"Horse is fine. Ain't that right, buddy?" Virgil cooed as he gently patted its neck with one hand and brushed with the other.

"How are the leases doin?"

"We have about a dozen broke four-year-olds, and a couple of three-year-olds that might not give us too much trouble," explained Virgil, finding a professional tone once again as he settled into the work mindset. "Got a handful of yearlings that I wouldn't even get on myself. I wouldn't bother saddlin' them up."

"That gonna be enough?"

"Gonna have to be."

"What happened to the recips?"

"We sold them to pay the down payment on the loan."

"That's right," Angel sighed. "Wish we had a few of those ones."

"Especially those Metallic Cats."

"If the bank would loan on earning potential, we'd have paid off every debt years ago and still had plenty left over."

"Doesn't do any good to wish."

"Well, I guess it's that time." Angel put her brush down and walked out of the stall, closing it behind her and locking the mechanism with a key only she carried.

Virgil exited the stall he kept his gelding in and did the same, locking the gate with a flick of his wrist and tossing the key back into his pocket.

"Everybody else locked up?" Angel asked.

"Made the rounds before we left, we're good to go."

"Don't forget the lights behind you," Angel said as she walked out of the barn, pointing to the switch behind Virgil that he'd already forgotten.

With a quick flip, the barn fell into blackness, interrupted only by the clash of metal gates hitting against one another and the slamming of the locking mechanism to keep it safely shut. Virgil pulled twice on the gates to make sure everything was closed before he turned and ran off toward his wife, who'd already started making her way back to the front porch.

They rattled on, playfully pushing one another before the flirting turned more obvious. As they disappeared into the house, the Holliday Ranch fell to the same harmless blackness that overtook the acreage, livestock, and simple family each night since they first called it home. As Virgil and Angel found comfort in one another, something else was waiting just outside their door to be found when it was already too late. It sat in silent devastation, biding its time until the rising sun would expose what had been done to the family.

VIRGIL WAS the last to wake—he slept hard and struggled to crack his eyelids open. There was an incessant alarm in the distance that could not be quieted, no matter how many times he wildly swung his arm and groaned in annoyance. It played over and over again, echoing in the room until it was impossible to ignore, blaring and sudden and urgent.

"Virgil! Virgil!" The call came again and again.

"I'm gettin' up, I swear."

"Virgil!"

"I'm up. I'm up."

He finally looked around the room to find he was alone. Angel was already gone, but it was her voice still calling to him. It came again.

"Virgil! Virgil! The horses!"

He scrambled to his feet and threw himself out the door before he'd even put a shirt on. The sun had only just started to cast its light across their corner of the earth in Texas, but it was enough to see the deathly panic and fear in his wife's eyes.

"Angel! What's going on?"

"The horses are gone. Everything's gone!" She was screaming at the top of her lungs. "The gate was wide open when I woke up. They're all gone, Virgil. All of them."

"I shut that gate! I know I did."

It was all Virgil could get out, and it was the last thing Angel wanted to hear. It didn't matter that he knew he shut the gate. The only thing that mattered was the fact that it was wide open and every damn horse they had was gone.

"I swear, Angel. That gate was as closed as it's been for the last decade every single night. It was locked up. The whole barn was locked up."

"I know," she said, finally coming face-to-face with her husband. "It wasn't you. Someone was here last night."

"What do you—" Virgil stopped talking when he saw what was in his wife's hands. She was holding a branding iron, half covered in mud and manure, but as brand new as the morning this world had wrought upon them.

"It's the Clantons."

Chapter 11

The sun rose above the tree line covered in blood.

There are days where violence is inevitable, where those who are desperate to inflict pain will do so one way or another. If you are lucky enough to live an entire lifetime without finding yourself on such a day, you are luckier than most could ever hope to be. Humanity tears and claws at itself on these days, impossible to escape, or even make sense of.

As soon as Wyatt opened his eyes and rolled over in his sleeping bag, he knew it was a day where his revolver would do more than hang at his hip. He could feel it down in his bones, even as he pried himself from the ground in search of a sip of coffee. His hands fumbled for the pot. Before the steam from his first cup could reach his face, his morning was interrupted by hysterical screams of a distraught woman.

For a man like himself, there was no easier way to wake up than to be compelled to the pursuit of justice. It boiled inside him, waiting to be released. He sat his cup down without so much as a sip, strapped his belt across his hips, and handled the revolver that was tucked into the leather holster. He thumbed the cylinder, spinning it to see each of the brass rounds perfectly nestled inside. With a drop, it sank back into the holster. Wyatt adjusted the drooping, worn cowboy hat on his head and stamped out the campfire.

He overlooked the Holliday Ranch, covered in goldless holes that so urgently begged for more of his attention, and listened as the woman's screams continued for the better part of five minutes. Angel was going through something, that much he could tell. There was no debate in his head or confusion about what should be done next. With the horse he'd been loaned still stalled in the barn, he took a deep breath and began the long trek in the direction of where the screams had come from.

Wyatt dodged every hole in the pasture and kept his mouth shut even as he closed the distance enough to see Virgil embracing his wife. A lifestyle that depended on the land beneath his feet seemed to always boil down to heartache in one way or another. Every empty hole he shoveled was yet another in his heart, in his dreams, and he could see plain as day that the family who'd given him a chance to earn a fortune was feeling something far too familiar.

His eyes glanced to the side, and he noticed the gate swung wide open on the barn. He still didn't say anything. He went to extend a hand to Virgil, but thought better of it. Instead, he kept his distance and asked the same question anyone would've asked in such a situation.

"What's wrong?"

"Someone broke into the ranch while we drank and argued," said Virgil without making eye contact.

"Do you know who?"

All Wyatt's question brought was a glare born of hellfire itself. Virgil was still holding a sobbing Angel, as the two refused to part even an inch. Wyatt saw his knuckles shaking, and he could feel the burning in Virgil's stomach even from a dozen feet away.

"What did they take?"

"Our livelihood, Wyatt. They took every damn horse we owned, and all the ones we don't own."

"Do you know where they went?"

"I have an idea. We both do."

"It's the fuckin' Clantons!" Angel finally screamed through tears and sweat. "How long are we gonna pretend it ain't those assholes? They took everything from us! They'll be back, too. You hear me? They'll be back."

"We'll be ready next time, darlin'," said Virgil, trying his damndest to reassure his wife despite the doubt and uncertainty filling his belly.

"We ain't waitin' around for all that." Wyatt rested his hand on the revolver tucked at his waist. "I'm gonna get my brother. Virgil, go find yourself a gun."

He didn't wait to hear any backtalk from either Virgil or Angel, he just turned around and walked right back the way he came. It took half an hour to get back to camp, now on the south side of the ranch, as they continued a fruitless endeavor to find gold somewhere, anywhere on the property. Morgan was panning a bucket of worthless mud when Wyatt finally returned. Sweat lined both of their brows for different reasons.

"You hear what happened?"

"Heard the screams," said Morgan without looking up from the pan. "Figured it was somethin' bad."

"It was."

"Seems like there's always somethin' bad happenin' out here. You notice that?"

"I do."

"Let me guess. You went lookin' for whatever trouble was out there, you found said trouble, and now you come back to me lookin' for a hand to deal with it. That about sum it up?"

"Pretty much," said Wyatt with unwavering stringency. "Get your gun."

Morgan let out a sigh that could be heard as loud as Angel's screams. He dropped the pan of dull gray mud and turned to leave, just missing a shimmering glint in the sunlight that would've kept him squatting and hovering in the same spot the rest of the day.

Their return to where Virgil and Angel were still coping with the loss of their horses would see their situation turn from bad to worse, particularly for Wyatt. Horseback was where he wanted to be. It didn't matter if it was a thirty-minute ride or a three-hour ride, he'd choose it damn near every time compared to any other form of transportation. He'd put his time in on the railroad and knew what it was like to travel down the tracks for hours on end. It wasn't something he would ever look forward to doing again. What waited for them in front of the empty barn was far worse.

Virgil didn't even bother to ask him or his brother what they wanted to do next. He just rolled up beside them, tossed open a creaking, rusted steel pickup door until it swung as wide as it could, and hollered two words, "Get in."

The ride inside the old Ford pickup was about as uncomfortable as Wyatt had ever been. It was the same dull, lifeless roar in his ears that the tractor brought, but at speeds he hated, strapped into a belt he couldn't wait to pry himself out of, and forced to endure an awkward closeness with Virgil and his brother that he never would have chosen willingly. They bumped and bounced down the dirt road as the air conditioning struggled to keep up with the Texas heat, and the springs in the seat gave way to potholes large enough to bruise their tailbones. It was a miserable ride filled with miserable conversation. Virgil vented about the Clantons, unleashing the kind of desperate conspiracy that only a man whose entire livelihood was under attack could conjure.

"From the day that man stood on our porch and tried to steal everything we own with a smile on his face, it's all gone to hell," he said, facing the windshield with eyes locked on the road the whole time. "We're gonna put a stop to this whole thing today. We're gonna get our horses, tell the Clantons to keep their filthy fuckin' hands off our property, and never stoop a single foot over our fence again. If I ever see them again, I ain't callin' the cops. I'm dealin' with it myself."

During Virgil's complaining, all Wyatt could think about was how soon he could finally climb out of the forsaken truck and never get in it again. There wasn't a single thing better about riding in a pickup compared to a good horse. He did his best to understand the stress Virgil and his wife were enduring, to keep his thoughts focused on how he could settle this unraveling dispute and get back to work, but the rattling V8 in the hood made him only want to fistfight the first man he came across when they made it to the Clantons on the other side of town. Until then, Wyatt could feel that all-too-familiar burning deep down in his belly. It boiled his blood and made his knuckles turn bright red. It brought sweat to his brow and a grumble in his chest. There was no other way to say it.

Riding in that truck was pissing him off.

There wasn't anything he could do to change his situation, either. He had to sit there and wait until they drove clear across town at seventy miles an hour down every farm-to-market road and back road imaginable. For someone who doesn't have much interest in traveling faster than a steady gallop across an open field—that someone being Wyatt—it was a nightmare in every sense of the word. It would be his brother to offer even the slightest distraction from the misery he'd found himself stewing in.

"We don't need to do anything we might regret. You can't take back what happens when you start shootin'. Ain't that right, Wyatt?"

"You sure can't," he agreed. "For some sorry sacks of shit, it's all they can understand, though. I don't want to be the one who's gotta sort 'em out, but I will."

"No one needs sortin', just a friendly word of warning is all."

"That word don't mean nothin' if it ain't in their language."

Virgil finally cut into the brothers' conversation. "I like the way you think."

"It's just survival," said Wyatt. "But my brother is right. We don't need to go bargin' into some man's home all hot-headed and get out of hand."

"We're here for the horses," said Morgan.

"And a friendly word of warning," Virgil reiterated.

They finally came to a driveway lined with aged

and storied oaks gently leaning over to shade their approach to the family home. Wyatt saw nothing but time and money and resources wasted on maintaining anything that might point toward the family's true nature. It was a plantation-style home, one built long before the Clantons ever purchased the deed in their name. Wyatt remembered Virgil mentioning something about the guy who owned the place previously and decided it was better to know more about what happened than go in blind.

"You said it was Johnny's old place a while back. Why did they lose it?"

"It was," Virgil answered as they slowed the pickup down to a crawl. "Johnny Franklin owned that place as long as I knew him. Inherited it after his daddy died, who got it from his daddy, one of those situations."

"It sold recently?"

"About a week after Johnny went in the ground."

"Sounds like they don't mind playing the long game."

"They got another thing comin'."

The pickup rolled to a stop ahead of what seemed to be a dozen men, each one perched on the front porch as if they'd been told to wait on Virgil, Wyatt, and Morgan's arrival. They looked bored. They sat still, even as both the driver and passenger side pickup doors swung open. Most were in denim and worn flannel or t-shirts, were unkempt and looked like they hadn't bathed in days. Every one of them watched intently as the three trespassers exited the pickup and lined up in front of the house.

It wasn't the dozen men bigger than him waiting on the front porch, or the threat of what might come out of the front door that worried Wyatt most about their increasingly precarious position. It wasn't even the gunpowder and lead waiting to be unleashed where they stood. It was the sinking feeling that he'd just stumbled onto the same old stubborn injustice that only he could root out.

Morgan could see the realization wash over his brother's face, and he knew immediately, there would be no gold unearthed at the Holliday Ranch until this came to an end. Forcible or not, justice would find its way to the Clantons and their men. It was determined right then and there, the fires of consequence would lick at the boots of any man who stands in the way of the man who introduced himself as Wyatt Earp.

Humidity and a stifled breeze gave way to sweaty palms and darting eyes as silence overtook the front yard of the Clanton home. It stayed like this for an awkward few minutes before the silhouette of a gangly man pushed the screen door forward and stepped out onto the front porch.

The first thing Wyatt noticed was how the handful of men waiting around quickly perked up. It didn't take long to piece together the fact that their boss had just come back into view, and they were all meant to at the very least appear to be at attention. Everything changed from the very moment the man named Joe Clanton protruded from the house with a look in his eye that could make every person under his employment drop dead. His lip curled, his eyebrows squinted, his hands scrunched into fists, and his chest heaved. It was as if the sight of Wyatt, Morgan, and Virgil standing in front of the home was enough to make him lose his temper, but the words that came out of his mouth were the farthest thing from such.

"Neighbors! What a pleasant surprise this is," he exclaimed. "What can I do for you on this fine day?"

There were no competing opinions on how the situation should be handled by the three men standing in front of Joe. No one sought to offer the benefit of the doubt or approach the matter with a more delicate sensibility. Virgil may have been the one to respond, but for the first time since the three had met, they were lockstep in their fury.

"Give me back my horses," said Virgil. "Every single one of them."

"Whoa, whoa now, wait a minute. Surely you didn't drive all the way here, pull into my own front yard, refuse to say so much as hello, only to accuse me of horse theft. That is a serious accusation."

"I know they're here. I want them back," said Virgil.

"Did you know they used to hang men for stealing horses? It's true."

It was Wyatt's turn to speak this time. "You've done nothin' but run from consequence your whole life. I doubt you'd know what was worth hangin' over, because you'd never stick around long enough to see it through."

"Not many men were killed over horse theft," Morgan chimed in. "Plenty went to jail for it, though. Plenty more carried a brand around the rest of their lives, too. Just so the other ranchers knew who they were dealin' with."

"Since we drove all the way out here and couldn't even afford you a good day, as you said, maybe you could at least let us know who we're dealin' with here," said Wyatt. "I don't see a brand."

"Word to the wise, you should stop while you're ahead, farmhands," Joe shot back. "Because what happened might have been your fault after all."

"What does that mean?" Virgil asked.

"It means, my extremely trustworthy men, whom I have known for the better part of a decade, just so happened to be traveling here just in the nick of time to catch sight of more horses than they'd ever seen walking down the side of the highway. They were loose, and there wasn't anyone around to watch them. I didn't know who to call, so I did the neighborly thing, and I rounded them up myself, hauled them back here, and waited for their owners to show up. Looks like our waitin' is all done, boys."

A dull, uniform chuckle erupted from the men waiting on the porch. Their smirks faded as fast as they'd formed, leaving Virgil just about ready to throw a haymaker at every single one of them.

"It would seem as though someone down at the Holliday Ranch left a gate open!" said Joe, eliciting more, if not sparing, laughter from the men at his pay.

"That ain't somethin' we do. We've been at this long enough, there ain't a gate open down at the ranch. But they will open mighty easily *if* someone has the intention of doin' so," said Virgil, taking a step toward Joe as he spoke. "Now, I'm only gonna ask this question one time, so think real hard about your answer, you hear me?"

"Crystal clear, sir."

"Did you step foot on my property without my permission?"

"Only once, being completely honest, and you were there to witness my trespassing. It was when I made the awful mistake of introducing myself and offering a welcome into the Clanton farming family. I can see now that would not have gone well at all, but I have not put a single toe on the Holliday Ranch since then, and neither has any man on my payroll. Hand to the Almighty above."

Virgil took the last step he could, bringing himself inches away from the face of the man named Joe Clanton. Cigarette smoke lingered in his breath, and he looked like he could've used a shave last week, and in his eyes was the deadly intent Virgil himself carried, staring right back at him. For a fleeting second, one that Virgil would've taken back if given the chance, he imagined the scenario that would unfold if he'd been armed. He'd draw on Joe first, in an attempt to cut off the head of the snake. The men behind him would do the same, though. He'd have to hope Wyatt and Morgan were who they claimed to be. There was more doubt in him than he cared to admit regarding their ability to gun down a dozen men before one was lucky enough to put a bullet through his own heart. Even so, crazier things had happened. As the chaos that could've been played out in his head, he watched Joe's glare twist into a warning before the man took a step back and lifted his hands.

"Both hands to the Almighty above, if it helps," he said and raised them even higher. "We are but good neighbors, doing the neighborly thing, and we are more than welcome to help haul those glorious equines back to where they belong. All you need to do is ask."

"We'll be back with a trailer," said Virgil. "I don't want to see you around the Holliday Ranch, and I ain't ever gonna tell you again."

Joe extended a hand, reaching out as if he was grasping an olive branch that never existed, ready to place it in the palm of Virgil himself in exchange for everything he and his wife had ever worked for. Joe's hand landed on Virgil's shoulder, followed by a coy smile and a halfhearted sentence that would echo in Virgil's head long after he would leave.

"Maybe one day, we can all sit back and drink some sweet tea and have a good ol' laugh about all this."

Wyatt spat on the ground right in front of Joe before the sentence could be completed.

Before anyone else could react, the dozen men behind their boss rose in unison with pistols in their hands and death in their hearts, and they were willing to wield both without end. Joe tried to raise his hand in time to quieten them, to encourage them to stand down, but one was more eager than the rest. A two-hundred-fifty-pound bearded man with a potbelly let his trigger finger slip.

Bam.

A bullet went right through Wyatt's foot, slamming into the dirt beneath his boot, sending the earth itself flying up into an impenetrable plume. To everyone's surprise, Wyatt didn't even flinch. He just stood there, staring at Joe with a glare that no man could match.

"Do it again and I'll kill you myself right here and now, Billy," shouted Joe without turning to face the gunman. "You'll have to excuse my overzealous compatriot, there." Joe leaned in to examine the hole in Wyatt's boot and decided to speak again when he saw no blood coming from the wound and no pain in the stoic man's face. "No harm, no foul, right? If you'll be on your way, I'll prep the horses for their return home. We can leave it at that."

"You and I can," said Virgil as he started to walk back to the pickup that brought them to the conflict. "But I sure as shit can't speak for Wyatt."

Chapter 12

It was a bruised dusk skyline that hovered over the Holliday Ranch upon Virgil's return home.

He found himself standing in the kitchen window, calloused hands gripping the sink almost harder, enough to leave indents on the stainless steel. He looked out over the pasture to the west of their home, taking in the torn-up pastures dotted with empty holes where no gold had been found. Sitting at the bottom of the sink—next to two empty plates and a couple of forks with traces of last night's pot roast still stuck to their ends—was the brand they found half buried in their barn, the brand in the shape of the same Clanton Family Farms, Inc. logo he'd noticed earlier that day.

His stomach twisted every time he thought of the lies Joe spewed right to his face. He held all the cards, and the proof of their thievery was right in front of him, but he was still too cautious to overplay his hand. It was a slippery slope, one that could lead to a war between the two families, but he was increasingly coming to the unfortunate understanding that such a fight was inevitable. The song of the cicadas rang through every room of their home, providing a chaotic backdrop that matched the thoughts racing through Virgil's head.

"Are you going to tell me what they said?" His wife's voice pierced the silence like a ghost in the night. "Why were our horses there, Virgil? What is goin' on?"

He wanted to answer her, he really did. No words came to mind, though, only more buzzing of frantic worries, scurrying from one improbable end to another. Their life was on the line, their children's entire inheritance, their way of life. It was all at stake, and the walls were closing in more and more. The Holliday Ranch was teetering on ruin. The bank was nipping at their heels, the Clantons were circling overhead like starved vultures, and even worse, the men digging up their land were starting to scare him down to his core. Nothing was going right.

He felt the hands of his wife slide gently around his hips and interlock over his belly, then he felt her rest her head on his back. Suddenly, all the stresses weighing on him, the buzzing in his head, all came to a halt. Angel had always been his piece of mind, his moral compass, his entire sense of sanity, and she never faltered in that role. He sighed and finally found the words to answer her.

"They shot Wyatt out there."

"They what?"

"One of Joe Clanton's men took a potshot off the front porch, damn bullet went right through his left boot."

"Oh my God. Is he all right? Do we need to take him to the hospital?"

"No, Angel. He didn't even notice it. He was just standing there."

"Oh," Angel said, allowing her voice to trail off for just a moment. "Maybe it missed? Maybe you missed something."

Virgil finally turned to look at his wife, showing the tears staining his cheeks and flooding his eyes.

"It's gonna be okay, honey." She immediately hugged him. "We can't get distracted right now, though. There is too much evil at our doorstep, too many forces trying to rip away everything we've worked so hard for. We need to stay focused on the Clantons."

"You're right," he said, pulling his face off of her shoulder no more than two seconds after he had just laid it down.

"The Clantons are real. Their threats are real. We need to deal with them before it's too late."

"We can't fight them without any money, Angel. We've already spent the advance Wyatt gave us to mine the ranch. Until this next batch of calves drops, we can barely eat dinner every night."

"It's just another problem to figure out. It ain't like we've never done it before."

Virgil turned again and grabbed the branding iron from the kitchen sink. "It's like we're under siege. The nitrate poison we found on those rustlers, the bank trying to take what isn't theirs, and now this," he held up the branding iron between them as he spoke. "They aren't trying to send a message anymore, they are comin' after this place with everything they got. And you know what we have on our side? Not a damn thing."

"We aren't going to break, no matter what. We can do this, just like we've always done it—together."

Virgil looked into her eyes and fell in love all over again. It must've been the thousandth time he'd felt this way over her, and no matter what happened in their life, a simple look could solve all his problems and put him at ease. But the swelling he felt in his heart wouldn't solve all the issues they were facing.

"Do you have any ideas?" he asked, hoping against hope that his wife had a plan alongside her calming presence.

"I met a family a while back. City folks, lookin' to come out and get away from the rat race. They seemed like real nice people. They had a couple of kids and a dog, told me they were stayin' in an apartment until they could find somethin' worth buyin'."

"Are you talkin' about selling?"

"Just a small patch, something just big enough to homestead a family on. That will give us all the money we need to take the fight to Clanton's front yard, and get them out of ours. They want the farm life, the open air, a place for their kids to grow up outside of the pressures of a world that don't care about them. We could do some good while savin' our own asses."

"There's no goin' back once we sell a piece of who we are, Angel. We've talked about it until we were blue in the face. It's a permanent decision to—"

"Temporary problem, I know. I'm just sayin' it's an option."

"Remember when we first brought the kids out to the ranch?" Virgil asked, relishing even a single moment outside of the stress they'd found themselves in. His thoughts finally drifted to a better time, one where he thought the ranch was teeming with unlimited potential, where the future was as bright as the stars that hung over the Texas night sky, and where his kids could grow up to become anything they wanted. Then he smiled. "Nat and Nellie pretty much hated everything about it."

"I think they still might," said Angel with a smirk curling on either end of her lips.

"I was right there with them, too. It took a while for this place to grow on me. I didn't understand what you saw in this patch of dirt. Then I watched the kids play in the dirt, work cattle, and learn to take care of themselves, and now I'd just about lay down my own life to keep it in the family." Virgil's chest tightened, his breathing became more shallow, his eyes fell to the floor, and he struggled to get his next sentence out without choking up. "To sell even a single acre of this place feels like I'm cuttin' off one of my own fingers."

"Listen to me. The Clantons are betting that we'd rather die than give up a piece of the ranch, much less the whole thing. They won't expect us to sell a corner lot. It won't be enough to hurt us, but it'll be enough to get the bank off our backs and fight back against the Clantons. It could be enough to save our skins."

"It's a slippery slope, Angel. Giving up even an inch could mean we lose it all."

"If we don't, we could lose it all anyway. I'm all ears if you got any better ideas. But at least this way we could keep the heart of Holliday Ranch, and it'll only cost us a few acres. We can make it work. We have to."

She placed her trembling hand on Virgil's chest and immediately felt the thumping of his heart against her palm. He was struggling, and her solution didn't put him at ease, but they didn't have many options. They could only play the cards they were dealt.

"What about Wyatt and Morgan? What are we supposed to do with them?"

They both turned to watch out of the kitchen window, noticing two ghoulish silhouettes treading across the pasture, one carrying a shovel tossed haphazardly over his shoulder and the other carrying a bucket heavy enough to force him to hold his other arm out for balance. They drifted further into the fading light of the horizon, their hunkered forms of the two brothers slowly becoming more and more indistinguishable.

"They are gonna be the ace up our sleeve."

Virgil's eyes widened, and a criminal laugh escaped his chest before he could hold it in. The thought was so bewildering, he couldn't help but find the humor in his wife's suggestion. She didn't bother to question what was truly happening with the two men they'd granted rights to dig up their land, and she didn't care what Wyatt and Morgan really were. The only thing she was concerned with was the Holliday Ranch. Anyone who'd fight alongside her wasn't to be questioned, only utilized.

"Think about how they've fought for us already. They chased those rustlers away and even killed to protect this place. I know you are scared of starting some kind of war with the Clantons over this place, but I'm tellin' you, it's already here. The fight is at our doorstep, and we need all the help we can get."

"We don't know if we can trust them."

"Right now, they're on our side. Let's keep it that way."

Virgil's thoughts drifted back to the day both Joe and Wyatt were standing on their front porch, ready to make an offer and plead their case. Wyatt was a man who seemed rigid in his principles, offered a firm handshake and a promising pitch about gold and opportunity and a brighter future. But after the incident with the tractor, after watching Wyatt take a bullet without moving a muscle, he didn't know what to believe anymore. There were too many problems bearing down on them, but he couldn't allow himself to become lost in superstition or fall victim to things that weren't even real. He had to stay focused on more pressing issues.

A low, guttural creak on the front porch distracted his already drifting thoughts and forced both him and his wife into action. He went for the revolver resting on the counter, a gun he'd never kept so close to his side in his entire life. Angel bolted for the door, revealing a double-barreled shotgun tucked behind the crevice. They weren't sure if it was a gate opening or someone climbing the steps to their home, but both of them were too on edge to allow it to go unnoticed. They lifted their firearms as one, aiming at the front door in a slow approach to find out what was going on. They didn't exchange a word or even a glance. Virgil simply twisted the aged doorknob and swung the front door open, following immediately with the barrel of the revolver.

The porch was empty.

They were living in fear, anxious and uncertain. Not even a creak in the night could be ignored at this point. The air outside was different, though. It was heavy, charged with an unsettling feeling that made the hair on their necks stand upright.

"Wyatt?" Virgil called out, his voice consumed by the encroaching darkness. "Morgan?"

No one answered. A breeze picked up in the

distance, and the pines shook in response, their needles waving and rustling in the dimming light. The cattle, still making their way to the trees for the night, called out into nothingness.

"The wind?" Angel whispered.

"Or Clanton's men still sneaking around like the snakes they are. I don't trust it."

Last time, they had no idea the Clantons were on their property stealing their horses. He thought of the brand again. They'd left it intentionally, knowing what would come of it. They wanted a war, and the way Virgil was feeling right now, gripping the revolver even tighter between his fingers, he was becoming more and more ready to give it to them.

He stepped out onto the front step, leaving his wife Angel standing in the doorway, still pressing the shotgun to her shoulder like she'd been taught. For a moment, he thought he'd just overreacted. He let out a sigh that alleviated only a small portion of the stress that had built up in his neck. When his eyes fell to the deteriorating floorboards on the porch, any bit of relief he felt dissipated, giving way to alarming panic that made his blood boil.

There was the brand again, burned black into the boards, mocking him and his wife.

"They were here again," he said, using the end of his revolver to point to the brand seared into their home. "This is a threat."

Angel was staring at the same contorted letter *C* that was formed at the end of the branding iron still inside the kitchen. The Clanton family brand was staring right back at her. It was a confirmation of everything they'd just talked about, like a wax stamp on an envelope, sealing their fate inside the home they were willing to give their lives up for.

"They think they can mark their territory, scare us into abandoning this place," Angel spoke with a tremble, finding its way into her voice. "I know that's what they're up to."

"They got another thing comin'," her husband answered. "Tomorrow, we're gonna meet that family, secure the money we need to fight back, and then we're gonna make sure this never happens again."

Chapter 13

The Holliday Ranch was changed the next morning.

The sun's rays cut through a foggy haze with towering pines casting long shadows over the pastures riddled with prospect holes, so far yielding only more disappointment. Shovels bit into the earth's surface in rhythmic tandem. Wyatt and Morgan focused on the work at hand. Sweat dripped down their noses and into their eyes, and the texture of their hands matched the wooden handles of their tools. The air filling their lungs was humid, laden with dust. They had lost count of their fruitless digs and knew only to keep digging, to keep searching for what had to be buried just out of sight, and finally claim what they knew was waiting for them.

It was only Wyatt who knew something else waited for them, though. It wasn't a carefree fortune waiting in his future, it was unadulterated justice, delivered by his own hands, biding its time on the horizon each time he gazed up from a hole in the ground. It called to him, louder than it ever did before. He felt its urgency. He leaned on his shovel and allowed his eyes to look up again, and this time they followed Virgil and Angel's battered old pickup as its tires sent rooster tails of dirt clouding their air behind them. They turned left at the county road, headed toward town. Whether it was the unusual speed or the feeling in his gut that pulled at him the most, Wyatt couldn't shake the uneasiness that worked its way up to his chest.

Morgan didn't pay it any attention. His shovel sliced the dirt with ease as he worked in a nonstop fluid motion, trying his best to hide the desperation beginning to creep into everything he did. His shirt was soaked in sweat already, and his muscles ached with every shovelful of dirt he tossed aside. Mechanical movements overtook him. In the midst of his own tunnel vision, he failed to notice the shift in his brother.

The clunk of a shovel hitting the dirt snapped him out of it. Wyatt dropped his spade when the truck in the distance had turned to nothing but an unrecognizable speck. It smacked against the ground with a dull thud, followed only by heavy boots hitting the dirt as Wyatt began making his way toward the barn.

"Where you goin'?" Morgan called out.

His brother didn't answer. He just kept walking, each step carrying him a little further away from the work that had to be done.

"You need some help?" Morgan called out a little louder this time.

Wyatt still didn't answer.

Morgan let out a sigh and dropped his own shovel, then started walking after his suddenly mute brother. "You could at least tell me what's goin' on, you know. If we have to fight someone else, I'd rather know what I'm gettin' into first."

Without a conversation to be had, Wyatt and Morgan made their way to the barn, freshly restocked with the horses that had been stolen from them only a couple of nights ago. They each saddled a half-broke colt and made it out of the barn in what felt like seconds. They trotted down the driveway and broke out in a full gallop once they hit the county road. In less than two minutes, they saw Virgil and Angel's truck in the ditch, surrounded by yaupons with gnarled hickory trees hanging overhead.

Both the husband and wife were still inside the pickup, but they were not alone. They'd left their own trails of destruction in the past, and they could recognize a stickup when it was happening in front of their face.

Wyatt knew to trust the burning in his gut. He heeled the chestnut colt to push forward even harder and gripped the reins a little tighter. His hand reached for the revolver at his hip, and he withdrew it with a slow, steady precision. He slowed the horse to a trot.

Two figures were standing in front of the pickup. Wyatt could make out only a masked silhouette, but their outstretched hand grasping a firearm was all he needed to see to know something had gone terribly wrong. He didn't wait to ask who they were, or what their name was, or what they were doing to Virgil and Angel. He simply put the front sight of his revolver at the center mass of the guy aiming his gun at the driver's side of the truck and squeezed the trigger.

The first man could not be identified. He had a cap pulled down over his eyes and a bandanna wrapped around his face. The second looked just the same, but with a hood pulled up over his head. Their masks were blank faces, white and empty, without any eyes or defining features. It was like Wyatt was shooting at a ghost.

When the first bullet struck the man's shoulder, all hell broke loose. Morgan followed up with a series of blasts at the hooded man but missed all of them. They scattered.

Virgil and Angel ducked into the seat of the truck, trying their best to get out of the line of fire as bullets started to pop off in every direction.

Wyatt dismounted and shoved his horse back the way they came. He didn't run. He put one foot in front of the other with the business end of his revolver spewing flames and gunpowder and lead.

Bam. Bam. Bam.

A bullet whizzed by his head, whistling and humming loud enough to ring in his head before the bullet lodged into a tree, sending splinters flying in every direction. He didn't duck. He just kept walking. Only two bullets left. Both of the hijackers had made themselves scarce, hoping to find cover and safety behind the hickory and oak trees just beside the ditch where the truck had landed. Each one exposed only a single hand holding a pistol, firing off at random and only coming close to striking their targets with pure, blind luck.

Wyatt and Morgan needed no such thing. This wasn't their first firefight. They split up at once, moving with care to flank the gunmen without saying a word to each other. Wyatt sent two more bullets to pound into the tree where the first man was still hidden. Chips of tree bark and wood split and fell to the ground, surrounded by a powdery blast. The bullets continued to pop off as Wyatt flicked his wrist to send the cylinder falling to the side and the empty brass casing tumbling to the ground. As they clicked and bounced off the pavement, Wyatt gently inserted five more bullets into the cylinder. With another flick of his wrist, he reached out once again and grit his teeth.

This time, he held his fire.

"Y'all wanna talk about this?" Morgan shouted as he crossed the ditch just behind the truck. "We could swap words instead of bullets, it'll hurt a heck of a lot less."

Bam.

The hooded man fired off a round that went into the air, far from endangering anyone in the area.

"Bullets it is!" Morgan cried out as he let the last three rounds in his own revolver loose at the tree where the man hid from sight.

"Wait!" Wyatt finally hollered. He was trying to see if Virgil and Angel had been hurt. Two silhouettes were hunkered down in the truck, refusing to lift their heads out of fear of the bullets flying back and forth all around them. Wyatt realized what was happening when it was already too late, though.

Bam. Bam. Bam. Bam.

The shots went off like firecrackers from inside the pickup. It wasn't Virgil and Angel hiding to save their lives inside the truck, it was two more gunmen, hiding until the time was right to strike.

Wyatt didn't hesitate. He fanned the hammer of his old, trusted revolver at his hip and sprayed lead through the window and door panel until the trigger no longer blasted out, and what was left of the men inside painted the cabin crimson. The silence that followed was broken only by the dying groans of the would-be killers inside.

Wyatt was still standing. His vision slowed, his thoughts came to a stop, and he acted on instinct alone. Each new two-hundred-thirty-grain bullet dropped like an anchor inside the .45 Schofield. Even the handle was screaming hot, but he didn't lose his grip. He simply turned his attention to the gunmen still hiding behind the trees, and hoped with everything he had that Virgil and Angel hadn't been gunned down by them just yet.

"Ain't them, Morgan!" he shouted to his brother and wagged the end of the revolver toward the line of trees obscuring the remaining gunmen.

His brother fired again at the tree in frustration. "No shit!"

Silence hung over them for the next few seconds as each man debated their own fate. All the while, Wyatt never stopped pushing ahead. The closer he eased forward, the more he could hear whispers from the other side of the treeline. They were faint at first, but if he stepped quiet enough, he could just barely make out what they were plotting. Their voices were muffled, but laced with frantic violence.

"Clantons won't stand for no deal with anyone but them."

"You can sell."

"But only to Joe."

"Now hand over them keys, lady. Or the only thing you're gonna do is bleed out."

Wyatt was only a few feet away. The gunmen couldn't see through the yaupon and greenbrier swarming the treeline, but he could see them. He could see the sweat on Virgil's brow, and the way Angel's fingers twitch nervously, aching for a fight she knew she couldn't take on alone. In the blink of an eye, he stepped around the trees and lifted his revolver, waiting for the firefight to pick up as soon as they caught sight of him, but they hesitated.

"Drop 'em," he called out to them. "Now."

Each one more reserved than the other, they reached their arms out, holding the gun in their fingers as if they were going to drop them to the ground and surrender. One held Virgil by the collar, who knelt at once, urging his wife to follow his lead. The other gunman relinquished his grip on Angel as she complied and fell face-first into the dirt.

"Don't do it!" Morgan's untimely demand—one he hollered out of fear for the two being held at their mercy—broke any notion of surrender.

The hooded man spun, startled by the sudden appearance of Morgan at their back, his weapon swinging to meet him first. The first gunman in the cap managed to fire off a bullet first, though. The next few seconds played out in a blur that only Wyatt could stay ahead of.

The gunman's wild shot slammed into the dirt at Wyatt's feet, kicking up a cloud of dust that shielded the coming bloodshed from sight. Wyatt met his speed with more accuracy, firing off two more rounds that tore through the masked gunman's shoulder.

His scream told Wyatt he'd done damage, but before he could move onto the second one, charging his brother with guns blazing, the first gunman lunged forward with a gut-wrenching scream. He was met with a strike to the nasal bone from the steel handle of Wyatt's revolver, spraying blood into his eyes as he fell face-first into the dirt. Before he could scramble to his feet in fury, Wyatt extended out his hand and fired a single bullet, holding a gaze as cold as hell frozen over just long enough to watch the man die.

The second gunman did his best to capitalize on the distraction his dying buddy present. Even though the unraveling situation was quickly leaning out of his favor, he doubled down his efforts and lowered his head as if to tackle Morgan. Maybe it was something that'd worked for him once before, or maybe he just saw someone else do it one time and thought he could pull it off, but unfortunately for that second gunman, he wasn't faster than a bullet. In a split second, Morgan fired off one more round into the top of the skull of the man blindly charging him. The sound of his corpse colliding with the earth was the last he'd ever produce.

"That could've went worse," Morgan said, shoving the holster in his rifle as he tried to step over the man whose life he'd just taken.

"That went about as bad as it could've," Virgil commented, picking his wife up off the ground and brushing her off. "The Clantons just tried to murder us."

"This is going too far," his wife said, as she finally made it back to her feet. "These assholes have to be stopped before we're all killed."

Wyatt took a step closer, examining both Virgil and Angel before choosing to speak.

"Y'all all right?" he asked, holstering his revolver while a calm expression washed over his face.

"Thanks to you, we are," said Virgil. "How many times have I said that now?"

"One too many."

"Ain't that the truth."

Angel's gaze drifted to the two dead men lying in

front of her, then over to their pickup, now riddled with bullet holes. She flicked her wrist in a halfhearted, exhausted gesture to the bodies. "How'd you know we were in trouble?"

"Had a feelin'."

"Good thing you acted on it."

Before they could let out any more words, a rustle in the brush behind them made Wyatt's hand twitch toward the revolver now slung at his hip. A fifth gunman, younger than the rest, but a Clanton nonetheless, showed his face at last and spewed one final threat before producing a polymer throwaway pistol in his white-knuckled, trembling grip.

"You're dead, Mr. Earp!"

Bam.

The bullet slammed into Wyatt's shoulder, muffled only a little by the clothes he wore. Wyatt didn't flinch or stagger backward, he just stood there, eyes locked on the young man hiding in the bushes. The final Clanton man's jaw dropped to the dirt, followed soon after by the gun he had just failed to kill Wyatt with.

"Run," Wyatt warned with a low rumble, then took a step forward.

The young Clanton man heeded the warning, scrambling to his feet, unable to coordinate his body to flee as quickly as his mind had chosen to do so. He bolted, clashing through the trees and thorns, leaving the bodies of his own men behind right where they lay. Wyatt, Morgan, Virgil, and Angel watched in silence as he made his escape.

"We should follow suit," said Morgan. "There could be more."

"That one might've been too scared, but Clanton's

men will be here to collect their dead before the law does. Best to be on our way before that happens."

"Maybe we should just wait for the law to show up," Virgil admitted, letting the words out as if he'd been holding his breath all day. "Maybe we're in too deep."

"They can't help us." Angel took her husband's hands in hers. "They may clean up this mess, they may give us empty promises about putting wrongdoers behind bars, but this will keep happening. One day, we won't be so lucky, and then it won't matter what the law finally decides to do, because we'll be dead."

"We aren't killers, Angel. We're ranchers. Look at what's happenin' to us. I'm scared. I can't lose you. Not even the ranch is worth that."

"You won't lose me."

Virgil took a step toward her and whispered, "You saw him get shot. Right in front of us. He's not even bleeding. We're in over our heads, Angel. I'm tellin' you."

His wife locked eyes with his, but she didn't say anything.

"Now's not the time for this." She leaned in close. "We gotta get out of here. There will be a time, though. I promise. Right now, we need to get back in that truck and make it to town. There's a deal that has to be made."

"You're right," Virgil said.

The husband and wife turned to Wyatt and Morgan and thanked them both again for saving them, then urged them to return back to the ranch and wait until they could make it back later that evening.

Wyatt watched as Virgil threw the driver's side door open, allowing sunlight to pierce each bullet hole he'd blasted into the pickup, then slide in behind the steering wheel. Angel climbed in beside him and rested her palm on his leg. The engine roared to life, unharmed by the gunfight that had just played out. It was only dust and promises he was left with by the time they were gone again.

The two brothers gathered their empty brass casings and trekked down the two saddled horses that had carried them into the fight. Their return was solemn. They had formed an unspoken bond in their many confrontations together. They'd faced down a dozen drunks and twice as many gunmen in their days. For reasons neither could explain, they could never bring themselves to stand down from a fight where justice was on the line.

Morgan rode up to Wyatt's side, his horse lathered from the hard ride that got them there. He took in what had just happened, acknowledging the men still lying face down in the dirt. It was only a sigh that he could offer them before turning to his brother. He nodded at Wyatt, turning his attention to the hole in his shoulder.

"You good?"

"Always am," said Wyatt.

Wyatt's mind churned, no different than his stomach, the entire ride back to the Holliday Ranch. He didn't dwell on the firefight they'd just endured, but instead the fight that was still to come. He knew Virgil and Angel were fighting for their ranch, their way of life, and he and Morgan had become too close to that fight, drawn to it like a moth to a flame, just like they had to every other injustice in need of their bullets. Sometimes he didn't understand why they still drifted in search of dreams that had never been fulfilled, or why they couldn't bring themselves to rest, no matter how much money they had. Right now, he could only think about one thing. He could not stand by while the Clantons continued their onslaught. They would feel the cruel hand of justice one way or another, he was sure of it.

The sun climbed in the sky as the road stretched on and on, burning away any desire to continue digging for gold by the time they'd returned. There was something redeeming about the owners of the Holliday Ranch, something that had forced him to reckon with his own past. Virgil's grit and stark understanding of a world they couldn't control reminded him of himself long ago. Angel's fire, burning deep in her belly, her refusal to break, reminded him of a woman he'd known from another lifetime. She was the kind of woman who could hold the world in her hands and give it to the one she loved, if only in exchange for a fair shot at enjoying it together. They had found their way into his good graces, and the attacks they were trying so hard to defend against were taking their toll. They were good people. They were worth fighting for.

"You heard what Virgil said, didn't you?" Morgan finally broke their silence.

"I did."

"You think they know?"

"I do."

"Why haven't they said anything yet?"

"Complicates things," said Wyatt.

"Hell, it's already complicated."

Wyatt didn't reply. He glanced down and noticed the hole in the frayed fabric over his shoulder, then he saw three more gunpowder-stained holes dotted around his torso. He'd need new clothes, that much was certain. His eyes darted to his brother, and he realized Morgan would, too. There were several bullet holes lining his ribs and chest. Neither mentioned anything.

The truth was a weight only he carried, it wasn't meant to be shared, at least not fully. Echoes of the past resided in his traipse through this life, binding him to a world without purpose. Good men would always face bad odds, that much he'd learned not long after he fired his first bullet. But after so many years, nothing had changed. The deal those two were chasing must've felt like their only lifeline in a world that no longer cared whether their way of life was dead or not. Wyatt felt the pull again. That same instinct that had driven him to the gunfight, was now forcing him to see this through to the end.

His eyes finally met his brother's. Morgan gave a slight shake, urging him not to speak out loud. He obliged, heeling his horse a little harder to pick up the speed to the old family barn once again. It didn't matter if Virgil and Angel had seen what happened to them, they weren't in a position to refuse any help that might put a stop to the Clantons before it was too late, and he wasn't in a position to allow injustice to go unnoticed beneath his very nose. Not while he could still wrap his hands around its neck and wring it so hard it may never see the light of day again.

From what Wyatt could see, Virgil and Angel were up against as bad odds as he'd ever seen, and if he hadn't been able to find purpose up until this point, it had now become impossible to ignore.

The Clantons were gonna pay for what they've done.

Chapter 14

The same dust that had swirled around Virgil and Angel's bullet-riddled truck clung to Wyatt's boots as he stomped around their makeshift campsite.

The Holliday Ranch had returned to its most normal state the following day, baking beneath the midday sun, taunting every move Wyatt and Morgan made with empty holes pockmarked in every direction. Wyatt's clothes were covered in gunpowder-stained holes, but he felt fine. The bullets that passed through him were nothing but a memory, leaving him unscathed, but pissed off. He wasn't the type to dwell. He prided himself on mental fortitude, the ability to stay focused on what was to come, and in this case, there was nothing to do but fight. It was all he could think about. He didn't sleep. He couldn't eat. Sometimes the only thing you could do with your problems in this world was face them head-on, and that's exactly what Wyatt intended to do.

It was a fight that had been brewing long enough. They'd stood back longer than they should have, refusing to enter a fight they helped to start. The Clantons had set their greedy eyes on the Holliday Ranch, but they were not opportunistic killers, and they did not act according to what was just in the world. That made them vulnerable to people like Wyatt and his brother.

Wyatt scanned the horizon, noticing the barn looming ahead with weathered planks, resting like a silent witness to the violence that continued to spill onto the lands of the ranch. Wyatt's boots crunched against dried grass and gravel, his gaze following alongside the county road that stretched into the distance. Wyatt's thoughts centered on the gunman they allowed to run free. He wondered where he may have gone, but not too long. The answer was clear. It was Clanton's men who'd tried to intimidate Virgil and Angel into selling the ranch to Joe. Wyatt could still remember the look of broken yaupon branches and scuffed earth as the young man fled the woods in a panic. No doubt his trail was still fresh.

Wyatt cleared his throat briefly, abandoning any attempt to suppress the tug of justice. It was too sharp, too unyielding, and like a spur digging into his own side, it couldn't be ignored. "We're gonna follow that trail."

"Trail?" his brother asked, caught off guard by the sudden demand.

"That gunman we let live. We're gonna go after him."

"Why in Sam Hill would we do that, Wyatt?"

"I got some questions for him."

"Not with that Schofield strapped to your hip, you don't."

"I ain't askin' you. I'm tellin' you." Wyatt's voice

was low and steady, like the hammer of his own revolver clicking back, ready to fall and take a life. "This needs to get done before we see Virgil and Angel again. We're gonna straighten this all out once and for all."

Morgan wiped the sweat from his brow with his forearm. "You sure about this? That boy is probably in Mexico by now, and the Clantons don't seem too keen on writin' us an invitation to come see them."

"They wrote their invitation already."

Morgan dug his heels in a little deeper. "Virgil and Angel ain't payin' us to be lawmen. You do remember our deal, right? We're here to dig up the gold, and hit the road. That's kinda hard to do if we don't ever actually do any diggin'."

"It don't matter if we dig or not, nothin' we find is gonna be safe until we keep this ranch in Virgil and Angel's hands. If you don't care that good people are gonna get killed for protecting what's theirs, maybe you'll care when the first thing the Clantons take is every bit of gold before we've had a chance to dig it up."

Morgan kicked at a clod of dirt, his jaw tightening more and more by the second.

Wyatt took a step closer to his brother and extended his hand. He placed it on Morgan's shoulder and gripped it tighter than he should have.

"The Clantons mean to burn this whole place to the ground. Are we ready to sit by and let that happen? You saw those two back there. They're scared. They don't know what's comin' for them like we do."

Morgan let out a sigh. "If you're fightin', then so am I, brother. But you gotta know we're walkin' into a wasp nest. Joe Clanton ain't just some two-bit rustler.

He's got men and money and a mean streak to back it all up. He ain't someone we need to be pickin' a fight with if we can't cut him down to size."

"Then that's what we'll do."

"I shouldn't have said a damned word."

"Let's get goin'."

Inside the barn, the air was thick with the scent of hay and manure. Wyatt ran a hand along the chestnut colt's flank he'd ridden before, feeling the animal's heart under his palm, sensing its accelerating heart-beat. The rhythm of saddling a horse grounded him, a tether to a life he could still touch from so long ago.

He and his brother led the horses out, just as Virgil's battered pickup rumbled up the driveway. The engine coughed, and sunlight glinted through the bullet holes Wyatt had left in the door. They exchanged a halfhearted wave as they passed by one another, each one uncertain of what the other had done, despite both doing what they thought was best to save the ground beneath their feet.

The ride to Clanton Family Farms was longer than they'd expected. Traveling by pickup had conveniences Wyatt was typically willing to sacrifice without a second thought, but instead of a twenty-minute drive, it was several hours on horseback, and without spurs and without so much as a drink of water, their ride turned miserable in a hurry.

"Got any big ideas in that brain of yours for when we see Joe?" Morgan decided to break the silence with an almost accusatory question.

"Maybe we should just follow his gunmen's lead. Take a couple hostages. Bark some orders. See what comes of it."

"I never did much care for your sense of humor."

"Who said I was joking?"

That was about the end of their conversation. Morgan may have known Wyatt would never do such a thing as to ride in guns blazing, taking prisoners and leaving a trail of destruction in their wake, but he still couldn't help but worry. The things he'd seen Wyatt do scared him down to his bones. When it came down to it, there was no telling the lengths he'd go to chase down evildoers and wring them out with his own hands.

It wasn't difficult to follow the trail left behind by the escaping gunman. Broken twigs, haphazard boot prints, and a discarded bandana snagged on a greenbrier all pointed the direction for the two Earp brothers.

The sun had started its descent in the west by the time they'd reached the Clantons. A familiar driveway snaked its way through the countryside to lead to the home they'd only just visited. As they approached, Wyatt took the time to see what it was the Clantons were really building. It was a flat stretch of land, with barbed wire fences glinting under the sunlight, separating discrete barns built of matching sheet metal that hadn't aged a day. There were enormous depictions of the same Clanton logo—a jagged letter *C*—on every building, men and equipment scurrying in every direction, and every reason Wyatt could think of not to do what he was about to do. Even so, he pushed on.

Wyatt reined in his colt and kept his eyes on a figure moving beside the nearest barn. It was too far to identify who it was, but close enough to know they were being watched. It wouldn't be long until the welcoming party they'd hoped to find on their arrival would start to take shape.

Morgan leaned forward on his saddle. "They're waitin' for us, Wyatt. You feel that?"

"Sure do."

Wyatt rode with the reins gripped in his left hand and his right hand resting on the handle of his Schofield revolver. Its weight was familiar, as was its intent, unchanged in a world that knew only constant change. All he had to do was withhold its usage until the time was right. Air filled with smoke curling from the house's chimney began to fill his lungs, mixing with the stench of dirt and sweat and a whole litany of terrible decisions that had summoned Wyatt and his brother.

It took only seconds for the front porch of the home to come into clear view, alongside its owner, Joe Clanton, who was puffing on a tobacco pipe perched in a rocking chair. A cloud of smoke poured from his cheeks and rose into the air before he stood upright. He was a gangling man with a broad frame. He wore overalls without so much as a speck of dirt on them, and a bent-out-of-shape Stetson tilted lower than any man should. He wasn't alone, either.

Two men flanked him, rifles slung across their chests like weekend warriors vacationing with their militia. Their eyes were hard and their demeanor stern. As Wyatt and Morgan approached on horseback, they left the side of their boss, walked down the steps in unison, then lifted their rifles to their shoulders.

"Well, well, well," Joe said with a clap of his hands behind yet another puff of smoke. "The wild Earp brothers have rode into town, we better watch our mouths, boys. These men could own the place if they so please. Or ain't you found all that gold yet?"

"Joe," said Wyatt, with a tip of his hat.

He and his brother paid no attention to the men still aiming rifles at their chests. They each tugged at their reins to come to a stop, twenty feet away from the porch, and ten feet away from the ends of the barrels pointed in their direction.

"You two lost?" Joe asked.

"We're here about your men," said Wyatt. "Those ones you sent to scare Virgil and Angel into selling the ranch to you, maybe even kill them if things didn't start goin' your way."

"My men? Killers? You must be mistaken, sir. I run a clean, legal operation here. Not a single killer on my payroll," Joe rattled on with a smile as big as Texas across his face.

"Maybe not after I got done with them," Wyatt said.

Joe's smile faded in a hurry. He stared at them with tight lips and piercing eyes.

Wyatt's comment had stirred some rather uncomfortable feelings regarding the sudden deaths of his men, that much had been made clear in a matter of seconds. What Wyatt didn't know was how he'd react to such brutal honesty. Men like Joe hadn't seen much of it in their lives. Wyatt went ahead and dismounted. His boots slammed into the dirt with a thud, and he took a step closer, keeping his gaze locked on Joe's. He could hear his brother do the same.

"One of 'em hightailed it back here, scared I was gonna gun him down, shoot him in the back for what he done. Can you believe it? I wonder where he learned about that sort of thing. Either way, he left all his buddies dead in a ditch, didn't even look back. Now, I don't know about you, but I slept pretty damn good last night. The only problem, I woke up wondering what he was in such a hurry for. What was so damned important that he just had to sprint back here to squeal to you?"

Joe's laugh was sharp, like a blade on a whetstone. "You got yourself a vivid imagination there, Earp. Maybe it's the age, I would certainly be the first to empathize with your delicate situation, but maybe you really are just seein' ghosts, old man."

Morgan bristled, but Wyatt's hand shot out, signaling him to dial it down. "We found your brand. We've taken enough of your men's lives to know better. We know exactly what's goin' on here. This ain't our first range war, partner. I'm here to tell you that it was your name on the tongues of those gunmen, until their very last breath."

"The cojones on this guy, am I right?" Joe couldn't keep his hatred focused for long, as he brushed it off with yet another joke and gestured just long enough to gather a laugh from the men still waiting on his call. "You ride up on horses like a couple of good ol' boys, accuse me of runnin' a bunch of killers and thieves, then try to tell me I'm startin' a *war*? That sure is a dangerous game you're tryin' to play."

"Ain't a game," said Wyatt. "You sent those men. You tried to poison the cattle on the Holliday Ranch. You tried to kidnap Virgil and Angel. I'm here to tell you all that ends now. I've seen your kind before, Clanton. You think the world is yours for the takin'. You don't stop 'til someone makes you."

Joe finally took a step off the porch and lulled closer and closer to Wyatt and Morgan with every word spoken. His face was now a scowl, twisted and distorted out of pure rage. He was taller than both of the Earp brothers, but neither of them knew what it meant to stand down.

"Come on a little closer, so you can hear everything I'm about to tell you," said Wyatt. "Leave the Holliday Ranch alone, or else."

"A threat? You're really threatening me? The drifter who stole the great name of Wyatt Earp right out from under the grave, comes to my home to threaten me," Joe began to preach to no one in particular. "With a flick of my wrist, you would both be lying dead in the dirt at my feet. You see, I can threaten with the best of them, and I have more men, guns, money, and grit than the lot of you combined." Joe walked in front of his two men, still shouldering their rifles, his smirk begging Wyatt to punch it right off his face. "You got guts, I'll give you that. But you're out of your depth. You need to take your brother and your fool's hope for gold and leave town. Leave the Holliday Ranch to me. Leave while you still have your lives."

Wyatt didn't move. "Not happenin'."

Whether it was the hand of God or the kiss of kismet, Joe faced down his own life after Wyatt's stubborn refusal. The figure from the barn sprang forward, hollering and running, unmistakable at first, but the man's admissions would soon become too damning to ignore.

"It's them! It's them!" he hollered over and over again. He ran through the field with high knees and arms waving. The panic in his voice was startling, the fear palpable. "They killed 'em! Killed every one of 'em! I told y'all!"

"What the hell is this all about?" Joe lifted his arms in disgust at the man's intrusion.

"Don't listen to me," said Wyatt. "Listen to your own man tell you what I will do."

"They killed them like dogs in the street!" The man shouted, following up on Wyatt's comment as if it was planned long beforehand. "They killed 'em all, I'm tellin' you. It's them! I barely got out alive!"

"You're the one?" Joe's face darkened, his eyes turned black and pointed. "*You* killed them."

"They drew first. And they'll keep dyin' if you don't back off."

"Leave!" said Joe. "Get off my land, or I'll bury both of you where you stand. You think you're the law? You're nothin'. The law does what I say, and so will you."

Wyatt's fingers traced the butt of his revolver. The wood grain of the handle, the steel core, the leather holster it called home, it yearned to be free, to spew forth hellfire and brimstone, to deliver justice by means of gunpowder and lead once again. Instead, he swung a leg over his saddle and planted his ass back on top of his horse. He reached up with a single finger and tipped his hat with a slow, deliberate gesture before leaving one last thing for Joe to think about. "This ain't over," he said.

"You're a dead man walkin', Earp!" Joe cried out after them, borderline hysterical. "You and your brother both! This'll be the last time you ever look in my direction without staring down death itself, you hear me?"

Chapter 15

Virgil stood alone on the land he'd come to know as his own.

Morning dew had given way to the unbearable, sweltering heat overhead. Virgil's flannel shirt clung to his sweat-soaked back, the fabric becoming heavier and heavier with dirt and despair. The idling tractor to his right was the only soundtrack to his racing mind. Thoughts of failure and loss, of life and love, and of the coming end no one could avoid, they plagued him. It was all so unavoidable. He only wanted to be able to wrap his hands around a single problem in his life and squeeze until it solved itself. Everything seemed so futile now. Protesting the inevitable had simply lost its luster.

His wife was proud to have received the money to pay the bank's sudden debt. Without explanation or a shred of proof, the bank granted a loan for a corner of the Holliday Ranch, receiving the funds as payment for something they couldn't even explain. It was a bitter solution to a sour problem, and it was all becoming more than Virgil had the stomach for.

He'd made it out into the pasture after seeing Wyatt and Morgan leave on horseback. Angel asked where they were going, and he didn't have much of an answer for that either, so instead, he hopped on the old mean green 1050 diesel and crept out into a pasture that had been untouched so far. They were a month away from the next round of branding and weaning calves, and the cattle had moved down to the south side of the property as they followed the shifting greener grasses of the season. It was peaceful out. There were so few opportunities to truly embrace the life they were trying so hard to protect.

As much as he hated to admit it, the ranch was slipping through their fingers. Every time they squeezed a little tighter, a little more desperate the situation became, and it seemed they slowly just lost more of the place they called home. Debts came and went, cattle markets rose and fell, but the Clantons circled overhead like vultures waiting on a dying steer to lie still, all while the banks kept calling, and the police would be of no help. He did his best to avoid thinking about those problems, but when his mind drifted to the ghost stories beneath his nose—whether the promise of gold he sold to two strangers could even be true—he wondered if there was anything good worth thinking about.

His wife was always the best part of his life. She'd given him everything, despite thinking the opposite. And it was times like these where he'd so typically rely on her strength and perseverance to inspire his own.

He pushed the hydraulics and slammed the bucket of the tractor into the earth, letting the impact rattle his bones, absorbing the pain still lingering from the bullet that nearly took his life in the woods not too far from where he stood. He still remembered the words of wisdom Angel had given him after she stitched him up, words that stood like a promise they had made together. He should've been allowing himself to find a night's peace after having paid yet another debt. He should've been holding Angel. He should've felt grateful. Instead, he was out digging holes in the yard like a madman.

He jammed the clutch and shifted gears, yanking up on the hydraulics to scoop enough dirt to make the diesel worthwhile in the process. The tractor hummed as he drifted to the right and tilted the bucket to remove the soil from his work area.

He paused just long enough to wipe the sweat from his brow with a dirt-streaked forearm. The pasture stretched out around him, its lilted, drying grass brittle under the relentless sun and suffering from too many months without fertilization. The Holliday legacy had rested on the edge of a knife for longer than he cared to admit. It was once a beacon of the West, a testament to the enduring promise of freedom. It was built on unyielding determination backed by a bullet for anyone who stood in its way. From Angel's ancestors tracing back to the famed gunfighter of old to the echoes of prosperity that lingered to this day, it wasn't just a patch of dirt—it was the realization of opportunity in all its glory.

As the sweat dripped into his eyes, and he struggled to keep his focus, such glory felt like a fading dream. His chest vibrated in sync with the tractor as it growled across the pasture and carved another trench into the dirt. The worn-out bucket tore through the earth's surface over and over again, each scoop another futile hope dashed beneath the sun, another betrayal from the land that'd already given so much.

For a moment, he found a bit of humor in the fact that Wyatt wasn't here to witness the amount of work that could be done in such a short time. Wyatt had hated the tractor, his face twisting with disdain every time Virgil fired it up, even when he thought no one was paying attention. Virgil stopped the tractor as the faintest bit of a smile escaped his lips. The 1050 idled with ease as he climbed down, his boots sinking deeper into the soft dirt than he expected. The air smelled of diesel and dry grass, a faint metallic tang lingering from the earth he'd disturbed. The tractor may be efficient, but it was also difficult to see, or find any sense of precision. As much as Wyatt may have hated the tractor for all its worth, there was one thing he understood as plain as day—you can't beat a shovel.

The wood and metal tool grounded him in something real. He drove it into the soil right in the middle of the hole he'd started, the blade biting deep, each swing a small act of defiance against the weight of his failures. The hole grew deeper, the dirt piling up beside him taller and taller. His shoulder ached and stung, the wound tugged with every movement, but he ignored the pain. He just dug faster. The rhythm became hypnotic. Scraping of metal and earth drowned out his own thoughts. Sweat poured from his forehead, and his hands began to blister against the wooden handle.

His thoughts about Wyatt began to sour. Each shovelful of dirt he hauled away brought his mind back to the haunting nature of the men he'd sold a claim to. Wyatt had been shot right in front of him, and he never even second-guessed it. Maybe he had gone mad. It would be the only sane explanation for what was happening. Virgil had seen it, had felt the chill of it in his bones. There was something unnatural about him, something that made Virgil question everything he thought he knew. Maybe he had gone mad. It would be the only sane explanation for what was happening.

The shovel smacked something hard, the clang sharp enough to jolt him out of his thoughts, the recoil against his wrists hard enough to bring his focus back to the task at hand. His heart leaped, another warrantless flicker of hope ignited somewhere deep in his belly. He dropped to his knees, scraping away the dirt with his hands, the cool soil crumbling under his fingers, wedging beneath his nails until they were stained black. Whatever it was, it was small, no bigger than a pebble, and as he brushed away the last of the earth, it glinted in the sunlight. His breath lodged itself in his chest, his pulse hammering in his ears.

Gold!

He held it up, the Liberty Head glinting golden sunlight across its dirt-flecked surface. It was small and wouldn't be enough to solve any of the ranch's problems, but it was in his hands. It was real. He laughed, a raw, ragged sound that echoed across the empty pasture.

"Angel," he whispered, his voice cracking with exhaustion and excitement.

"Angel," he spoke again, this time just barely louder than a whisper.

He wasn't sure if he was expecting an answer or not. The excitement sent adrenaline pumping through his veins. He didn't know what else to do, so he just kept calling out for his wife. He'd sold the idea of gold at the Holliday Ranch to Wyatt, but he struggled to find the means to believe it himself. They hadn't seen anything worthwhile since his kids were still in elementary school.

"Angel!" he screamed out this time, scrambling to his feet, clutching the old one-dollar gold coin like a lifeline and sprinting to the house. "You ain't gonna believe this!"

They'd left the porch light on after the night they had. Its faint glow was overwhelmed by the harsh midday sun, but it was Virgil's lighthouse in the distance. He gripped the gold coin hard enough to draw blood into the palm of his hand, but that only made him grip it tighter. It took a few agonizing minutes to reach the front of their home on foot, but the adrenaline carried him the whole way.

His wife was in the kitchen, her dark hair pulled back in a messy bun, her hands moving over a pile of papers spread across the table. There were more bills than letters across its surface, and more doubts than hope running through her mind. She looked up as he burst through the door, his boots tracking dirt across the worn, creaking floorboards. Virgil's face would become burned into her brain until the day Angel died. The sheer shock emanating from his eyes would be something she'd simply never forget.

"Virgil, what—" She stopped, her eyes locking on the coin in his hand. "Is that…"

"Gold!" he said, holding it out to her, his grin wide and reckless. "I shit you not. Found it just now, out in the pasture. It's real, Angel."

She took it without thinking, her fingers trembling slightly as she turned it over in her palm. The light caught its surface, casting a warm glow across her face.

Hope filled her for a few fleeting seconds before reality weighed down upon her once again.

"It's beautiful," she whispered, her voice laced heavily with doubt. "But one piece, Virgil, it's not enough. It's not even close."

"I know," he said, the excitement fading as he realized his wife was once again returning him to earth as the realist she always was. "It's *something*, though. If this is out there, maybe there really is more gold buried on the ranch. Think about it. No one could ever come for us again."

"A few things, first," she answered, handing the golden coin back to her husband and clasping her hands. "You already sold the claim to the entire Holliday Ranch. If you dig up any gold, isn't it technically Wyatt and Morgan's to own?"

"Well—"

"Also," she cut in, "those two have been digging for weeks and haven't turned up anything. Half the ranch is one big pothole at this point. I wouldn't be getting my hopes up about there being much more where that came from."

Virgil deflated. The weight of her words pressed down on him, flattening his hopes until he could see straight enough to be honest with himself. She was right. A single coin wouldn't be enough to fend off a single monthly note, much less return the ranch to prosperity like they'd hoped.

Even so, he couldn't ignore a spark in the darkness. It was so difficult to let go of its importance, of the potential that still waited just beneath the earth's surface, somewhere out there. He knew his wife didn't want to hear it, and he didn't even want to utter the words, but it was something he had to do.

"I can't stop," he admitted, his voice barely over a whisper. "How could I? Look at it. It's a fool's dream, but it's right in front of us. Begging to solve our every problem."

"Do you hear yourself?" Angel responded. "You think there is some endless gold vein running beneath our feet? The coin you hold was stolen by an outlaw lost to history, and dropped mistakenly on our property. There is no vault below waiting to be unearthed."

"We wouldn't ever have to set foot inside that dang bank again, Angel. It could carry us through every winter, keep our bellies full until every new calf crop hits the ground. The ranch could return to what it was meant to be. I don't know about you, but I damn sure like the sound of that."

"I'm tellin' you, if it's too good to be true, it usually is. But I also know you're more stubborn than a mule and there ain't nothin' I say that's gonna change that. All I ask is that you don't lose your head in all this. I need your help, Virgil. What we did today only buys us so much time. The bills keep comin' and we're spendin' more than we're makin'. That math works out for everyone but us."

"Just a little while longer," he said, still eyeing the coin flickering in his fingertips.

"What are you gonna say to Wyatt? What if he says that's his gold, not yours?"

"He'll just have to understand."

"That ain't right and you know it. You made a deal. You shook on it. You need to talk to him. It's the least you could do."

Yet again, his wife was right. He hated to admit as much, but he would have to come clean to Wyatt and Morgan about what he'd found. Even worse, he'd have to show them where he found it. They would almost certainly never leave him alone until he spilled the beans.

"They went out this morning," he told Angel. "But as soon as they get back, I'll let them know what I found. I promise."

"Then it's settled."

"For now," Virgil continued, "I gotta keep digging."

"Please don't be out too late," said Angel. "We have some celebrating to do tonight."

"I haven't forgotten," her husband said with a coy smile. "Who would've thought we'd be celebrating one less banknote."

"That would've been easier to predict than you runnin' in here like some Californian prospector."

They shared one last laugh before Virgil was basically running out the door as fast as he flew in only minutes ago. He was back in the pasture before the sun had begun to turn orange and set in the west. The air was humid, the sky a pale blue, with clouds threatening to bask him in cool shade just along the horizon. As much as they needed the rain, Virgil knew it would not arrive before he was done for the day. The tractor sat right where he'd left it, its green paint chipped and faded, a relic of better days, a promise that its diesel engine could still tackle anything Virgil threw at it. He considered firing it up again, but something held him back, a voice that wasn't his own. Maybe it had been Wyatt's, because he found himself unable to resist the urge to grab his trusted shovel.

It was the same shovel that'd struck gold only a little while ago, and he hoped it would do so again. He drove it into the soil, the blade sinking deep, and began to dig, each swing a small rebellion against the darkness he had once believed was closing in all around him. The hole where he'd found the golden coin was marked with nothing but a handprint where he'd found the one thing he thought he'd never find. He couldn't help but feel as though his discovery was a small act of defiance against the doubt that gnawed at him. He dug deeper, the soil damp and heavy now, each scoop revealing nothing but more dirt.

A small part of him hoped Wyatt and Morgan might never return, then he could spend his own days digging up the treasures that waited for him. But he knew that was a fate worse than death. The gambler's fallacy would eat him alive, take everything he'd ever known, and pull him further and further from reality in the process. Nothing was due to him. He could only take whatever presented itself. If the land was testing him, testing to see just how far he'd go to save his family's home and keep his wife's generational legacy in the right hands, he made it his life's mission to pass that test.

As the sun continued to fall and his endeavors turned once more to fruitless efforts, handfuls of empty dirt began to return his thoughts to a sense of normalcy. His shirt was soaked with sweat once again, his hands bloody and blistered, the hole large enough to swallow multiple cows with room to spare. But no matter how much more he wounded the earth, it never produced another piece of gold.

None of that mattered anymore, though. He already held hope in his heart. The weight of the golden coin in his pocket was more than enough to keep him searching. It didn't matter if he dug for another day or another month, this was the kind of hope that could sustain him. As the sunlight began to dwindle in the distance and the heat began to die down, replaced by a gentle breeze sweeping in from the north, he thought of his wife's words. They had something to celebrate today, that much was true. If he didn't return soon, he'd be in trouble, too.

Fighting the urge to continue tearing the earth apart, he dropped the shovel where he stood and turned to leave his work behind for the night. When he lifted his eyes from the holes in the ground, he saw Wyatt and Morgan watching him, standing silently no more than ten feet away. Their faces were blank.

"Any luck?" Morgan asked.

Virgil didn't respond, he simply reached into his pocket and produced the single golden coin he'd dug up earlier. A smile crept onto his face. "It's real," he said, basking in the weight of the gold in his fingers.

"No shit? How did you—"

"We need to talk," Wyatt cut off his brother.

"I already spoke with Angel about the claim we sold you. We know that this is technically—"

"It's about the Clantons."

"What do you mean?"

"They're coming," Wyatt said, his voice rattling like a snake about to strike. "And they mean to kill us all."

Chapter 16

The Holliday Ranch was a sight to be seen, sprawling into the horizon beneath a sky dotted with bright stars.

The only sound was a faint breeze rustling the grass and limbs near the old family home, a restless warning to those who waited for something far worse than a chill in the air to sweep in. Wyatt stood on the porch, his boots planted firm on the weathered floorboards, like a tree growing through an abandoned home, waiting for something, or someone, that may never exist to return. His eyes darted back and forth, never focusing on any one thing for too long. His thoughts did the same.

The gold coin Virgil had dug up earlier weighed heavily in his pocket. The small, glinting promise pulled from the earth spoke to him. It told him of secrets past and riches to come, it begged him to get back to shoveling, but it also warned him of the dangers it would almost certainly beget. After everything was said and done, the golden coin was nothing more than a reminder of what was at stake for both Wyatt and his brother, as well as the family that called the Holliday Ranch home. It may not have been worth nearly enough to secure the future of the ranch, but it was a spark of hope that would at least carry them for one more day.

None of it meant anything if the Clantons weren't stopped, though. It would be the only golden coin to their name if Joe had his way. They could dig up a dozen more, and they'd all be useless against the vultures circling overhead, looking to strip the land bare.

Wyatt's eyes scanned the horizon, where the county road vanished into the blackness. He remembered the fire in Virgil's eyes as he hoisted the coin into the air, and the tremble in Angel's hands as she watched Wyatt take it for himself. There was something about them that told Wyatt they were both ready for what was to come, even if he was desperate for any other solution. He'd spent the better part of two hours explaining what happened when they arrived at Joe Clanton's place. It was a mix of confusion and terror that Wyatt saw in their eyes when he explained what would likely happen next.

Joe wasn't the kind of man who knew how to hold back, but as far as Wyatt could tell, he also wasn't the kind of man to get his hands dirty.

Morgan stepped out from the house, his boots scuffing the boards, a familiar brown bottle swinging in his hand as he walked. "You plannin' to stand out here all night?" he asked, his voice low but carrying that same old drawl that always edged on a challenge.

"Till I know they're safe," Wyatt said, refusing to

break his gaze on the driveway stretching through the front yard. "Clantons ain't done. You saw Joe's face today. How many times have you and I seen that kind of look? Or heard that kind of threat? He'll be here, sooner or later."

Morgan set his sweaty beer on the rail of the porch, then propped his foot up on the bottom rung. "I don't doubt you a bit, Wyatt. We have seen that face before, but we don't usually have people standin' in the way of our bullets, you hear me?"

"These people won't be in our way," Wyatt said, and finally turned to face his brother. "They'll be on our side."

"If you say so."

The silence that fell over them lasted only a few seconds before Morgan broke it with another question.

You really think that gold coin means somethin'?"

"It's more than we've found so far."

"What if he's lyin'?"

"Why would he do that?"

"Why does anyone do anything?"

"Because they get somethin' out of it. Virgil and Angel already sold us the claim. They don't get nothin' out of this."

"Money changes people, Wyatt. You know that. That claim might not mean anything if there's enough gold down there."

"It means more than you know. It might not be enough to keep the lights on, but there ain't much that'll spark some hope like a piece of gold bein' dug out of the ground. If they believe in that, they'll fight. And that's exactly what we need right now."

"Why would they fight for a piece of gold they've already signed away?" Morgan couldn't help but ask.

Wyatt fell silent again.

Morgan tried to make eye contact, but Wyatt avoided it. "Tell me you didn't," he said.

Wyatt still didn't answer.

"You did, didn't you? You promised them a cut of the claim they already sold? Why would we ever do such a thing?"

"They're good people, Morgan. I didn't promise all of it, just enough to give them a head start if everything works out."

"Unbelievable. Why should we even keep diggin'?"

"This place is different. There's somethin' about it. It's like a memory of something that died out long ago. It's not about gettin' rich anymore. It's about protecting it when no one else will."

"You're startin' to sound like a preacher. All this talk of signs and justice. Don't start goin' soft on me now, dangit."

Wyatt's lips twitched, not quite a smile.

"Ain't no preacher. Just a man who knows what happens when you let wolves run loose. From what I see, there's a lot of wolves out there."

Wyatt's mind drifted to the confrontation at Clanton Family Farms, Joe's smug grin, the rifles aimed at their chests, and the panicked gunman spilling his fear like a confession. Joe had called him a dead man walking, and Wyatt didn't have any reason to doubt his threats, even if the man had no idea what he was getting into. He'd stared down the fiery pits of death itself before—hell, he'd walked through it—and he had yet to find anything that'd make him back down on something he believed in. The Holliday Ranch was more than dirt and cattle, even to him, it was a way of life, a piece of the West that still breathed, and he'd be damned if he let the Clantons choke it out.

"There's only one way to solve this mess for good. But we're gonna need to get 'em both on board."

Morgan nodded, his jaw tight. "Virgil's halfway there already. That gold's got him thinkin' maybe there's a future here. Angel's tougher than she looks—she'll stand with us. But they're scared, Wyatt. They've been beat down too long."

"We just need to show 'em the Clantons can bleed, is all."

He pushed off the rail and walked into the house without saying another word, the screen door creaking behind him as he barged inside. The kitchen was dim, the only light coming from a single bulb above the table where Virgil and Angel sat, their heads bent over a map of the ranch. Virgil looked up as Wyatt entered, his eyes shadowed with exhaustion but burning with something new—hope, maybe, or just stubborn defiance. Wyatt didn't talk at first. He dragged his feet until he was standing in front of the table, shoved his hand into his pocket, and flicked the golden coin between his fingers. As he locked eyes with both Virgil and Angel, he reached out and placed the coin on the table between them.

"Wyatt," Virgil said, his voice rough. "Thought you'd be out keepin' watch."

"Time for talkin'," Wyatt said, pulling out a chair and sitting across from them. Morgan followed not too long after, leaning against the counter with his arms crossed.

"That coin right there you found, Virgil—it's a start. Could be more down there, enough to save this place. But none of it means a damn thing if the Clantons take it first."

Angel's eyes narrowed, her fingers tightening around the edge of the table. "You think we don't know that already? You think the Clantons are the first to come after us like this?"

"No ma'am, I don't," answered Wyatt. "I do think you're gonna need some help fightin' back against this guy, though. As it sits, you're outmanned and outgunned. And they're comin' in hot, that much I can guarantee."

"You sure got good at statin' the obvious all of a sudden," Angel popped off. "If you got somethin' useful to say, now's the time."

"It ain't just about fightin'. It's about makin' sure they don't come back. None of the Clantons. If we hit 'em hard enough, they won't think twice about tuckin' their tails. That's the only language men like Joe understand."

"We're not gunfighters," Virgil chimed in. "We're ranchers."

"What he's saying is, we're not so sure we can't fight like you. If we lose, we can't just up and leave this place, abandon our whole life," his wife backed him up. "We have to do something now. All of this is just getting out of control. We've spent all day talkin' about what needs to happen, and we both think it's time to be honest with ourselves. It's easy to talk up a storm, but when it comes down to it, Virgil is right. We're ranchers. And I think we're in over our heads with all this."

Wyatt got the feeling this conversation was going somewhere he wouldn't like. "What are you tryin' to say?"

"We called the cops and reported the Clanton's crimes. They are sending someone out here to get our statement."

"You called—"

"We gotta go, Wyatt," Morgan spoke up in a hurry. "Right now."

"Hold on." Wyatt lifted his hand.

"No!" Morgan walked over to the window leading to the den, overlooking the front yard of the family ranch, and pulled the blinds apart with one hand.

Red and blue lights sliced through the dim kitchen, followed by a low rumble of an engine and the crackling of tires rolling over gravel.

"We gotta go."

"You shouldn't have done that, Virgil. This is a mistake. We have to fight them ourselves, or you'll never be free of it. This ain't the kind of justice that needs to be dealt."

"Thank you for your help," Virgil replied. "That coin is yours to keep, by the way."

Headlights flooded the inside of the home as the police car pulled further into the driveway. Morgan grabbed Wyatt by the arm and forced him out of the room, making their way to the back door to escape the view of whoever it was that had just pulled in. Virgil and Angel stayed put, refusing to say a word or move a muscle until a knock came on the front door. It was firm and rapid, as if the person on the other side was in a hurry.

When the door swung open, Virgil was met with a man who had a familiar face. He didn't know him, but it sure felt like it. Something in his eyes told him that they'd made the wrong decision before a word was ever exchanged. They should have listened to their gut, to Wyatt and Morgan.

Angel nudged his elbow, knocking him out of the spiral of regret he'd immediately fallen into. Virgil could feel something off with his wife's behavior, and it didn't take long to figure out what was happening.

His eyes fell to the badge pinned onto the officer's chest and the name etched into gold, glinting in the approaching moonlight, just as the man of the law spoke.

"I'm Sheriff Clanton," he said. "But you can call me Joseph."

"What happened to the other guy…" Angel's voice trailed off as she tried to recall the name of the previous sheriff.

"Ol' Stevens finally took the plea bargain," Joseph answered for her. "He retired a month back, and the department decided to go with *mister outside* hire. So, looks like you're stuck with me."

"My name's Virgil, this here is my wife, Angel."

"Ma'am." Joseph tipped his Stetson with two fingers. "Heard there's been some trouble out here."

"Is this the first you're hearin' of it?" Angel blurted out.

"We got some reports of disturbances in the area, people goin' into places they shouldn't, maybe even some shots fired here and there. When they came in, I thought to myself, now there is no way all that is goin' on with those good folks of Holliday Ranch."

His tone dripped with false concern, and Wyatt caught the glint of calculation in his gaze. Another Clanton, another piece of Joe's machine. It was all he could think about.

"The days haven't been kind to us lately," Virgil

said, his voice tight. "Our backs are against a wall, and we're afraid our lives are on the line. This place is under attack, damn near every day it seems."

Joseph let out a devilish smirk, his hand gently sliding over his belt until it hovered above his holster.

"That so? Funny, because I also heard you've been stirrin' up trouble yourselves. Got yourself a couple of fellows diggin' up the place, causin' a ruckus with my kin. You know, my little brother Joe's real upset about that little visit you paid him today."

Virgil's fingers twitched at the sheer thought of the sheriff being Joe's brother. He was itching to yank a revolver from his hip that wasn't there. "Your kin's been threatenin' our livelihood, poisonin' cattle, stealin' horses, and tryin' to kill good men for no reason. You wanna talk about trouble, let's start there."

Joseph raised an eyebrow, unfazed. "Big accusations, stranger. Got any proof?"

"We got proof, all right," Angel said, stepping forward, placing herself between her husband and the sheriff. "First, we found the nitrate poison meant for our cattle. Still got it tucked away in the barn. And you know what else we found in the barn? The Clanton brand. You know, that big farm your brother finally brought to town. And if you have the urge to turn around for one quick second, you'll find that son of a bitchin' brand burned into our home. You gonna do somethin' about that, Sheriff, or you just here to cover for Joe?"

"Careful there, ma'am," said Joseph. "I'm just tryin' to keep the peace out here."

Angel scoffed as Virgil pulled her back to his side. "We don't want any trouble. That's why we called y'all."

"I hear ya, Virgil. Loud and clear." The sheriff nodded, then tipped his hat once again, this time making a mockery of courtesy, and turned back to his cruiser. "I appreciate the statement. I know it's late, and I've kept you long enough already. But don't worry, I'll be seein' you folks real soon."

He turned to leave the house, pausing for a split second to glance down at the Clanton brand seared into the floorboard. A faint trace of a chuckle escaped his chest as he shook his head and made his way back to the SUV he'd arrived in. He climbed into the vehicle, the engine roaring to life as he pulled away, the headlights cutting through the darkness until they were gone.

Virgil watched until the taillights vanished, his teeth grinding all the while. "He's one of 'em," he said, turning to his wife. "Clanton, through and through. Law or no law, he's with Joe."

"What are we supposed to do now?"

"We need to find Wyatt and Morgan," Virgil admitted. "Now."

"We're still here, don't you worry." Wyatt stepped out from the other side of the home. "Come on out, Morgan," he hollered down to the barn.

Morgan took one step out from behind the east-facing wall of the barn and gave a short wave to those standing on the porch. His smile could be seen even from their distance.

"We never left. We just kept gettin' ready."

"They're all in it together, Wyatt," said Virgil. "The whole damn Clanton family."

"They're comin' tonight," Wyatt answered, his voice low and steady. "That sheriff was scoutin' us out, seein' how ready we are. You gave 'em the perfect opportunity."

Virgil's stomach churned, the weight of his mistake settling like a stone sinking in a pond. He'd called the law, hoping for help, but instead, he'd let a Clanton walk right into their home. "I'm sorry, Wyatt," he said, his voice rough. "I thought—"

"No time for that," Wyatt cut him off, his tone sharp but not unkind. "Check every rifle, every round. Barricade the windows and lock every door. Morgan is already locking down the barn. We're holdin' this ground."

They scattered at Wyatt's final word, the ranch coming alive with purpose under the burning, starlit sky. Wyatt stayed on the porch, his revolver still in hand, his senses sharp as a blade. The gold coin was back in his pocket now, its weight a welcome distraction for the fight ahead. It was an unkept promise that he was determined to return to.

Virgil and Angel found themselves holed up in the kitchen with .30-30 rifles and more revolvers than either of them could hold. Boxes of bullets littered the countertop. It was like something out of a movie, but for the couple who only wanted to protect their home, they were living in a nightmare.

THE NIGHT DRAGGED on without end. Even the buzzing cicadas died out in the distance, drowned in the same darkness that engulfed the home where Virgil, Angel, and Wyatt held fort. It was the kind of quiet stillness that would make your hair stand up and your mind make up things that were never there.

There wasn't too much else to be said at this point. Their options had been exhausted, whatever may come was inevitable, the only thing that remained was to answer one last question—how would they stand against it?

Wyatt made himself a home on the front porch. He nestled into the rocking chair, illuminated only by a small, half-burned candle at his side. As much as he wanted to keep watch, there was nothing to see. His brother remained in the barn for what he had described more or less as obvious reasons, overlooking the largest landscape of the ranch. Wyatt was left facing the driveway, hoping they would be stupid enough to ride head-on into him. There were no sounds coming from inside the home, but he knew Virgil and Angel sat at the table, bracing themselves for what was to come. He was thinking about the gold coin in his pocket, about how he should have left it with Virgil as a moral compass for what they would have to endure, when he heard the attack begin.

Pop. Pop. Pop.

A brush rifle cried out from the barn, exploding through the night with flashes of fire, dancing through the Holliday Ranch like a summer lightning storm.

"They're here!" Wyatt screamed, jumping from his chair.

Pop. Pop.

It was Morgan. He'd hoisted himself up to the hayloft on the second floor and found cover in all the square bales stored away for the coming winter. Wyatt couldn't make out what he was shooting at yet, but he was firing in a hurry and hollering incoherently between every round. Wyatt didn't wait around to figure out what he was saying.

"I'm comin'!" he hollered.

Wyatt stepped off the porch, his revolver held low, his senses sharp. The ranch was a patchwork of moonlight and darkness, the barn a looming silhouette against the sky, sporadically flashing from gunshots spewing fire downrange into the pasture. He hadn't made it halfway to his brother before he caught movement near the fence line to his right—figures moving low, their shapes indistinct but purposeful. They were flanking them. He turned and sprayed his revolver, slapping the hammer over and over, peppering any living thing just beyond the trees at the fence line. A haunting silence between gunshots hung in the night for a few seconds. Wyatt took the time to drop fresh rounds into the cylinder of his revolver. Before he could finish, a blinding muzzle flash came from the trees, and a gunshot pierced the air.

The bullet whizzed past Wyatt's head, becoming lost in the nighttime behind him without another sound. He didn't flinch, didn't duck. He raised his Schofield and fired, the recoil familiar, the sound of a thunderclap in the night, its gunpowder-fueled flame a strike of lightning at his enemies. A scream followed, sharp and brief, as one of the figures dropped. The ranch erupted into chaos. Gunshots rang out, flashes of light punctuating the darkness as the violent summer storm unfolding at the ranch grew stronger.

Virgil burst from the house, a lever-action rifle in his hands, Angel right behind him with a six-inch stainless .357 magnum revolver, each one a cannon in their own right, ready to be wielded in defense of their home.

Wyatt turned just in time to see Virgil and Angel's bullet-flying entrance into the gunfight, and he knew right then and there, the Clanton men didn't stand a snowball's chance in hell of surviving the night. Wyatt's voice boomed throughout the Holliday Ranch, echoing through the pastures like a war cry from the heavens above, threatening any living soul close enough to bear witness.

"Kill 'em all!"

Chapter 17

There are few in this world who know the taste of gunpowder and blood in the air, the way it fills your lungs and expels from within you.

Wyatt was crouched behind a splintered H-brace in the fencing that connected the Holliday Ranch barn and the family home. He stared up for a few seconds, relishing the adrenaline surge beneath a sky of relentless stars, where gunfire exploded into the night like fireworks. The Schofield revolver was warm in his hand, having spat enough fire to burn a house down within a matter of seconds. He should have been thinking about the dozen or so rounds he had left in his pocket, or the still-approaching Clanton men with their minds set on only one thing—death. He couldn't bring himself to worry about such worldly matters, though. As the shots popped off, thunder in the night punctuated by bolts of lightning, his mind dwelled on the ravages of time.

Surviving a firefight wasn't about strategy or skill, or at least that wasn't Wyatt's experience. It was about fate. Hands that were not his own would guide the conflict to whatever end needed to be. Wyatt had been involved in so many situations that most would describe as life or death, that he finally understood the reason for his own walking away each and every time. There would never be any outcome other than what was supposed to happen. In this, he found sanctitude, a kind of selflessness that could carry him through a fight where any other man would be too afraid to move.

Clanton's men continued to skulk behind the shadows, their shapes darting between trees and cattle pens, only showing themselves long enough to fire a sporadic, ill-aimed bullet in the general direction of someone who wasn't on their side. The barn was being peppered from every corner, holes blasted into its side like a hundred tiny sticks of dynamite popping off at once. Morgan's rifle cracked from the barn's hayloft, each shot producing a muzzle flash bright enough to light the pasture in fleeting bursts.

Virgil and Angel hovered on the front porch, taking cover where they could, behind the dilapidated framing and ducking inside just long enough to reload. Virgil fancied himself a screamer during a fight, something Wyatt couldn't help but take notice of. Every curse word under the moon was shouted out at those Clanton men as Virgil emptied round after round into the woods, hoping to tag one of them.

Wyatt patted his pocket one more time, reassuring the weight of the last bullets he carried with him. They weren't enough to win a war, but they would keep him in the fight long enough for fate to have its way.

The Clantons were relentless. They weren't marksmen—most of their shots went wild, punching holes in the barn or kicking up dirt near the porch—but their numbers made up for their recklessness, their lack of precision. Wyatt counted at least ten, maybe more, their voices carrying low and guttural across the pasture, barking orders or cursing when Morgan's rifle answered from the hayloft. Each crack of Morgan's Winchester .30-30 lit the night, causing a strobe of fire which revealed the rustlers' positions for a fleeting second before darkness swallowed them up whole all over again.

"Wyatt!" Virgil's voice cut through the din, hoarse but steady, from the porch of the family home. It was the first word he'd uttered that wasn't some form of cussing since the firefight broke out. "They're circlin' round the west side! Get 'em!"

Wyatt didn't answer, just nodded to himself, his eyes scanning the shadows. Virgil was holding the porch with Angel, forming an impenetrable line of fire from lever-action hunting rifles and revolvers past their prime, spitting lead whenever a Clanton got too bold. Angel's rifle had roared right after Virgil's demand, its blast scattering a pair of rustlers who'd crept too close to the house. Wyatt had seen one of them limp away, clutching his side, but the others hadn't slowed. They were hungry for the Holliday Ranch, for its land, its cattle, its future. And now, maybe, for blood.

He darted from the H-brace to a chipped concrete water trough, keeping low as bullets whined and whistled overhead. The trough was poor cover, but it gave him a clear line of sight to the west pasture, where Virgil had spotted movement. Sure enough, three Clanton men were creeping along the fence line, their oversized cowboy hats pulled low, carbines glinting in the moonlight. Wyatt steadied his revolver, exhaling slowly, and squeezed the trigger. The Schofield bucked, and the lead man crumpled, his rifle clattering to the dirt, followed only a second later by his corpse. The other two ducked behind a stack of hay bales, returning fire, their shots splintering the trough's edge.

"Morgan!" Wyatt shouted, his voice barely carrying over the gunfire. "West side! Two behind the bales!"

Morgan's rifle cracked twice in response, and one of the Clantons screamed, a high-pitched, animal sound that pierced the gunfight, lacing it with the kind of desperate violence known to soldiers and desperados. The third man broke cover, sprinting for the trees in a futile attempt to save his own life while his partner continued his bloody screams, but Wyatt was already moving. His boots pounding the dirt as he closed the distance. He fired on the run, the shot grazing the man's shoulder, sending him sprawling. Wyatt loomed over him, the Schofield leveled, but the rustler raised his hands, babbling pleas for mercy.

"Don't shoot! I don't wanna die! Not like this!"

Wyatt's finger tightened on the trigger, his eyes cold and unforgiving, like he was staring down at a life he'd already taken. But fate, that unseen hand working in such mysterious ways, stayed his own hand. Instead of squeezing the trigger, he growled a warning in the hopes of ending the fight before things turned worse. "Crawl back to the hole you came from. Tell 'em this ain't their night."

The man scrambled away, disappearing into the shadows in an instant, and Wyatt turned back to the fight. The gunfire refused to slow down. Morgan was hammering away, moving through what seemed like an unlimited amount of ammunition tucked away inside the barn. Virgil and Angel's screams were the only other sounds to be found. Clanton's men had abandoned their strategy and resorted to an every man for himself tactic. They were spineless and cared only about their paycheck, this much Wyatt knew for certain. With enough dead bodies becoming manure for the fields, they would start to second-guess their actions. They only had to hold out long enough for such a realization to hit.

Wyatt returned the way he came. This time, making his way to the barn where his brother stood alone. He did what he could to keep them from circling him, but five of Clanton's men were closing in. His Schofield was hot enough to give third-degree burns by now, but Wyatt didn't hold back.

Bam. Bam.

Two men fell where they stood, never to move again. Wyatt stepped by them without pausing to see their endless glare into the stars above. He paid no attention to the metallic scent filling his nostrils, the blood pooling into the earth inches away from his boots. He simply lifted his right arm, gripped the revolver a little tired, and went back to work.

The third man, trying to close in on the barn, charged at Wyatt unexpectedly. He abandoned his rifle and yanked at the pistol tucked into his waistband as he ran. It was an unfamiliar polymer pistol, and it contained a heck of a lot more than six rounds. That poor man sent every bullet he had right into Wyatt, cursing with every squeeze of the trigger, becoming more and more stunned by the revelation that his opponent would not go down. Wyatt absorbed blow after blow during the man's charge. He lost count after ten rounds, then the man tried to scream.

"What are—"

His brother must've heard the cacophony ringing out, because it was a sudden bullet to the spine that ended up halting the man's charge prematurely. The unknown Clanton man faceplanted into the dirt and laid still.

The last two men had seen enough. They circled to the north side of the barn and did their best to collect themselves. Wyatt watched them confer briefly with the one that had just escaped Wyatt's own bullet —their words were indistinguishable, but their panic was palpable. It was the turning point he was hoping to force into existence. He watched as the three men shook their heads and turned around to hightail it out of the Holliday Ranch, their tails tucked so far between their legs they looked like they ran bowlegged.

One of them must have been the de facto leader, because it took only a few minutes for the firefight to begin to die down. The Clantons slowly started pulling back to regroup, their shapes fading into the tree line until it was only the breeze sweeping in that could be seen. Morgan's rifle fell silent, and for a moment, the only sounds were the low moans of the wounded and the distant bellering of spooked cattle likely still fleeing the sounds of gunfire. Wyatt made his way to the porch where Virgil and Angel were still in the process of reloading every gun, their faces streaked with sweat and grime and fear.

"They're backin' off," Virgil said, slamming a fresh round into one of the many rifles he had in rotation during the fight. "But they ain't done. There was too many of 'em out there to just quit."

Angel nodded, her hands trembling. "They're

waitin' for us to slip. We're low on ammo, and they know it. We can't stop now."

Wyatt glanced at the barn, where Morgan was already trying to climb down from his makeshift watchtower in the hayloft. "They've had their fill for now," he said, barely above a whisper.

Virgil snorted, wiping blood from a shallow cut on his cheek, caused by a bullet that was only inches away from taking his life. He couldn't believe what he was hearing. "Had their fill? And we're supposed to just sit here and wait on them to come back to try and kill us again? There's gotta be somethin' else we can do. Waitin' on a miracle is what got us in this mess."

Wyatt's lips twitched, not quite a smile. "Miracles ain't my style, Virgil. I don't reckon this is over by a long shot, but for tonight, it is."

Before Virgil could reply, a sharp whistle pierced the night, followed by the thunder of hooves. Wyatt spun, his revolver raised, as five riders burst into view from the east pasture, their silhouettes black against the moonlit horizon. He hesitated. They weren't shooting—not yet—but their intent was clear, charging straight for the house. They were coming for Virgil and Angel, making one last Hail Mary attempt to sway the fight in their favor. Wyatt fired, dropping one rider, but the others fanned out, their horses kicking up clouds of dust that shielded them from view in the swirling darkness.

"Get inside!" Wyatt shouted, shoving Angel toward the door.

She hesitated, her rifle raised, but Virgil grabbed her arm, pulling her into the house. Wyatt dove behind the porch railing, bullets splintering the wood as the riders finally opened fire, hoping to cut off the couple's escape into the home. Morgan's rifle answered from twenty yards behind Wyatt, but the riders were too fast, too spread out, circling the house like wolves. The Earp brothers fired in succession, sending round and round downrange, but no bullet found their target.

Virgil reappeared at the door, his Winchester barking like a rabid dog.

The riders were closing in. Their bullets came too quick, forcing Wyatt and Morgan to cast all doubts aside and charge head-on. All five converged at one point, just before the barbed wire fence cut off their charge. Wyatt half expected them to jump the fence on horseback, but Morgan knew better. With one brother already on one knee firing his lever-action, the other lifted his revolver and began to fire.

What they didn't see, however, was the sixth rider who had used the distraction to his advantage and slipped behind the house in the night. They were alerted too late by the sharp, piercing scream of Angel, who put the pieces together.

"Virgil!"

A broad-shouldered man with a bandana masking his face, leaning low in the saddle, a lasso spinning in his hand, appeared like a shadow in the night. Wyatt saw it too late, the rope snaking through the air, looping around Virgil's shoulders before he could react. The rider yanked hard, and Virgil stumbled backward, dragged off his feet and into the dirt with a grunt that would be burned into Angel's brain forever.

From his back, Virgil watched his wife lunge forward, but Wyatt caught her, pinning her against the wall as bullets raked the porch. Virgil thrashed, trying to free himself, but the rider spurred his horse, dragging him toward the pasture. Two other Clantons caught up to the lone rider in the chaos, trying and failing to keep Wyatt and Morgan pinned down.

With Angel safe, Wyatt broke cover, his Schofield blazing, but the riders were already fading into the darkness. Virgil's struggling form, fighting the rope with everything he had, became a dim shape in their wake. Morgan's rifle cracked, and one of the Clantons slumped in the saddle, falling off his horse to lie still in the pasture. The others didn't slow, didn't hesitate. They disappeared into the treeline with their prize.

"Damn it!" Wyatt roared, slamming his fist against the porch post.

Angel wrenched free of his grip, her face pale, eyes blazing with fury and fear. "They took him," she whispered, her voice breaking and cracking before any tears could well up in her eyes. "They took Virgil. They took my husband."

Wyatt stared emotionlessly into the night. His clothes were riddled with bullet holes, but he stood without a scratch, no different than his brother. They were unharmed, but distraught all the same.

The hoofbeats had faded, the stars offering no answers or consolation. Fate, it seemed, had played its hand, and it wasn't the one anyone had expected. The Clantons had turned the tables, striking not just at the ranch but at its heart. Virgil, beaten and bound, was gone, and with him, the fragile hope that had held them together.

"We've gotta get him back," Wyatt said, his voice sullen and faltering, though his grip on the Schofield was white-knuckled. "They ain't won this thing yet, Angel. I promise."

Angel didn't answer, her gaze fixed on the darkness as her worst nightmares were realized in an instant.

The night was quiet now, the Clantons gone, their horrid kidnapping marked only by the dust still settling in the pasture and the haunting memory that was already playing over and over in her mind.

Wyatt reloaded his revolver, each click of the cylinder a promise. The hand that wasn't his own might've guided the fight, but it wasn't over yet. He'd carve his own path to its end before he let the Clantons have their way. Virgil was out there, and the people who took him would soon learn what it meant to cross a man who'd already walked through death's door and come out the other side.

Angel fell to her knees at last, her sobs and heaving and cussing and threats were all that remained of the fight for the Holliday Ranch.

Chapter 18

To have a loved one torn from your grasp is a kind of pain no living person should feel.

It was the kind of hurt that led to despair, followed by rage, abandonment, and dissociation, before the spiral culminates in cold, unyielding death. There was a knot in Angel's stomach, it twisted and turned and threatened to upend everything inside her. Tears poured from her face until there was nothing left, only dry heaves and bloodshot eyes. Her fists bled from slamming them into the ground, her knees from forcing herself to crawl home, unable to bring herself to her feet. The loss of her husband wasn't a gut punch, it was like her heart had been ripped from her chest and filled with the lead of every bullet that had been fired during their shootout at the ranch. It was unbearable.

Angel stopped crawling in the dirt just beyond the porch, her hands reaching out to clutch the wooden stock of the last rifle Virgil held—a lever-action Winchester once shot by her grandfather—her breath ragged, escaping from her lungs in uneven gasps. The rifle was still warm from the firefight, its barrel streaked with grime and the faint burn of spent rounds. She gripped the rifle a little harder with fingers trembling from the weight of what had just been ripped away.

Her husband was gone.

Virgil had been dragged off into the dark by Clanton's men, his curses and threats and screams fading into the darkness. Her partner in life, her anchor, her reason to keep fighting for a patch of land she was starting to believe was cursed, was gone in an instant. She was left with nothing but the echo of his name in her throat.

She pressed her forehead to the rifle's stock, the wood biting into her skin, grounding her for a fleeting moment, as she lay on her stomach in the dirt just in front of their home. The ranch was silent now, with the low moan of the wind through the bullet-riddled barn and the distant bellow of cattle the only things left for her to focus on. The Clantons had vanished, their hoofbeats swallowed by the night, leaving behind only the bodies of their fallen and the wreckage of her life.

Angel's eyes burned. There were no more tears left to give, only the relentless fury that swirled inside her gut. Such ferocity could only be sprayed without aim, and it just so happened that Wyatt and Morgan were still standing behind her.

"You're not ghosts," she whispered, her voice a cracked, hollow thing, before a shout exploded from deep within her. "You're demons!"

The thought of the Earp brothers standing in her yard, bullet holes riddling their coats yet not a scratch on either of them, was insanity. She'd watched Wyatt endure inhuman bullet shots with her own eyes, and she remembered her husband's warnings after working with them both out in the field. Ghosts, Virgil had whispered before the Clantons took him. Phantoms, or memories of the past, hell-bent on haunting them. She called him stressed at the time, unable to escape the reality that ghosts don't carry revolvers or bleed a man dry with a single shot. Demons did, though.

Angel pushed herself to her feet, her husband's Winchester heavy in her arms, and turned to face Wyatt at last. He stood silhouetted against the porch light shining in his face, his hat tilted low, his coat flapping in the breeze, covered with gunpowder-stained holes that should've ended him ten times over. His eyes met hers, steady, unyielding, like he was staring through her to some truth she couldn't grasp. She wanted to scream, to put another bullet through him, to hurl the rifle at him, then finally to demand answers about who they were and where they came from. Instead, she asked the impossible.

"What have you done?"

"Angel, just—"

"No! You don't get to do that. *You* caused this. You and your stupid son of a bitch brother."

"I know you're—"

"Shut the hell up, Wyatt. Just shut the hell up."

Angel limped her way back onto the porch, stumbling over each step and doing her best to remember to breathe. Her knees shook, and the knot in her stomach never subsided. All she could think about was the view of her husband, bound in rope by men with hidden faces, being dragged through the pasture into the night. There was only one thing left to do—she had to go find him.

A lump formed in her throat at the thought of chasing down those Clantons. She knew she couldn't do it alone, as that'd be a death sentence. She needed help, but she wasn't sure if she could stomach asking the two men who had been party to her husband's loss. For all their tricks and guises of immortality, they could not save Virgil, and every ounce of her yearned to blame them for it. She turned around again, her eyes puffy and her voice quivering, and told Wyatt what had to happen next. "We have to go after him. We have to find him."

Wyatt holstered his Schofield, the click of the leather loud in the stillness, and stepped closer, his boots crunching on the grass and gravel of the yard. "Angel," he said, his voice low, like he was calming a spooked horse. "We're gonna get him back. I promise you. My brother and me, we're here to help. You gotta know that by now."

"Help?" Angel blurted out, halfway laughing and halfway crying, cutting through the night with frightened desperation. "This is what you call help? My husband's gone, Wyatt. They dragged him off like a damn steer to the slaughterhouse. But not you. You're standin' there, not a mark on you, tellin' me you're here to help."

She jabbed the barrel of the rifle toward him, not aiming to fire, but to point out the obvious. Her hands shook with the urge to do something, anything, to make sense of the chaos. "I saw you take those bullets. I saw you stand there like it was nothin'. You and your brother, walkin' through all that hellfire like a Sunday stroll. Y'all ain't human."

Morgan came to the side of his brother, his hand resting on his rifle, but he stayed quiet, his eyes darting around as if he was looking out for any leftover Clanton men. There was something in that look of his, a shared secret he couldn't let slip. Wyatt briefly cast him a look that told him to drop it right then and there.

Angel had trusted them, let them into her home. But at the end of the day, what was happening was her fight, her life. With Virgil gone, she felt like a fool for believing in them at all, even if that was nothing compared to what she felt like having to ask them to pick up arms again and track her husband down.

"Now ain't the time to be worryin' about us. The Clantons took Virgil, but I guarantee they ain't plannin' to kill him, not just yet. They're tryin' to break you, and take the ranch in the process. They will offer him up in the hopes you will trade your livelihood for his life. You let that happen, and they win. You can't let them take everything you and Virgil built."

"Don't you dare talk about what was built here. You don't know what this place means. You don't know what it cost us, or what it's done to us." Her voice broke, and she hated herself for it, hated the way her hands shook as she clutched the rifle tighter. "He's all I got left, and you let them take him."

Wyatt's jaw tightened, but he didn't flinch. "I didn't let them take him, Angel. They got the drop on us. I swear to you we'll get him back."

"Swear?" She laughed again. "What's the word of a demon actually worth, Wyatt? Tell me, what could some shadow of a man who died a hundred years ago promise me? We were out of our minds to even give you the time of day. All the stress must've finally driven us mad. It's the only explanation that makes any sense."

Morgan finally spoke, his voice quieter than Wyatt's, but carrying the same weight. "We're here for a reason, ma'am. Maybe you don't understand it. Heck, maybe we don't either, but we're here. And we ain't leavin' till this is done."

"For once, I agree with my brother," Wyatt spoke, locking his eyes onto Angel. "This ain't over yet. You still need us."

Angel stared at him. Her chest was heaving, her mind a storm of grief and doubt and pure, unfiltered anger. She wanted to sprint into the woods, to chase after her husband. She wanted nothing more than to put one foot in front of the other until she was standing at the Clanton farm with a gun in her hand and a target to unleash the hate in her heart. She wasn't stupid, though. She knew it would be her own death sentence. Although Angel would never admit to such a thing at such a grief-stricken moment, Wyatt and Morgan were right. She needed them, but how could she trust something she didn't even believe was real? Her thoughts spiraled in on themselves until they left her crippled, unable to even stand. It was too much, too heavy, and she was drowning in the inaction that had taken hold since losing her husband. She dropped the rifle, letting it clatter to the ground as she sank to her knees again, her hands clawing against the floorboards, splintering beneath her nails. There was no way forward she could accept.

"It's over," she whispered. "There's *nothin'* left." Her voice trembled, and she wanted to cry, but there were no more tears left to shed. "The Clantons won. Or the bank will. Or those damn industries they're workin' for. It don't matter. They're gonna take it all, and I can't stop it, just like I couldn't stop Virgil from bein' taken. All I ever wanted was to give this place to our kids, but I've been a damn fool."

Wyatt crouched in front of her, his coat brushing the ground, those bullet holes staring at her like accusations. "You're still breathin', aren't you?" His voice cut through her whimpers like a blade lodged into her spine. "You listen here, if there is still dirt beneath your boots and a deed with your last name on it, then the fight ain't over yet. The Clantons ain't won nothin', we'll see to that. You just gotta fight with us. Besides, they don't know what they're up against."

"I can't," she said, never looking back at him. Angel shook her head, saying no over and over to nothing in particular. She wanted to scrape the floorboards up with her bare hands and bury herself beneath the home, to escape the torment of what she couldn't change. "You don't get it. I believed my husband when he said these crazy men and their plot to dig up a bunch of gold could save us. I let him bring you into our lives and it's done nothin' but go to hell ever since. You did this, you inhuman piece of shit."

Wyatt's eyes darkened, and he lowered his gaze, refusing to look away from her even when she was hinting at something so sinister. "Call us whatever you want, ma'am," he said. "The Clantons ain't gonna stop. They took Virgil only to offer him back up to you, askin' for the same price you wouldn't pay before, but with more leverage this time. You think they'll just give that up? You think they'll let him walk away just because you're scared? They'll burn this place to the ground, and they'll laugh while your whole life is destroyed. I promise you that."

Without her husband at her side, she couldn't shake the feeling that it was all just too much. Virgil was her tether to strength. He was her rock. Without him, the ranch was only dirt and debt, remnants of a dream born long before everything relied on a shovel and gold stolen from the Wild West.

She looked at Wyatt, at the holes in his coat, at the unearthly peace in his eyes that no living man should have at a time like this. She looked at Morgan, his rifle still in hand, his face unreadable but resolute. And she thought of Virgil, out there in the dark, fighting to live, if only to get back to her. The only thing she could rely on was herself in such a train wreck. The two men standing before her offered nothing but problems. They'd turned her life upside down, and she had nothing to show for it. For a split second, she thought of the golden coin Virgil had dug up, and she remembered how Wyatt had snagged it for himself.

"That coin," she said without thinking. "You still have it, don't you?"

Wyatt reached into his pocket and held it up, pinched between his fingers. The golden reflection glinting against the porch lights.

Angel couldn't look at it for long. She flicked her wrist and turned to walk away.

"There's your payment. Take it and get out. I never want to see your faces at the ranch again," she said without looking back. "It's time I figured this out for myself."

Chapter 19

Once a testament to the enduring legacy of the Wild West, its grit and determination to withstand the tests of time, the Holliday Ranch had become a graveyard of shadows and death and despair.

There were no more trails of cowboys coming to work the land or ranchers looking to buy stock for their herd. Cows and their calves roamed without direction on unfertilized pastures without hay to graze. Horses stood without saddles to carry or cubes to eat. It was a ghost town in the truest sense of the word.

The only souls left haunting its pastures were the Earp brothers, and even they intended on doing what they were told and hitting the road come daylight. Despite the storm brewing on the horizon, the air thick with churned earth and lingering gunpowder, Wyatt and Morgan found their solitude in a place that'd never failed them before—inside a bottle. Whiskey was the poison of choice, and it was a welcome escape from the night they'd had. Wyatt sat on a rickety chair inside the makeshift campgrounds, listening to the crackling logs of the fire no more than a few feet in front of him, his fingers grasping tightly around a half-empty bottle dangling over his thigh. Morgan sprawled himself out on the ground, lifted above the dirt by only a few pieces of fabric stretched taut beneath him.

The brothers were untouched, not a scratch on them, despite the lead that had torn through their bodies and clothing all throughout the night. Yet even then, they felt a different kind of pain. They felt for what the ranch was going through, for what Angel was suffering, and for the fate of her husband, Virgil. They were leaving empty-handed, but what was worse was the fact that they could be leaving behind death and destruction in their wake, not cold-blooded justice.

Wyatt leaned back in his chair and took another swig of whiskey, listening to the creaking of the chair's legs beneath his weight. His blank stare made it look like the fight he'd just been caught in the middle of was nothing more than a bad dream. He savored the liquor burning his insides for a few seconds before speaking up.

"We really gonna let it end like that?"

"I don't know you to quit anythin' in your life," Morgan answered. "Never really mattered if someone told you to or not."

Wyatt flicked the gold coin into the air. It hummed and whirred until it smacked in the middle of the palm of his hand. "Ain't just about the gold. But I'm tellin' you right here and now, there's a whole fortune buried in this dirt. Feel it all the way in my bones."

"You're gonna make me ask, aren't you?"

"Ask what?"

"What you're doin' this for, is it the gold or do you have a thing for that family?"

"A little o' both, I guess. I know she asked us to leave, but we both know this ain't a fight she can win alone."

"That's true."

"And if we give up now, we'll never know what we missed out on, either."

"There it is," Morgan said, finally looking up from his whiskey-fueled daze. "Capitalist to the core, aren't you?"

"You got a problem with bein' richer than a railroad baron?"

"I don't think people measure wealth by those standards anymore, Wyatt. World's changin'."

"It's always changin', but everyone still speaks the same language. World will change until the end of time, but it was built on men takin' what's theirs, and because of that, it'll always run on money," Wyatt said as he pushed the bottle to his chapped lips and turned it upside down. "This place isn't just worth a fortune, it's hidin' one too."

"I wish I shared your certainty, brother."

"Virgil and Angel are fightin' for their home, and their legacy. They are well aware of the same fact I'm hintin' at, let me tell you that right now."

Morgan shook his head, a grin creeping up on his face through it all, but his gaze drifted beyond his brother, where the night continued to engulf their camp until nothing was left on the horizon. "You think Angel's gonna let us stay after that fit she just threw back there? Kinda hard to come back after bein' called a damn demon."

"She's just scared, is all."

"Hell, Wyatt, she ain't wrong to wonder. I saw the

look in her eyes. She looked half-ready to burn this place down herself just to get rid of us."

Wyatt's lips twitched, not quite forming a smile just yet. "Think about what she's goin' through. Lost her man, her future, now she thinks she's lost her hope. Them rotten Clantons ain't done with her, either, and she knows it." He pressed his lips to the bottle again, the whiskey's bite formed a faint echo of the gunfire that haunted his thoughts. "We'll stay outta her hair tonight and check back with her in the mornin'. She'll come 'round by then, and then we can figure out how to get Virgil back."

The campfire crackled and popped, shushing the two brothers, just long enough for them to fall into an introspective silence. The fire cast long shadows that merged into the darkness surrounding them, dancing across the ground like specters celebrating their misfortune. Wyatt tried not to dwell on what had happened. His thoughts swirled from the hail of lead that he walked through without a flinch to the flicker of memory of sagebrush and gun smoke of a lifetime ago, and he forced himself to concentrate on the moment at hand.

Whiskey hit his tongue again without a second thought. He swished it around his mouth, letting it burn his gums and the back of his throat before forcing it into his gut. He took another swig, then another. His thoughts slowly began to wrangle themselves under control. He could see the hurt in Angel's eyes as she lashed out at them.

"I got my doubts, but you never let me down before," Morgan said between drinks of his own.

"This is *ours* for the takin' now," Wyatt answered, halfway speaking to Morgan, trying his best to reassure himself. "We help Angel, we get Virgil back, and we walk away with enough to set us up for good. That's the game."

Morgan raised his bottle in a mock salute. "To the game, then."

They drank in unison. The whiskey was no different than a ritual they shared together, a moment of defiance against the hellish night and the scorn of a woman who'd told them to leave. The campfire flickered, casting a shadow that moved eerily wrong, too slow, too deliberate. Wyatt's hand stilled on the bottle, his fingers grasping it just a little tighter, his eyes narrowing.

Morgan froze, his bottle halfway to his lips, his gaze snapping downwind to the north. Their makeshift camp was set apart from the main house across the pasture to the west. Angel had already retreated inside.

"You hear that?" Morgan whispered, his drunken slur gone in an instant.

Wyatt nodded, setting the bottle down in the dirt silently. His Schofield revolver lay at his side, close enough to grab. The wind whistled in the distance, carrying nothing with it to be seen. A shift in the shadows sent the Earp brothers scrambling to their feet, firearms in hand and at the ready. A snap came next, louder than the wind, followed by the creak of leather, deliberate, unhurried. Whoever was out there wasn't trying to hide their presence by any means.

"Clanton?" Morgan mouthed, his finger inching toward the trigger of his lever-action rifle.

Wyatt shook his head and lifted his revolver at nothing. They'd learned more than enough about Clanton's men in the firefight. They were cowards who refused to show their faces. They skulked in the dark, choosing to shoot you in the back and run away before anyone knew any better. This was different, like a challenge.

The shadows split in the night, and a silhouette appeared, at first shapeless and void, then towering and menacing. The figure stood motionless, broad and hunched, with a face covered in darkness, shrouded beneath a bent, dented cowboy hat. It was a man, but Wyatt couldn't tell anything else about who was standing before them.

The man took a step forward.

Wyatt clicked the hammer back on his revolver, locking it into place. Morgan followed by racking his rifle, chambering a fresh round.

The man seemed older than the ranch itself. His skin was leathery and creased, his eyes glinted wild and feverish in the light of the campfire flickering across his face. In his right hand was a double-barreled shotgun, still broken in half in the crook of his arm. The air itself around him curdled and twisted, heavy with the stench of tobacco and grime. His voice carried the traces of death itself, like a corpse left in the sun too long.

"Don't shoot, don't shoot. I don't want to fight," the man said. "Been lookin' for you boys. You been stickin' your nose where it don't belong."

"Give it a rest, old man," Wyatt said, still holding his revolver up, ready to fire in a split second.

The shotgun clicked into place and was jammed against the intruder's shoulder before Wyatt and Morgan could realize what was happening.

"You don't wanna do this," Morgan urged.

"This ranch ain't yours, never was. Shoulda minded your own business."

"This is our business," Wyatt answered. "We bought the claim here, fair and square."

"I thought you didn't want to fight. You a Clanton, mister?" Morgan's question landed like a ten-pound weight in a pond.

The old man let out a laugh that sent a chill down the Earp brothers' spines. It was dry and punctuated by wheezing and hacking. "You don't know what I am…" his voice trailed off into a whisper.

Morgan afforded himself a glance at his brother. Wyatt tilted his head and darted his eyes back to the man in front of them. "Why don't we—"

"Just like I don't know what *you* are," the man uncurled his hunch, standing tall and upright, confidence settling into his stance. He leaned forward, keeping the shotgun trained directly on Wyatt.

Three firearms were a hair away from unleashing gunpowder and lead on one another. Two were trained at the strange man interrupting the Earp brothers' drunken tirade, with one double-barreled shotgun trained right back at them.

Wyatt was the first to break the standoff. He lifted his finger and motioned for Morgan to take it down a notch, then he spoke, "Sounds like this man has a story to tell."

"Sure does," said Morgan, without pulling his rifle away.

"You gonna oblige us, sir?"

"Ain't no story," the old man told them. "You two might've crawled out of the pits of hell for all I know, but one thing's for certain, I'm gonna send you right back by blowin' you both to kingdom come."

The first blast came without warning. A cloud of gunpowder-filled smoke bellowed out, followed by a muzzle blast spewing out a thousand lead balls with only one goal—to maim and murder without hesitation.

The second blast followed immediately after. Another *boom* from the double barrel, another plume of smoke, another thousand lead balls back by fire pouring out.

Wyatt and Morgan remained where they stood as the smoke cleared.

"So, it is true," the old man said, lowering his shotgun at last.

The three men stared at one another for a few awkward seconds. A stillness fell over them, one that felt like it was from a century ago. The wind died down, matching the creatures of the night, until there wasn't so much as a blade of grass swaying. A chill sank into their bones.

The quiet didn't last long. A sudden thud of the old man's shotgun hitting the ground sent them into a flurry of deadly action. The old man yanked at his hip, producing a seven and a half inch .44-40 Colt revolver from its holster.

He only managed to fire off one bullet this time.

Wyatt and Morgan were ready for what was to come. Wyatt squeezed the trigger once, and his Schofield howled in response. The muzzle lifted just as the old man clutched at his chest. Before he could topple over, Morgan fired his lever-action, and a bullet slammed into his shoulder, sending him flying backward until he was flat on his back, staring up endlessly at the pitch-black night sky.

There was no blood pooling beneath his body or

ragged breaths of a man struggling to cling to the final few seconds of his own life. There was no twitching or last curses to be uttered. There was nothing but a shadow of a man lying dead in the dirt.

"What the hell just happened?" Morgan couldn't help himself.

Wyatt kept his revolver aimed at the man. He approached him slowly and steady, never ready to surrender his advantage until death was certain. When he looked down at the stranger who'd opened fire at them, his heart lodged in his throat, and his stomach twisted in knots. The man's eyes were locked on Wyatt, but he was not alive. It was the kind of stare that would haunt a man until his dying day, and it would be burned into Wyatt's brain forever. He recognized the man lying in the dirt, but he could not say the name. They'd known each other in another lifetime, when the world wasn't so small and disconnected.

"Who is it?"

Morgan's question fell on deaf ears.

"It had to be one of Clanton's men. Right?"

Again, Morgan was met with no response.

Wyatt nudged the body with his boot to make sure there were no more surprise bullets coming his way, then he knelt down beside the man. The campfire flickered just behind them, sending shadows crawling over the man's face, glinting in his unmoving eyes still fixated on Wyatt like an old oil painting. Whether it was justice or just another man gunned down was a question for another day. For now, Wyatt would be satisfied just by figuring out who had come to attack them. A torn edge of paper was protruding from the inner coat pocket of the old man. Wyatt reached down gently and plucked it from the corpse. He could just barely make out a name scribbled in cursive on what turned out to be a deteriorating, old, folded letter.

"*Billy Clanton,*" he whispered.

Chapter 20

The Holliday Ranch would never be the same again.

It was a battered thing, its bones creaking, desperate to snap under the weight of violence that came in like waves battering the shoreline. The pastures were scarred and destroyed, and bullet casings littered the front yard and around the barn. Fortune and happiness were a distant memory in such a hellscape.

Angel was standing at the foot of the staircase that led to their bedroom. Her breath was shallow and sharp. The lever-action Winchester was propped against the wall behind her, its barrel cold, its trigger numb to the trauma she was enduring. Her fingers dug into the trim around the doorframe, causing white paint to build up beneath her fingernails.

It would only be a couple of hours before the sun burned away the night that she hoped to forget for the rest of her life. Tragedy was something that happened in the movies. Tears would fall, and people would hug, then life would move on. Her reality was different. In the faint traces of comfort she found in the four walls of the family home following the firefight that saw Virgil, her beloved husband, taken hostage, her sense of security was shattered once again.

She reached down and winced as she peeled back the gauze on her arm, revealing a gash deep enough to warrant stitches, coated in dried blood.

She'd almost died. Not in the firefight, not when Clanton's men rode in like thieves in the night to steal her husband during a hail of gunfire, not even as she watched Virgil get dragged away by a rope tied to a horse like he was a victim of frontier justice gone wrong. It was after the nightmare, when the stillness of the night overtook her, after she'd stumbled back into the house and collapsed into loneliness with tears staining her face.

It wasn't long before Angel had found herself sitting at the kitchen table, her thoughts racing to find a solution to get her husband back. His chair was next to hers, empty and desolate, no different than the pain she felt in her chest. She was staring into oblivion, coming face-to-face with the worst of her own imagination when terror struck her yet again.

The kitchen window exploded inward, a stray bullet from an unseen shooter tore through the glass and grazed her shoulder, leaving a searing kiss in her arm. Blood soaked her sleeve and dripped down her wrist before she even knew what was happening. She fell to the floor, crawling on her knees as her heart pounded and her body was flooded yet again with adrenaline. She'd sobbed without making a sound, waiting for the next bullet to find its way into her home. It never came.

The silence that fell over once again mocked her.

Another near-death experience when she could barely stand upright as it was. Fate had taken another swing at her, and it had missed again. Now, standing at the staircase, feeling the sting of blood crusted on her arm, she felt more fragile than ever. She held onto hope that her husband was still alive, maybe even breaking a few bones of his captors while they struggled to keep him bound in rope. She wanted to find anything inside her that she could cling to, anything that would help her to recover Virgil. The ranch was a stubborn patch of dirt, demanding more out of her than she ever had to give. It was the home of her and Virgil's fight against a world that only wanted to chew them up and spit them out.

She wasn't sure how long she'd been standing at the staircase, unwilling to take the first step to climb up to their bedroom and rest her head. She just stood there. Her hand rested on the rail, and her eyes looked up to the second floor, but she never moved her foot. There was a fire in her chest, kindled by what she'd just survived, sparking a revelation that burned brighter than any fear she'd ever felt before. She stood long enough for the darkness to begin to dissolve around her home and the sun to shine its unwelcome morning light through the shattered window, glinting off of pieces of glass scattered across the floor.

Boots hitting the steps on the front porch came and went. She was lost in her own daze and didn't pay any attention. Knocks came next, but she still couldn't break away. A bang on the door and a shout from the other side finally snapped her back into reality, and it would be the last time she ever allowed herself to fall to pieces again. Not while her husband still needed her.

Angel turned around just as she heard her name being called from the front porch. She lifted the rifle from the floor and tossed it casually over her shoulder before swinging the door open. Wyatt and Morgan were standing in front of her, riddled with bullet holes. Her eyes traced dozens of holes in their clothing, making them look as though they'd just left the front-lines of a war unharmed. Their faces were unmarred by the fight that should've taken their lives a dozen times over. Wyatt's Schofield revolver was nestled in its holster at his hip, and Morgan cradled his own rifle in his arms like it was taking a nap. Their eyes carried the same unnatural calm she came to resent, unbothered by the horrific things they were caught in the middle of.

As soon as she locked eyes with Wyatt, she cringed at her own words. *Demons.* She didn't know what they were, but she knew she shouldn't have treated them like that, not when they were trying to help her. No one deserved that. Her shoulders sank, and her eyes welled up with tears once again, even though she hated herself for crying, she let the tears fall.

Wyatt took a step forward and scooped her up, squeezing her shoulders just long enough to make a difference. Morgan patted her on the shoulder before they all stood face-to-face once more on the porch.

"You're still here," she whispered, her voice scraped raw. "Thought I told both of y'all to go."

Wyatt pulled his dented straw cowboy hat from his head and ran his fingers through his hair. He sat it on top of his head again and spoke plainly to her. "Ain't never been too keen on takin' orders, Angel. Not when the fight ain't done yet."

Morgan reached for her arm, but Angel jerked back. "You hurt?"

"I'm fine," she answered. "More than fine, actually."

"Is that right?" Wyatt questioned.

"I was sittin' there last night, wallowin' and cryin' my eyes out, wonderin' what I am supposed to do next to get Virgil back. Next thing I know, a bullet shatters the kitchen window and tears through my arm. That's when I knew, I wasn't any different than both of y'all. I'm supposed to fight for this place, it's always been me."

"Now, that's the spirit," said Wyatt. "I knew you were too tough to break."

Angel pushed past both Wyatt and Morgan, her boots scuffing the floorboards as she walked right over the Clanton brand still burned into her home. "It ain't about bein' tough, it's about this." She lifted her arms up, gesturing to the ranch, the barn, the pastures, even the horizon she just watched Virgil vanish into when the Clantons took him. "This place is everything. We've given it everything, and it damn sure has no problem taking every bit of it. I convinced Virgil to leave his job a long time ago, to move the kids out here so they had a proper childhood. We planted dreams in this dirt, and we watched them grow and change and become what we always wanted them to be."

She adjusted the rifle still leaning on her shoulder and looked up at the morning sky, taking in the sun climbing in the east and the clouds gathering in the south. She felt the breeze wick the tears from her cheeks and the sweat from her brow, and she allowed herself to feel something other than crippling doubt.

"Those bastards are gonna get more than they

bargained for. The Clantons won't get away this time. I don't care if they control the banks, the police, or a thousand men. Death is comin' for all of 'em. They don't know what this ranch means, what it stands for," her voice carried across the incoming breeze with the weight of a woman who'd stared death in the face and refused to back down.

Wyatt and Morgan stood silent, like soldiers coming back from the brink of death, waiting for their final orders. Their eyes never changed, holding that same eerie serenity that made Angel's skin crawl.

"This ranch is our blood, and those sons of bitches are hell-bent on spillin' it until there ain't nothin' left." She turned to Wyatt as she spoke, her eyes blazing, the fire in her chest burning hotter than the gash on her arm. "I was ready to give up last night, Wyatt. I sat at that table, starin' at Virgil's empty chair, thinkin' it was all over. Then, that damn bullet came through the window and sliced open my arm, but it woke somethin' up deep inside me, somethin' I didn't even realize was there. I'm done clingin' onto hope. Hope for my husband, my poor Virgil, hope for this ranch, hope for everything we've bled for. I'm done with hope. It's time I took matters into my own hands while I still got breath in my lungs."

Morgan shifted, his rifle cradled like an extension of himself, a faint grin tugging at his lips. "You're talkin' like a general, Angel. It's a good thing you got us."

"About that," she answered, "I should apologize to you both. I know what I said was wrong, especially since you were willin' to take up arms for me and my family, for this place. I called you demons, and even though I don't know what you are, truly, I do know that you both have stuck your necks out further for us than anyone has in more than a decade. I'm sorry."

"You can go ahead and cut that kinda talk out right now," Wyatt wasted no time in responding. "There's still a fight waitin' on us, and Morgan and I are determined to see it through to the end, one way or another."

"I know you aren't exactly riskin' your lives doin' all this, but I want to tell you I appreciate it nonetheless."

"So, what's the plan?"

"The plan is simple, lots of fuckin' guns," she answered with a newfound sternness settling into her voice. "Guns, ammo, and whatever we need to track those Clantons down and bring Virgil home. We don't wait for 'em to come back. We take the fight to them, hit 'em where they live. We burn their world down before they can strike the match on ours."

Wyatt's eyes glinted, a familiar trace of a smile curling on his lips. "You're talkin' my language, Angel. But the Clantons ain't small-time. They got men, money, and someone pullin' their strings. You sure you're ready for that kind of fight?"

"I don't have a choice," she stepped closer to the Earp brothers as she spoke. "I know I was born for this fight, though. And I got a couple of aces up my sleeve that sure won't hurt, either."

Wyatt and Morgan couldn't help but crack a smile at her remark.

"I don't know how you two walk through bullets like they're rain, and the way I'm feelin' right now, I was wrong to care. You're here, and you'll fight with me. That's all that matters."

Morgan completed his low, dragged-out chuckle,

tipping his own hat when he'd finished. "Hell, Angel, you're makin' me wish I'd met you a hundred years ago. We could've raised some serious hell."

"Still can," she said, without missing a beat. "We find their trail, we find Virgil, and we end this whole dang thing once and for all. Clanton will bleed out before he steps foot on this ranch again."

She turned to the horizon, where the sun was becoming a blazing disc, painting the pasture gold. This time, as she overlooked her family's legacy, she couldn't shake the feeling that the Holliday Ranch looked like a battlefield—torn earth, shattered fences, the barn all shot up, but still standing. The fire in her chest grew. It was a beacon now, guiding her through the grief, the doubt, the fear. She could almost hear Virgil's voice, his stubborn laugh, telling her to keep going, to hold the line. She would.

As if the devil himself heard Angel's threat, a thunder rose in the distance. The rumble could be felt before it was heard, like it came from deep beneath the ground. It was a low growl that shook the earth like a storm rolling in. Angel froze where she stood, her grip tightening on the Winchester as the rumbling grew louder and louder, distorting itself until it became a mechanical roar that drowned out even her own thoughts. She squinted into the distance, where dust clouds bloomed along the property fence lines, swallowing the golden light of the rising sun. Her heart sank. She knew she would not have to hold the line for long.

Wyatt and Morgan turned, their unsettling calm still refusing to be snapped, but their hands drifted to their weapons, instincts honed by more than a century of gunfighting and backstabbing.

"What the *hell* is that?" Angel muttered, her voice barely audible over the roar of her invaders, hidden in a cloud of dust.

Wyatt tilted his hat back, his eyes narrowing. "Trouble, ma'am."

The first of the eighteen-wheelers crested the hill, its chrome grille glinting against the Texas sun like a predator's teeth. Behind it came another, then a third, and a fourth, their trailers rattling with emptiness, waiting to haul away Angel and Virgil's livelihood. The ground trembled as they tore down the driveway leading to the Holliday Ranch, kicking up gravel and dust that choked the air. Following close behind were flatbeds hauling massive mining equipment—excavators with steel claws large enough to dismantle skyscrapers, bulldozers that could rip the heart out of the earth, and the makings of a wash plant capable of running every ounce of dirt on the ranch. The Clantons were coming to do more than just steal their home, they were going to take everything the Holliday Ranch could ever offer, and leave its bones in their wake.

Angel's throat tightened, but the fire in her chest burned hotter. "They can't do this," she said, her voice coming like a dagger to cut through the chaos. "Not today. Not ever."

"Look at all that," Morgan shifted his rifle in his hands uncomfortably as he spoke. "Reckon they think this is a done deal."

"Let 'em think it," Wyatt said, his Schofield revolver already in hand, spinning lazily in his fingers. "Ain't none of that devilry gonna save them from what's comin'."

The convoy of blacked out SUVs and pickups

rolled to a stop at the edge of the ranch, led by a single 1980s model Cadillac Sedan DeVille with cattle horns as wide as the hood strapped to the front end, their tires crunching over the bullet casings still scattered in the dirt from their fight only a night ago. Each vehicle bore the same ominous Clanton family logo. Men spilled out of the trucks—Clanton's hired gunmen, an untrained mix of roughneck cowboys and overall-wearing farmhands, all armed to the teeth. Rifles, shotguns, and pistols of every caliber gleamed in the sunlight. A gangly, well-dressed man was the last to climb out. Joe Clanton rose above the sedan like a giant among men, a half-smile curled at the corner of his lips, and eyes hidden behind sunglasses far too big for his face. He wore an untarnished jet-black felt cowboy hat despite the ninety-degree heat and humidity, a black jacket, jeans, and square-toe boots to match. There wasn't a firearm to be seen on him, but he wasn't the kind of man to bring a knife to a gunfight. He reached up, placing the stub end of a cigarette between his lips for one final pull before flicking it into the dirt and exhaling a haze of smoke into the air.

He stepped forward—flanked by two men in tactical vests, each cradling an AR-15 like they were born holding it—and smashed the still-lit cigarette beneath his boot. "Angel Holliday! If that really is the name you claim!" Joe's voice boomed across the yard, dripping with false courtesy and self-righteous fury.

Angel took a step forward without thinking, then stopped herself. The Winchester hung at her side, but her eyes were locked on Joe, unyielding and unforgiving. She wanted to call him every curse word under the sun, she wanted to start unloading every bullet she had right at his head, but all she could do was stare.

"You've had a *rough* night, I hear. Thought we'd come on by and lighten your load."

"That son of a—" Angel started beneath her breath.

"I'm a fair man with simple needs," Joe's hollering cut her short. He was walking slowly down the driveway toward her, speaking with wild hand gestures and a condescending tone that irked every nerve Angel had. "I have tried to be nice about this whole thing, honest to God, I have. I didn't want it to come to this. If there was any other thing to be done about my situation, it would have been done already. I come bearing an unfortunate message for you, Angel, and if I may be frank, also your ancestors."

Angel allowed herself to walk forward, matching Joe's pace. Her thoughts spiraled, and she fought against the hopelessness that was always haunting the edges of her mind. By the time she reached no more than thirty feet away from the man who'd caused so much suffering in her life, her eyes were burning with tears of rage.

"You got some nerve, Clanton, showin' your face here after what you done," she said. "Where is my husband?"

Joe spread his hand and showed her his palms, making a mockery of innocence. "Now, now, let's not get ahead of ourselves. I'm a businessman. You know that. And I think you also know that you're sittin' on a literal gold mine here at the fine institution known as the Holliday Ranch. To put it simply, I'm here to make sure it don't go to waste. Those trucks back there?" He jerked a thumb toward the eighteen-wheelers.

"They're for your cattle, your supplies, anything worth a dime, or even a nickel for that matter. And that equipment?"—he nodded at the excavators, their steel arms looming like vultures circling a corpse—"that's to dig up what's rightfully ours. You can walk away with a fat check, or you can make this harder than it needs to be."

Angel's laugh was bitter and filled with hatred. "*Rightfully* yours? The only thing rightfully yours is the lead waitin' inside this Winchester. It's got your name all over it."

Joe's smile faded, his eyes as cold as a snake ready to strike. "Hollow threats and empty promises are all you've got left, I'm afraid. Your husband is rather indisposed at the moment, wouldn't you say? And judgin' by the sight of you, you ain't ready for what's to come. I'd say now is as good of a chance as you'll ever have to walk away alive. The ranch is gone, you can go ahead and wrap your head around that. If you can, maybe you can see that sweet face of Virgil again while he's still breathin'."

The mention of Virgil hit like a punch, but Angel didn't flinch. She felt Wyatt and Morgan at her back—the aces up her sleeve. "You're a *coward*, Joe, a murderin', cheatin', no good coward," she said. "Always hidin' behind your men, your money, but I see who you really are. I see behind that fancy hat and those freakish boots. You want everyone to think you're rollin' in cash, don't you? Well, if you want this ranch, you're gonna have to pry it from the cold, dead hands of those who stand in your way."

Joe chuckled, but it was hollow. "Have it your way."

He raised a hand, and the men behind him fanned

out, forming a loose semicircle around the front yard of the Holliday Ranch. The excavators roared to life, their engines snarling as they lurched forward, tearing into the pasture with ruthless precision. The ground shook as steel claws ripped through the earth, uprooting grass and dreams in equal measures. The eighteen-wheelers idled, their drivers ready to load up whatever the Clantons deemed valuable.

Wyatt stepped forward, his revolver glinting in the sunlight. "You're makin' a mistake, Clanton," he said. "This ain't your land. Never will be. You need to give it up while you still can."

"You'll have to explain to me how you're still livin' when this is all done," Joe said as he turned his attention to Wyatt. His eyes lingered on the bullet holes in their jackets and the way their fingers twitched for the trigger of their guns. He buried what he saw beneath his bravado and spoke again, "If you still can, of course."

Morgan let out a laugh that came from his belly, long and drawn out, louder than it should've been. The interruption earned him a pair of stern, demanding glares from Angel and his brother before he decided to cut it short.

The Clanton men shifted uneasily while the Earp brother let out his laugh. Their guns were still raised, but their confidence wavered visibly. It was a turn in the tide against the Holliday Ranch, and it was just what Angel needed to see. It was also a shift that Joe Clanton himself could feel, all the way down to his bones.

"I got nothin' to hide," he said as he turned his attention back to Angel and the only leverage of power he still had. "Everyone knows you're hidin' a bunch of gold up here. The whole town says you're too much of a shut-in to spend it anywhere. They say you're just hoardin' it so your kids can do the same. They call it the Holliday family tradition. Did you know that?"

Angel was already fuming. Her eyes darted back and forth from Joe to the gunmen, making sure she didn't miss her opportunity when it came.

"Clanton Family Farms, Inc. is growin' every single day. It's a beast that ain't hard to wrangle, even on an easy day. With all the regulations comin' out of Austin and twice as many comin' out of Washington, DC, it's a wonder any of us still has a job. When you factor in all the inflation and immigration and middlemen and—"

"You're broke, too, aren't you?" Angel couldn't help herself.

"Don't you *dare* put words in my mouth, you filthy piece of—" Joe caught himself, brushed his jacket, and hiked up his pants a little higher, flashing an exotic leather Angel couldn't identify on his boots, then spoke gently. "I have every bit a need for that gold in the dirt as you. How's that?"

"I knew there was a real person somewhere inside you. Glad you could let it out for all of us to see. I will say, all of that minin' equipment sure does make a whole lot more sense now."

"You struck a deal with those men behind you," Joe shot back. "Ain't no reason why we can't work ourselves up somethin' even better."

"What's gonna happen if I say no?"

Joe Clanton lifted a hand, and his men all chambered a bullet in unison, the clanking of firearms erupting like an army waiting on their orders.

"Am I being clear enough?"

"I'd rather die," she answered without hesitating.

"I thought you might say somethin' like that," said Joe. This time, he snapped his fingers, and the door to his Cadillac flung open in an instant. "I know all about the stubbornness that runs in your side of the family. Who doesn't know the triumphant resilience of the legend known as John Henry *Doc* Holliday? Gambler, gunfighter, and ever loyal friend to the long arm of justice. Well, that's all fine and dandy, but what does that mean for the one you love?"

Virgil fell out of the backseat of the sedan, bound in rope and duct tape, covered in blood. His muffled scream punctuated the ringing in Angel's ears at the sight of her husband. A masked gunman followed, standing over the top of him. Virgil crawled toward her with his wrists tied, barely moving through his struggle. His eyes begging to be nearer to his wife. The gunman lifted a pistol, aiming it at the back of Virgil's head.

All Angel could do was scream.

Chapter 21

They say history repeats itself, that we live in a never-ending loop of tragedy briefly interrupted by moments of peace lasting just long enough to forget about what lies waiting in the shadows. Some people can never forget, though. Some things change people forever. Sometimes, tragedy refuses to be interrupted.

Angel's scream still hung in the air, raw and hoarse, with tears already streaming down her face as she watched her husband try to crawl away from a fate far crueler than anyone deserved.

Time itself slowed. The Holliday Ranch narrowed to only a ray of sunlight glinting off the end of a pistol barrel. Angel's heart thundered in her ears, pounding like a drum carrying the tune of a war dance soon to come. She saw Virgil's eyes, frantic and full of fear, locked with her own. There was no time to plead for mercy or fight back against the inevitable. There was no time to do anything but watch her world fall apart.

Wyatt's hand was an inhuman blur, his Schofield

revolver flashed in the Texas sun, and in a fraction of a second, justice was dispensed.

The gunman's head snapped back, a crimson burst sprayed directionless into the air, and his body crumpled lifelessly into the dirt. His pistol clattered harmlessly beside Virgil as confusion and shock took hold of the invaders. There was a strange few seconds of silence that followed, broken only by the pounding of boots against the dirt as three of Clanton's men abandoned the fight right then and there. No one said anything, likely because no one blamed them for doing what everyone was already thinking. But those few seconds of silence wouldn't last long. Wyatt's gunshot was a match struck in a powder keg ready to blow, and it ignited the ranch into full-scale, absolute chaos.

A line of weapons roared to life, an explosion of muzzle blasts poured out in a deafening cacophony of gunfire, producing a hail of bullets aimed right at the Earp brothers. Dirt and gravel flew into the air as the front yard was pounded with lead. The old family home just behind where the brothers stood splintered and shattered against a relentless storm of shots slamming into the wood siding and windows. Bullets tore through the air, destroying everything in their path without remorse. It was an ear-splitting, overwhelming outburst of gunfire that threatened to engulf everything alive or dead at the ranch in one fell swoop.

Angel was ready, though. She dove to the side, her rifle snapping to her shoulder in an instant as she fired round after round into the line of men attacking everything she'd ever loved in this world. She had the lever-action rocking back and forth, cycling new rounds as fast as she could squeeze the trigger in her scramble for cover. She found safety from the horrendous death promised by every bullet hurling her direction, but there wasn't much she could do on the other side of an old pickup that had already seen too many firefights in its life.

The gunman closest to her clutched his chest and fell, dropping the shotgun to the ground as he took his final breath. Two more dropped right where they stood. The exchange of gunfire seemed to rage on longer than what should've been possible. By the time Angel was able to grasp what was happening, the Earp brothers had already gone to work.

Wyatt and Morgan stood shoulder to shoulder against an endless onslaught. Their movements were synchronized, as if their hands were guided by the ghosts of their past, telling them where their enemy would be seconds before they moved. Wyatt fanned his revolver's powerful .44 caliber bullets with deadly calm, each one a blazing, unstoppable act of modern-day frontier justice. Morgan's rifle swept the Clanton line, forcing the hired guns to scatter for cover behind their trucks and SUVs. The Earps had been outnumbered before. They knew what it took to be unyielding, to face off against the kind of men who were hell-bent on killing anyone they thought stood in their way.

The Clanton line faltered, their bravery depleted before their magazines were empty, their will to die for a paycheck crumbled under the Earps' relentless assault. Those who tried to run away were not shot in the back, but those who pressed on, who thought they could kill Wyatt and Morgan with gunpowder and lead alone, were left to discover a fate worse than death all by themselves.

Amid the racket of the gunfire and brief pauses to reload, Angel crawled in the dirt to find a way to her husband. When she made it around to the other side of the pickup, she saw Virgil doing the same. They lurched forward, their knees and elbows bloody and screaming in pain as they desperately fought to get close to one another.

The duct tape came away in sticky clumps across Virgil's face, revealing bruises and cuts that made the terror in his eyes palpable. His eyes were glassy from the surge of adrenaline, but he never stopped.

The feeling of relief that washed over Angel when she finally grabbed his hand was indescribable. They were surrounded by men trying to kill them, ducking bullets flying inches over their heads, and leaving their own lives to chance in order to hold each other one more time. When they finally scrambled behind the pickup together, they fell into one another's arms.

"Hold on, baby," she whispered into the hair on the side of his head as she pushed her lips to him.

"I'm all right, I'm all right, I'm all right," Virgil repeated over and over again.

Angel pulled back, now having to shout at the swell of gunfire that came as soon as she made eye contact with her husband. "Did you get hit? Are you bleeding?"

"I'm all right," Virgil said again, his eyes tearing up.

She grabbed his face, one hand on either cheek, and squeezed him closer to her just long enough to plant a terribly timed kiss on his lips. "I thought you were dead, Virgil! I thought I lost you!"

"I'm here now," he told her with a raspy voice. "And just so you know, I'm sick of this shit."

"Me too, baby," she said through a smile she never should've shown. "Me too."

"Let's end it, then."

From the other side of the pickup, neither Angel nor Virgil could see the one who'd brought this down on them trying to flee for his life. Joe Clanton was sprinting back to the cattle-horn-grilled Cadillac that brought him into the ranch as his men unleashed hell. His boots slid on the gravel, forcing him to catch himself with his hands before he could slide behind the trunk of the car. Bullets lodged into the door and rear panel, then shattered the windows, almost masking Joe's high-pitched shrieks of fear with every close call.

"You're makin' a mistake, Earps!" he bellowed through the panic coursing through his veins. "This ain't your fight!"

Wyatt's response was a bullet that shattered the Cadillac's rear taillight, inches from Joe's head, sending blistering pieces of glass and plastic into his eyes.

Angel peered from beneath the pickup, her breath ragged but her resolve unbreakable. She could only see from the knees down of her attackers, but she knew the Clanton men were regrouping, even if their numbers were dwindling and their desperation growing. She spotted one of the overall-wearing farmhands making a break for it, but he wasn't abandoning the fight. He was sprinting toward one of the excavators. It must've been at least a thirty-ton piece of equipment, painted bright yellow with tracks that looked like a tank made for war and a bucket large enough to wipe out their home in one swing. Its diesel engine screamed when it came alive, and the hydraulics hissed louder than any gunshots ringing out. Angel's stomach sank.

"He's gonna use that to break us up," she told Virgil.

Through bloody teeth and bloodshot eyes, her husband responded, "He won't stand a chance."

The excavator crawled through the earth, ripping chunks as the trucks hurled it forward with monstrous growls. The bucket swung to the side, showcasing its steel teeth, each one larger than a man's head. Its operator sat nestled inside the cab behind tinted windows, maneuvering levers like his life depended on it.

Clanton's gunmen wasted no time in seizing the opportunity provided by the excavator's entrance into the fight. Ten men swarmed behind the machinery with firearms pushed to their shoulders, spewing lead in sporadic fashion.

"Morgan!" Virgil hollered before pointing out the excavator crawling forward in its unstoppable approach. "Stop that bastard!"

Morgan nodded, his rifle swinging toward the excavator. A single shot punched through the cab's window, and the farmhand slumped forward just as the machine ground to a sudden halt no more than twenty feet from where the Earps stood. The distraction cost Morgan, though. A Clanton gunman had flanked him in the few seconds it took to stop the excavator. He fired a shotgun blast that lodged itself right in Morgan's chest. The impact staggered him, nearly taking him off his feet, but he didn't fall. Bullet holes already riddled his jacket, and the new pellets joined the tapestry. He turned to face the gunman, showing his feral grin, and opened fire, dropping him right where he stood.

Angel's stomach churned at the sight. She still didn't understand what Wyatt and Morgan were, but she knew she needed them. She turned to Virgil, doing her best to put aside the thoughts of what consequences awaited her in eternity for relying on their help.

"Can you shoot?" she asked, but her voice became drowned out in the gunfire as soon as she spoke.

He coughed, blood flecking his lips, but he never lost his resolve. "Gimme a gun."

Angel reached behind her back and yanked a spare revolver from her waistband, then shoved it into his hands. It was an old .38 Special six-shooter that Virgil kept in the barn for emergencies, but it would have to do.

The firefight raged on all around them. It had been only fifteen minutes, but each second ticked by in agony, becoming a brutal dance of lead and smoke where the only ones left standing would own the ground they walked. The Clanton men, their ranks thinning, fired wildly, coming close only by accident in their frantic state. Some of their shots missed so drastically that they tore through the barn's walls opposite where they should have been aiming.

Angel spun from around the front end of the pickup and returned fire, her Winchester's lever-action a steady rhythm, each shot resulting in the rifle getting lighter and lighter in her grasp. The fight would soon turn desperate, and then they would all be sorted accordingly. She shook the fears from her focus and dropped another gunman. His body fell into the dirt behind a splatter of red. The cost was high, though. Bullets grazed her arm, reigniting the pain from the previous night's stray shot. A wound on top of a wound. She screamed out, gritted her teeth, and blasted off another round in anger. The fire in her chest was burning hotter than the sting ever could.

Virgil followed his wife's lead. He stood behind the

truck, reaching over the bed with the revolver in his grasp. For a split second, the terror that coursed through his veins when he was roped and dragged away from everything he loved found its way back to him. He remembered the rage that came when he was made to feel helpless, the heartbreak that weighed over him when he thought of his wife, and the twisted desires he had to end every single one of the Clanton men to protect his life. Then, he pulled the trigger.

Wyatt and Morgan pushed forward through it all. They moved like apparitions through a home they'd once wandered a hundred years ago. The hail of bullets passed through them like the breeze, each mortal wound that never came striking more fear into the ill-equipped Clanton gunmen. Wyatt's revolver cracked, taking the life of a cowboy hat-wearing man in his fifties who'd chosen to aim a rifle in the wrong direction. Morgan's shots kept the Clanton line pinned, preventing them from advancing.

Joe Clanton's voice rose again, shrill and distraught. The fight had already gone on much longer than he'd ever anticipated, and he let it show in his voice as he said, "The ink has already dried, my friends! This ranch is ours and there ain't nothin' that can be done about it now!"

"One of us is dyin' today, Clanton!" Virgil shouted back before shooting a demented smile at his wife.

Wyatt and Morgan continued carving through the Clanton ranks with deadly precision. Their firearms spewed flame and smoke, and bodies kept falling. What looked like dozens of men now seemed to be only a few, stubborn gun hands who knew just enough to stay alive. The Earp brothers stayed side by side, never faltering, never surrendering. Bullets tore through everything they wore, some even ricocheted off their firearms, but they just kept going, pausing only long enough to jam more bullets into their guns.

There were only three pockets of Clanton men still holed up in the fight, and not a single one of them made any effort to save their boss, Joe Clanton, who was still pinned down behind the Cadillac.

Angel and Virgil emerged from behind the truck just as the bullets began to die down, moving rapidly in unison to find cover before going right back to firing again. They focused on the few men still clinging to life behind the excavator idling aimlessly in the front yard, with one maintaining cover fire and the other putting a bullet in whichever was brave enough to stick their head out first.

Wyatt and Morgan finally saw it fit to split up. Morgan turned suddenly and sprinted toward the barn, moving to get ahead of three men doing their best to flank the fight. Wyatt moved the other direction, focusing his fire on two particularly difficult men with AR-15s and plenty of ammo to spare.

Wyatt could feel the wind off every bullet, hear its whistle as it passed by, but he never felt a lick of pain. The frustration from the two men he was approaching became more and more apparent. They shouted orders in a coded language and sprayed every bullet their modern killing machines could let loose, but it would do no good. It sounded like a buzzing hornets' nest by the time Wyatt reached no more than a few feet away. The men wore black safety glasses and gloves to match, with faces hidden behind thick beards. The only cover they could find was behind the trailer of an eighteen-wheeler. They alternated shooting from the rear and front ends of the trailer, exposing themselves only long enough to unleash a burst of rounds before ducking for cover again. The bullets came faster with every step Wyatt took toward them. They came like crackling fireworks, more frantic, more furious. Wyatt stood ten feet from the trailer when they gave up alternating and went all in with the hand they were dealt.

The gunmen broke cover and sprinted toward Wyatt, charging forward with rifles spitting fire fast enough to make the barrels glow red hot from the stress. They screamed together, knowing they were coming face-to-face with death itself. Wyatt reached out, almost close enough to touch the first man, and squeezed the trigger. He fell face-first into the dirt, his final act to make mud of the earth with his own blood. The second was only a fraction of a second behind. He'd emptied his rifle and resorted to charging with the butt of the rifle, ready to strike a fatal blow at Wyatt's head. Wyatt sidestepped and swung the handle of his revolver into the back of his head, sending him tumbling to the ground right next to his dead partner. Before he could return to his feet, Wyatt slapped the hammer of his revolver, and the second man dropped dead.

By the time he'd cleared the riflemen behind the eighteen-wheeler, Morgan had gotten the jump on those trying to outflank everyone at the front yard. Wyatt looked up just in time to see his brother rocking the lever-action back and forth at a tight-knit group of three men doing their damndest to live to see another sunrise. Morgan left no man standing by the time he'd finished firing.

With the gunfire finally beginning to slow, the hum of the trucks and excavator idling in the yard became a soundtrack to the groans of pain and gasps of death. The Holliday Ranch had become a warzone. Smoke rose into the air as if it were a wildfire that had scorched the front yard. Bullet casings littered the driveway and grass. It was a hellish scene that never should have taken place, and it wasn't over yet.

Angel and Virgil were still exchanging rounds with the last of Clanton's men. Their rounds came like stray explosions in a battle that had already been decided. Virgil was down to his last bullet, but Angel had a handful left in her lever-action. She jammed in another round and leaned her head down until her cheek rested on the butt of the rifle. It was the first time she'd had enough time to breathe and find her aim. She slowed her breathing, focusing her sight on one of two places her targets would reveal themselves, trying not to scan the horizon and give anyone an advantage over her. Time itself seemed to slow to a crawl as she sat there breathing, waiting to take a life. This went on for ten seconds, then twenty. Finally, Angel glanced around, just long enough to catch the glint of something at the end of the driveway. She saw red and blue, sitting on top of a car parked behind the convoy, waiting for the aftermath. To Virgil's shock, Angel suddenly let out a sigh and dropped the rifle.

"We can't stop now, babe," he urged her. "They'll kill us as soon as they get the chance. We gotta end it."

"Look," she said, and motioned to the car no one had noticed until now.

"It's Joe's brother," Virgil acknowledged. "He's watching."

"No," she answered. "He's waiting."

"What the hell for? Don't he see what's happenin'? It's worse than the O.K. Corral—"

Just as he spoke, a bullet slammed into the dirt no more than a foot away from where Virgil and Angel were standing. They jumped back, startled and uncertain where the shooter was hiding.

Joe stood up from behind the Cadillac, gripping a .44 magnum revolver as black as his heart, boasting a barrel ten inches long with smoke still trailing from its end. His face was stained with blood from a gash on his cheek, and his clenched teeth were pearly white. He stared at them just like a murderer looks at the jury that just convicted him. Death was coming, one way or another.

He lifted the revolver, gave a devilish grin, and squeezed the trigger.

Chapter 22

It takes a fool to believe death will solve anything. Ounces of blood spilled are not measured in what was gained, but what was lost. It was a fact of life that most were forced to reckon with.

Beneath the sweltering Texas sun, with sweat pouring into their eyes and adrenaline filling their veins, the stench of gunpowder filling the air, and trigger fingers still itching to let loose one more bullet —the Holliday Ranch found itself in a company of fools.

What should have been thirty seconds of gunfire had turned into fifteen minutes of bloodshed, where no one could ever imagine walking away triumphantly, only with a new, tragic burden to bear throughout the drudgery of life afterward. This harrowing realization hung over those who were still breathing, turning the chaos of battle into silence for a few stark seconds before evil reared its ugly face again.

Boom.

The first bullet in the gun fight shot by Joe Clanton

cracked like lightning striking down, cast not from above, but from the forces of darkness that are always at work from beneath the earth. It fired off like a cannon, louder than anything they'd heard during the fight so far. Joe looked like a beast backed into a corner. His hands shook, his teeth gnashed, his breath trembled, but he kept his revolver aimed in a tight grip that seemed to never falter.

The bullet passed through Wyatt, joining a dozen holes just like it, already burned into his clothes. He never flinched. The impact came like a gentle breeze, barely nudging him, nothing more.

Joe fired again, then again, and again and again. The final bullet to escape the end of his barrel was no different than the first. It made no difference to Wyatt. By the time the smoke cleared and Joe could see the man who introduced himself was Wyatt Earp, standing alone, unharmed and unbothered by all of his pent-up, deadly rage, all he could do was lash out.

"You ain't real!" he screamed, his voice cracking like dry timber going up in flames. "None of this is real!"

Wyatt's lips curled into a cold smile, the kind that had sent men running for more than a century. He cleared his throat but thought better of what he had to say and decided to keep his mouth shut. Instead, he raised his Schofield, but something inside him prevented his finger from compressing the trigger beyond the break that couldn't be reversed. He didn't fire—not yet.

The fight was ebbing, and the gunfire popping off had become sporadic. Morgan picked off one final Clanton straggler, the man's body jerking as he collapsed behind an SUV. Angel's Winchester clicked empty, and Virgil slumped against the pickup, his revolver spent. The ranch fell into an uneasy hush, broken only by the rumble of engines and the distant wail of wind through the torn pastures. It wasn't the first gunfight that had broken out within the property boundaries, and it certainly wouldn't be the last. Judging solely by the amount of bodies bleeding into the dirt, it might've been the deadliest one to date, though. The fight may have been winding down in the front yard of Virgil and Angel's home, but it was not over.

Joe reluctantly lowered his ten-inch-long revolver. His chest heaved as the realization began to take hold of his bloodshot eyes. He couldn't win. Not against ghosts, not against the unyielding will of the family who called the Holliday Ranch home. He'd swallowed up a dozen ranches in a conquest fueled by debt and despair, set against inescapable threats of ruin. He'd put himself in a bind by growing too quickly, consuming too many resources, and failing to secure any worthwhile income. The scales of justice were being weighed now, however, and it was clear as day to see he'd come up short in the end. He stepped out from behind the Cadillac, hands half-raised, the gun dangling loose in his fingers as if it would've made a difference any other way. His fancy jacket was torn, his boots scuffed, and the self-righteous fury drained from his face, leaving only a hollow shell of a man who'd bet everything on a losing hand.

"All right," Joe admitted, his defeated, bitter voice carrying across the yard. "All right, you win. Is that what you wanted to hear? You win."

"Look around," Angel hollered at him. "Ain't no one winnin' out here."

"You people don't get it," said Joe.

Angel shot a knowing glance at her husband, who returned one right back to her. They'd come to understand more than men like Joe probably ever could, but that wasn't something he wanted to hear at the moment.

"We were goin' under, drownin' in a sea of red," Joe began to explain, plopping himself down on the hood of the Cadillac just a few inches away from the horns gracing the front end. He was covered in sweat, and with the sunglasses no longer hiding his face, his defeat was painted on every expression. "I tried to keep it afloat. Did everything I could think of. Money was always comin', but for some reason, it just never got here."

Wyatt's finger tightened on the trigger, but not enough to fire off a round, letting the man spill his guts without the need of assistance. Angel and Virgil made their way over to his side, their weapons lowered but ready. Morgan leaned against the barn in the distance, reloading casually, his eerie calm a stark contrast to the wreckage that surrounded him in every direction.

Joe began to pace slowly, walking back and forth in front of the car. At first, he was silent, moving his hands as if he was rehearsing the speech to come in his head before speaking it aloud. Then, he stopped, turned his attention to Angel, and began the performance he'd just concocted.

"You met my brother, Newman Clanton, not too long ago, ain't that right, Mr. Earp?" Joe nodded toward Wyatt, calling to memory a scuffle in the same dirt they stood. "Newman made his fortune all by himself. And bein' my brother and all, he was kind enough to give me the loan to get me started. I took whatever I could, but turned out to be more than I should've. When I lost all of that money, I turned to my other brother, Joseph, for more. I think you two met him not too long ago," this time he turned back to Angel and Virgil.

"We know Sheriff Clanton," said Virgil.

"He's sittin' right out there," Angel commented. "In case you were wonderin'."

"Yeah, he is," Joe sighed as he spoke. "He came up with more money than he had a right to, all on a promise I gave him."

"What kind of *promise*?" Angel couldn't help herself.

"The promise of the Holliday Ranch, and everything it held. You think you're the only ones who know about the gold and brass seeds planted in this very dirt so long ago? Diggin' up that gold became my only hope to save what I'd built. Without it, I'm finished. The farms, the name, everything."

"That explains all the equipment," Virgil told his wife and Wyatt before looking back at Joe. "Let me guess, today was the deadline before someone came for everything *you* own."

Joe's head sunk, his eyes hitting the dirt. "You gotta understand—it's survival."

His voice cracked on the last word, and he even managed to show off a single tear streaming down his cheek. The monologue hung in the air, a pathetic unraveling of a man who'd cloaked his greed in family honor, his conquest in self-righteousness, and his desperation in sheer brutality. There was nothing left for such a man to cling to, except for the .44 magnum revolver that had yet to leave his grip.

Wyatt might've even felt a flicker of something, not

quite pity, but at the very least recognition. He'd seen men like Joe before, capitalists buried beneath their own choices, chasing fortunes that slipped through their fingers like sand. Understanding doesn't always equate to mercy, though. Men like Joe had a way of making their bed but never wanting to lie in it. More often than not, it was up to men like Wyatt to show the way. Justice has never been a negotiation, and that wasn't going to change today.

Before Wyatt could do what was necessary, Angel stepped forward to interrupt him with her Winchester hanging at her side. "You tried to poison our cattle. You stole our horses just to torment us. You kidnapped my husband and terrorized our home. Then, when you couldn't force your way in, you decided to shoot the place up and kill anyone who stood in your way. And now you think you can manipulate us into savin' your ass? We should put a bullet in you right now and be done with it all."

Wyatt knew the tone in Angel's voice, he knew the decency that made her and her husband the kind of people you could gun down a crowd of evildoers for and still sleep fine at night. They were what most people called the salt of the earth, but that also meant they didn't have what it took to do what needed to be done.

"We're gonna let you—"

Wyatt lifted his Schofield and aimed it at Joe. "We ain't gonna do any of that," he said.

"Put it down." Angel lifted her hand at Wyatt. "We don't wanna kill anymore. That sheriff is out there, waitin' on us to slip up. We can defend ourselves, but we can't gun anyone down in cold blood. You know that."

The hammer cocked back into place with an all-too-familiar click that sent the dominoes falling wherever they may.

Joe moved first—he bolted for the Cadillac driver's side door, yanking it open and diving almost headfirst inside. The engine roared to life, tires spinning gravel as he floored the accelerator.

"Wyatt, no!" Angel shouted.

Wyatt fired anyway, the Schofield recoiling in his hand as fire and gunpowder blasted out. The bullet shattered the passenger window, then the driver's window. Joe's panic-stricken face could be seen for a split second before the tires of the Cadillac began to spin aimlessly in the dirt and gravel. The car began to fishtail down the driveway, spewing dust into the air like a demon fleeing the pits of hell. Wyatt fired again, this time shattering the back glass as the Cadillac barreled toward the end of the driveway.

Angel and Virgil watched the car almost disappear in a cloud of dust with Joe's silhouette hunched over the steel wheel. They each committed the look on the man's face to memory, every fearful detail, especially the realization in his eyes that his own life may come to an end, not just the livelihood he was so desperate to kill to maintain. It was a warning that could only be given when life or death hung in the balance. As they considered the lesson learned in blood, they watched Joe Clanton race away.

He wouldn't get far, though. Just as he crested the slight rise in the driveway leading toward the county road, the Cadillac's rear lights lit bright red, and the rear end lifted as Joe leaned heavily on the brakes. The rear tires skidded violently through the dirt, causing the car to drift sideways before coming to a complete stop.

There, idling at the gate leaving the Holliday Ranch, was the sheriff's cruiser—red and blue lights pulsing lazily. Joe had never been the wiser about his brother, Joseph, waiting to see how the chips fell. Sheriff Clanton sat behind the wheel with his badge gleaming through the windshield. He'd taken bribes and given unfair shakes to people before, but he wasn't about to go down over his brother's failures, and Joe knew it.

Joe slammed on the brakes, but momentum carried him forward anyway. Panic seized him. He couldn't stop, as he knew what would happen. If he failed to secure the Holliday Ranch, he would have to pay with his life.

With a savage yank of the wheel, Joe veered left, the Cadillac lurched off the driveway, ripping through a five-strand barbed wire fence, carrying t-posts and dangling strands of barbed wire with it as the motor roared and the car sped away. It bounced wildly over uneven terrain, screaming as it plowed through overgrown grass and broken limbs and deep ruts. It was a blinding turn of events that saw the horned Cadillac seem to stampede through the west pasture of the ranch, heading toward an open field and a tree line in the distance.

Wyatt and Morgan were already sprinting toward the vehicle, with Angel and Virgil trailing close behind. The howl of the motor haunted them as Joe attempted to make a fateful escape.

It bounced and spun its tires and fought for every few feet it made through the pasture. The old sedan wasn't built for off-roading, but Joe's foot kept the pedal to the floorboard through it all. The exhaust sputtered, and the engine revved as the Cadillac found an open stretch to pick up speed. Joe's getaway vehicle climbed from ten miles an hour to twenty, then thirty, then forty. It was like waiting on a tornado to touch ground, knowing the devastation that was bound to occur, but unable to do anything to stop it.

Angel was the first to see it coming. "Oh my God!" she screamed out, covering her mouth with her hands.

The west pasture of the Holliday Ranch had become a minefield of holes in recent weeks. Deep craters dug by Wyatt and Morgan in their relentless search for gold, with the earth piled high like graves waiting to be filled, posed a relentless obstacle course for the madman on the loose.

Joe didn't see any of it until it was too late.

The Cadillac hit the first hole at full speed. It sank down, with the horns strapped to the front end of the car impaling the earth as the front end crashed violently into a wall of dirt. Two of the four tires exploded on impact before the entire rear end of the car hurled itself upward. Glass shattered as the motor revved up until it was knocking endlessly into the air. The hood bent in half, panels crumpled, a mixture of glass and metal and plastic flew into the air in every direction as the car flipped upward, end over end, until it came to a sudden, dramatic halt. The engine let out a final, agonized, sputtering groan before it died upside down in a massive pit, wheels spinning futilely in the air. Smoke billowed from the wreckage, acrid and black, mixing with the dust settling overhead.

Wyatt reached the scene first. He approached slowly, revolver aimed forward at the ready with the hammer already cocked back, but there was no need.

Joe Clanton hung limp in the inverted seat, blood dripping from his misshapen, crushed skull, eyes open but now forever unseeing. The crash had done what bullets couldn't. Justice had been delivered in a twist of irony, his greed leading him straight into a grave doubling as a prospective hole for the gold he risked his life for.

"Another of the crimson days," Wyatt uttered before turning to face Angel, Virgil, and his brother, Morgan.

Angel didn't need to ask any questions, she could see the result of what they'd just witnessed in Wyatt's eyes. "It's over," she said. "He's gone."

Virgil felt a mixture of horror and relief wash over him. Disbelief set in almost immediately as he finally began to put the pieces together of what they'd just survived. They were surrounded by bodies, and Joe's was only another one to pile on top of the atrocity that had just taken place, the atrocity that they had to stop by any means possible.

The Holliday Ranch stood silent in the wake of such devastation. It was battered, but unbroken. Holes as deep as the one that brought an end to Joe Clanton randomly dotted the pasture almost as far as the eye could see.

They were not alone, though. The sheriff car still lingered at the end of their driveway with red and blue lights quietly flickering in the distance. Sheriff Clanton was still waiting at the gate. Even though the fight had come to an abrupt end, shadows of corruption, deals made in the dark, and greed left unchecked, the world still stood against the ranch, just like it always had.

Chapter 23

Just like life and death, there is a fine line between greed and success. It comes in the definition, in what it means to have what matters most, in everlasting abundance. A life like that is only experienced by a select few in the world. Where most get caught up in the toils of their lives and what they can be compensated with for their troubles, some are able to bask in a simple, unchangeable fact—they already have what matters most.

The Holliday Ranch looked like a battlefield. Bullet casings reflected the sun's light, eerily similar to the muzzle flash that led to their final resting place. The front yard was littered with fallen gunmen, firearms, and a convoy of vehicles with no one left to drive them away. An excavator let out a low, deep rumble, idling in the gravel with nowhere to go. The Cadillac that held Joe's body still let out a trail of smoke into the air, becoming a beacon of distress at the ranch.

It was a beacon that had to be answered.

Sheriff Clanton sat at the end of the driveway. His cruiser sat still with red and blue lights pulsing like a heartbeat, still grasping at every chance of life. The lights flicked back and forth for a few seconds before the car shifted in place, then suddenly, they went dark. The car began its approach down the driveway without another sound, allowing the crunching of gravel to be its only warning.

Virgil was holding Angel, barely standing up together, right in front of their bullet-riddled home. Just like them, the ranch wasn't without its wounds, but it was still standing when all the gun smoke had cleared. Virgil's face was a map of bruises. Cuts still slowly wept blood from where duct tape had torn his skin raw. His ribs ached with every breath, the memory of being dragged by a rope behind a Clanton horse still searing his mind. Angel's arm throbbed through shredded grazes. Her Winchester rested in the crook of her arm, depleted but still ready to keep fighting, just like her. They wanted to collapse in the dirt where they stood, but relief was a luxury they couldn't afford yet.

Wyatt and Morgan stood nearby, untouched by the chaos that had just ravaged the ranch, keeping their distance from the couple as the sheriff's cruiser approached slowly and deliberately. Their gaze offered no insight into the destruction they'd wrought or what it had done to them, despite their clothes barely being held together by the few strands that hadn't been struck by bullets.

The cruiser stopped a few yards away from where Virgil and Angel stood. It sat for a few awkward seconds before the driver's side window rolled down halfway. A gray felt cowboy hat-wearing man sat at the steering wheel, the same man who'd shown up on their front porch just before the firefight started. Sheriff Joseph Clanton turned to look at the couple just as his badge gleamed dully in the sunlight leaking into the cruiser. His eyes were hidden behind dark sunglasses, but his mouth twisted into a smirk that carried none of Joe's bravado, only a cold, calculated disdain.

"Y'all sure made one hell of a mess out here," Joseph drawled, his voice cutting through the silence like a dull blade. "My brother always was the fuck-up in the family."

Virgil's jaw clenched, his fingers curling into fists. "You saw what happened. Your brother got what he deserved, Sheriff."

"Easy, I ain't here to start another fight, just to put this one to rest. My brother's dead, he saw to that himself. Clanton Family Farms is done for. Daddy was as dumb as a sack of rocks to give it to Joe, but what's done is done. Now the bank wants their money back, and so do I."

"We can't help you with that," said Angel.

"No," the sheriff said, shaking his head. "I don't expect you can. Everything my brother owned is goin' up for auction, now. Newman and me will get back what we're owed, and if we're lucky, a couple extra bucks for our trouble. It's gonna take every piece of equipment and every damn acre to get us whole again, but ain't nothin' gonna change that."

"What happens to us?" Virgil asked.

"I'll send some people to get the rest of Joe's mess cleaned up. Then, if you're lucky, you won't ever see me again out here."

"You think we're supposed to believe you after what your brother did to us?"

"I don't reckon you got much of a choice, to be honest."

"You sat there and watched those men die. You didn't do anything. You coulda stopped all of this," Angel cut in, her frustration beginning to show. "You were waitin' to see who was the last one standin', weren't you?"

Joseph looked out from over the top of his sunglasses, then gently lifted a couple of fingers to tip his cowboy hat down. "Good luck keepin' this place from fallin' apart, ma'am," he said, then rolled up the window and circled around in the driveway, taking care to avoid the bodies and equipment scattered around.

As the cruiser raced away down the driveway, Virgil let out a breath he hadn't realized he was holding. "Son of a bitch," he muttered. "Thought he'd try somethin'."

Angel leaned into him, her head resting against his chest, feeling the unsteady rhythm of his heart. "We can finally breathe again. It's over."

Even as the words escaped her lips, they felt hollow. It was a bittersweet victory. The ranch was saved, but the front yard was a graveyard, the pastures in ruin, the barn nearly destroyed, and worst of all, their home had been forced to endure the worst of it. Their life had become an ongoing nightmare they couldn't wake up from. Greed and fear and desperation had been the backdrop of their problems for so long, it was difficult to imagine what normalcy might ever look like.

Yet, as they stood there, embracing one another in the wreckage of what remained of their life, a truth settled over both Virgil and Angel at the same time, heavier than the smoke, clearer than the morning light. The ranch wasn't just dirt and cattle and a never-ending list of chores to be done. It was them, their family, how much they cared for each other, and their stubborn refusal to let the world break them, no matter what they faced. What made the Holliday Ranch special wasn't just the legends who came before them or the promise of prosperity in the future, it was what they felt for each other. It was what carried them through the gunfire and treachery—their love.

Wyatt and Morgan seemed to be content about being left out of the moment that had washed over the couple, still holding each other in front of their home. Wyatt's eyes scanned the horizon, almost as if he was already chasing the next fight. It was Morgan who decided to speak up first through a grin stretching across his face as wide as Texas.

"You two all right?"

Virgil nodded, wincing as he shifted his weight, refusing to let go of Angel. "We'll live. Thanks to both of you."

Angel kept her head on Virgil's chest and joined her husband in thanking them. "You kept your word. You fought for us, for this place. We owe you more than we can ever repay."

Wyatt shook his head, his worn cowboy hat casting a shadow over his face. "Ain't about debts. It's about doin' what's right."

"Y'all are more than welcome to keep diggin' on your claim," she told him. "It's the least we could offer you."

This time, Wyatt shot a glance over at Morgan before he could say anything. "We sure appreciate the offer, but I think it's about time for us to get on out of here. We got word of an opportunity we can't pass up."

"Too good to be true, if you ask me," Morgan chimed in.

"I didn't," said Wyatt before turning his attention back to Virgil and Angel.

"We're gonna spend the afternoon breakin' down camp and packin' up, then we'll be on our way come first light."

"So soon?" Angel questioned.

"Gotta get it while the gettin's good, you know how it is."

"Can you really fault us for leavin' after all that?" Morgan cracked.

Virgil let out a weak chuckle while Angel scoffed his remark off. "Hell no, I can't, Morgan. Can't say I blame you for wantin' to move on at all," he said.

"What's next for y'all?" Wyatt asked with a stroke of sincerity, finding its way into his grizzled voice.

"Rebuild," Virgil answered plainly. "This place has gone through worse, maybe not much worse, but we needed a new chapter around here. I think the Holliday Ranch is due for some tidyin' up and maybe a new coat of paint. It might not be much, but it's all we got left, and I'll be damned if we don't get this mess cleaned up. There's a bright future waitin' on us, we just gotta get back to work."

"Before we do any of that, we got a couple of people we need to reach out to," said Angel. "It's time to call Nat and Nel."

Virgil's eyes widened at the mention of their kids. Nathaniel and Nellie were none the wiser about what had just taken place at the ranch. When they found out, both he and Angel were in for a mighty big scolding. They were good kids, off on their own, creating a life for themselves. But they made it clear when they left, they wanted to know everything that was happening at the Holliday Ranch, as they still cared about the place they learned to call their home.

Angel looked up to her husband, finally pulling her head away from his chest. A smile overtook her when she least expected it, and the beginnings of a tear formed in her eye.

"It's time we invited them back home," she told Virgil. "It's been too damn long."

"It sure has," he told her. "I miss them."

"The whole family back together, sittin' down for a meal at the same table. It sounds like a dream."

"Sounds a lot better than the nightmare we've been stuck in, that's for sure."

Wyatt finally walked up to where they were standing, his calloused right hand outstretched, with a warm smile on his face. "Seems like you two have a lot to look forward to. It's been a pleasure gettin' to know you both. Sure is good to find decent, hard workin' people still carvin' somethin' for themselves outta this mean old world."

"The pleasure has been all ours, Mr. Earp," said Virgil, reaching out to clasp his hand in Wyatt's.

When he got to Angel, it was both arms open for the woman who'd been willing to take on every Clanton gunman by herself if needed. Angel leaned in and hugged him tight. "Y'all don't be strangers. If you ever need a place to put your boots up. You know where to find us."

"We sure do," said Wyatt before taking a step back.

Morgan followed his brother's gesture, giving a firm shake to Virgil before giving Angel a wink and a side hug. They stood together, feeling the wind take the sweat from their brow and the relief wash over their nerves. It was a quiet moment to reflect on what they'd suffered together, on what they'd fought for. They didn't take too long, just long enough to make it mean something, to give them at least a single moment to remember that wasn't filled with flying bullets and threats of death and destruction.

Wyatt felt an urgency that no one else could have in that moment. He reached into his pocket and pulled out a single gold coin, the same one Virgil had found in the pasture just before he was taken by the Clantons. He spun it in his fingers a couple of times, thinking about what he might be giving up by doing what he was about to do. Then, he let out a sigh and flicked the coin with his thumb. It spun through the air, catching the sunlight just right before it landed right in the middle of Virgil's palm.

"You should have it, that way you have somethin' to show for all your work," said Virgil, getting ready to hand it back to Wyatt.

"You dug it up. It's yours," he answered. "Keep it."

"You're a good man, Wyatt."

"I might even suggest goin' back to where you found it," Wyatt said, his voice returning to his usual seriousness. "There might be more where that came from."

"Maybe I will." Virgil closed his fingers around the coin, letting its weight ground him.

The Earps each tipped their hats in unison, different from how Sheriff Clanton had just seen them off. Their gesture was one lost to the pages of history, carried by the weight of something greater than the ranch or anyone who fought for it. Without another word, they each turned and walked away. They moved like relics of a bygone era amid the modern wreckage, never turning to look back at where they came from, focused only on what lay ahead. Their silhouettes began to fade into the swirling dust and hazy heat until they were too difficult to make out, as if the ranch itself was surrendering their service and letting them go free.

Virgil and Angel held onto each other as they watched the two men until they were gone. They were alone when it was all said and done. The men who'd saved them disappeared into the stories that birthed them. They didn't mind, though. Peace was something that had escaped them for so long. The sounds of the ranch began to return—cows bellering in the distance, the wind sweeping across the pastures, birds calling out now that the gunfire had gone away, even the wind chimes hanging from the porch miraculously unharmed by the flying bullets—it was almost enough to lull them into feeling safe again.

Angel reached down to grab Virgil's hand, a tender act of affection she relished now more than ever before. His grip was tight and reassuring, yet soft and telling, and he was as relieved as she was to be standing together. When her fingers clasped around his, she could feel the gold coin still in his hand, now pressed between them both, warm and heavy.

They stayed like this for what must've been an hour, just settling into the feeling of not having to fight for their survival, realizing that they'd been so close to losing everything in their life. Craters throughout the ranch opened up like chasms in the earth, some larger than others, each one an unkept promise of fortune and security.

Virgil couldn't help himself. He thought of what Joseph had told them earlier, about the Clanton Family Farms empire crumbling beneath its own weight. He thought of what would happen to its remains, about the land that had been stolen out from under people just like him and his wife. He allowed himself to form a dream most would call delusional under such circumstances, but he knew exactly how Angel would react. He held her hand tight, keeping the coin pressed between them, and walked with her back to the front porch. They climbed the steps in unison, taking a fleeting moment to acknowledge the Clanton brand still burned into their home. What was once a threat of their undoing was now a key to their future.

"I think I'll spend the evenin' gettin' my hands dirty," he said finally.

"You really want to go back to diggin' today? Do you think that's smart?"

"To be honest, Angel, I can't remember a time when I've been so excited to get to work."

"What if there ain't nothin' out there?"

"Then there's nothin' out there," he answered bluntly. "But what if there *is*?"

Angel laughed, a sound that sliced right through the grim air lingering around the ranch like a ray of sunlight in the dark. "All right, you got my attention, what if there is?"

"I got some ideas."

"You gonna share 'em with me or keep me guessin'?"

"Well," he started, thinking about his next words carefully. He separated his hand from hers and lifted the gold coin up between them, spinning it so they could both get a good look at its shining surface. "I do know of quite a bit of land that's gonna be comin' up for sale soon."

Angel smiled, yet another ray of sunshine to break the darkness. "You're serious, aren't you?"

"What if I am?"

"You're dreamin' big now," she told him.

"Maybe so…" he answered, letting his gaze drift from Angel's eyes to the pastures stretching out that made up the Holliday Ranch. Fortune or not, their livelihood, their entire world together had been saved, and that was more than enough. He tucked the gold coin back into his pocket, allowing it to remind him of everything that had gone into the dirt beneath their boots. All the blood and sweat and tears, all of the sacrifice and pain and stress, it was all going to pave the way to a better future, not just for him and his wife, but for every generation that may call the Holliday Ranch home.

"No one will say we didn't earn it, though."

Chapter 24

Gun smoke mingling with the scent of spilled blood and churned soil was a brutal reminder that justice, however hard fought, was keen to leave no riches in its wake for those who carried out its most ruthless demands.

Wyatt and Morgan had witnessed firsthand the resolute determination that had allowed the ranch to stand the test of time. They'd tipped the scales in their own favor with the weight of enough bullets to make sure it would never sway again. They chased fortune, and with it, a future free of the kind of hardships Virgil and Angel had endured for so long. They'd found no such thing. But even though they were leaving with less to their name than when they came, justice had come as its own reward.

The fading Texas sun over the west pasture would prove to be the last time either of the Earp brothers would see it set over the age-old pines and oaks at the Holliday Ranch. It was finally quiet, as if the land itself was sighing a relief after the storm.

Wyatt was standing at the edge of what they called their camp, but in reality was just a hole in the ground for a fire and a few bedrolls that could be dragged away in a hurry in case it rained. It was made for an uncomfortable stay, but it was certainly easy enough to pack up when the time came. Wyatt's cowboy hat was tilted up on his head, revealing sunken eyes that carried a century's worth of triumphs and failures, giving his weary appearance an edge of stoicism few men of the modern world would ever come to know. His Schofield revolver still hung at his hip, its barrel cool now, but its trigger as ready as it ever had been for yet another fight.

Morgan was leaning his rifle against a fencepost, getting ready to start rolling his bed up and securing what little possessions he had in the area. His ratty jacket had become a patchwork of bullet holes that told a story no mortal man could ever hope to survive. His work was mundane, and he moved through the motions like he'd done it a thousand times before, because he had done just that.

The two were wandering souls in a modern world of machines and money. They were echoes of what once was, tethered to a purpose fulfilled in the crimson chaos of the Holliday Ranch's salvation. The fight was over. With the bloodshed coming to an end, Wyatt felt a quiet satisfaction, not the fleeting rush of a gambler's win, but the steady weight of right triumphing over wrong. They'd found only one gold coin in all their digging—a solitary glint in a sea of dirt—but it didn't matter.

Morgan kicked at a clump of earth, his crooked grin warm despite the carnage behind them. "Well, brother, we ain't walkin' away with a fortune this time."

"Justice don't pay in coin," said Wyatt. "Never has."

Morgan chuckled and shook his head, returning to his work without another word. They each toiled away in silence, breaking the camp down with a rehearsed, practiced ease.

Wyatt rolled his bedroll tight, securing it with a worn leather strap, its edges frayed from years of use. Morgan gathered their meager belongings, including a dented tin coffee pot, a skillet blackened by countless fires, and a pair of canteens, only to stuff them into a canvas sack.

The horses, sturdy and dependable, were loaned by Virgil. They each snorted softly, sensing the shift. They were at least familiar with their Wyatt and Morgan after taking them to the Clantons not too long ago. If all they'd received as payment for their work and sacrifice were the pair of horses that had carried them through the fight, it would have been more than fair compensation.

Wyatt slung a shovel over his shoulder, its blade nicked from weeks of fruitless labor, a symbol of hope that had outlived its purpose here. Morgan followed suit, his shovel balanced beside his rifle, both tools of their restless trade. The sun dipped lower, painting the horizon in streaks of rich amber light. The two made for their horses, slinging what little they owned over the back of the saddles. By the time they had climbed up to put their own ass in the saddle, sweat had covered their faces, but exhaustion never seemed to take hold.

Wyatt paused, his hand resting on his saddle's

pommel, just long enough to glance toward the ranch house. Virgil and Angel stood on the porch, their silhouettes framed against the fading light. They stood together, hands clasped, a unit forged in fire.

"Don't need to worry about them two. They'll make it," Morgan said, swinging into his own saddle. "Got more grit than most. I'd hate to be anyone standin' in their way."

"I ain't worried," said Wyatt.

The brothers turned their horses toward the open road, the ranch fading behind them, its battered outline already beginning to disappear behind the tree lines swallowing the homestead. They moved like apparitions, drifting away as if they'd only just arrived a few moments ago, leaving behind carnage and its resulting redemption.

All Wyatt could feel in his core was the pull of the next horizon, the next chance to set things right, to find an opportunity to make something of himself in a world that had long forgotten its own ways. They rode in silence, listening to the steady clop of hooves and the faint jingles of uncomfortable spurs. The ranch driveways bled into the county road, which in turn bled into a dirt path through the woods away from the towns and traffic and people too busy to look where they were going.

Morgan hummed a tuneless melody, his rifle slung across his back, the shovel bouncing lightly against his horse's flank, his mind an endless train of useless ramblings. Wyatt's mind drifted to the whisper of a new opportunity, though, the one that had reached his ear when he least expected it. There were rumors of a claim too tempting to ignore, a chance to chase the fortune that had slipped through their fingers here, a chance to make a real difference. It was something he just couldn't pass up. After a few minutes contemplating the possibilities, Morgan finally caught on to what was happening and decided to inquire about what was next for them.

"You never did tell me why we had to up and leave the place so damn quick," he told Wyatt. "I used to say I'd follow you anywhere, didn't matter where, 'cause you never led me astray before."

"Used to?"

Morgan shot his eyes over to his brother, his look saying everything he couldn't put into words.

Wyatt couldn't help but let out a laugh at his brother pressing him for information. Morgan was loyal, sometimes to a fault, and brains weren't always his strongest suit, but he knew right from wrong. When it mattered most, there was no judgment other than his own that he respected more than Morgan's. He may not have owed him an explanation, but he would be wrong not to give him something.

"We got another claim," he told him finally. "Bigger than the ranch, bigger than anything we've ever done before."

"What we diggin' up now, Wyatt?"

"Silver."

Morgan let out a sigh. He wasn't too thrilled to get back to swinging a shovel, but there wasn't much else they could do these days. Whether it was his undying loyalty or an otherworldly impulse he couldn't ignore, he'd be right by his brother's side. The only thing he could do was get a laugh out of their situation.

"Silver, gold, it's all the same to me. The only question I got is, you think we'll find more than a damn coin this time?" Morgan asked, forcing his usual grin to cover the doubt that he was fighting to suppress.

Wyatt's lips twitched, almost a smile, almost something worse. He thought about his answer for a few seconds before responding. "When has that ever mattered to you?"

Morgan laughed, a low, easy sound that rolled across his lips. "You're gettin' philosophical, Wyatt. Don't go changin' on me now, not after all this time."

"I don't know about all that."

Morgan raised an eyebrow, his grin fading to curiosity. "Where's this claim at?"

Wyatt didn't answer right away, his gaze fixed on the horizon where the unknown still waited for him, like an elusive gun always aimed at wherever he was going, never where he was. He squinted, reacting not to the sinking sun bleeding red rays of light into his eyes, but instead to the rush of memories flooding into him. Some were his own, some weren't, all were of lives long gone, of a world long gone, and deep down, he knew there would be no return. He was destined to drift nowhere in particular. He was more than a deliverer of end times for men who had it coming, and he hoped to leave the people in his life with a simple truth of the world when he was gone—it's worth fighting for. He chased those foolish dreams like most men, with no choice in the matter, only pulled to the next shred of hope for something more than he already had. Instead of thinking about how he would tell his brother where they were going, he thought of every single place he'd ever fired a bullet, of every man's eyes he'd seen lose their light, of every jail cell he'd put evildoers within, and every promise of freedom from it all that never came.

The horses plodded on, their shadows stretching long across the dirt, soon to be swallowed in the coming darkness. Wyatt's shovel gleamed faintly, a tool of labor and hope, while his Schofield revolver rested quietly in his holster, a different kind of tool, one built for the consequences of judgment.

It had been long enough for Morgan to give up waiting for an answer. He flicked his hand in mild annoyance before returning to the ride, gripping his reins and reaching one more time to make sure his rifle was still secured at his side. He knew who his brother was, and he knew what went on in that head of his. For lack of better words, he'd found solace in the fact that he was simply along for the ride.

The Holliday Ranch was behind them, its memory now a testament to the stubbornness of its own survival. There were few places that had left such a lasting impression on the two, like it had restored something within them they didn't know they had lost. Virgil and Angel would rebuild, call their kids home, maybe dig deeper for that gold. Wyatt didn't need to see it to know they'd already found what mattered most. He envied them, in a removed sort of way, but envy couldn't hold him. It never could. The trail called, and he answered, same as always.

As the sun sank below the horizon, bathing the world in fiery red and sullen shadows, Wyatt finally gave the answer his brother had given up waiting on. His rumbling voice was distant and detached. Two words came like a whisper from the grave, clawing and thrashing into the world like a freight train hurling itself out of the depths of hell.

"Tombstone, Arizona."

Chapter 25

"You did *not* get kidnapped."

"Hand to God. They roped me like a calf at the rodeo and dragged me off, right out there in the front yard."

"And Mom saved you?"

"Sure did," Virgil said, wrapping his arm around his wife, Angel. "She saved this whole place."

"Can you imagine Mom actually shooting a gun? I remember when she was so scared of an opossum in our closet, she wouldn't come inside the house for hours."

"You better believe she did. Your mom was a real-life badass, guns blazin' and all."

"I wasn't alone." She looked at him with a smile and a blink-and-you-miss-it wink.

"So, are those men gonna come back?"

"We made sure they won't, not ever again."

A pause hung over the family, allowing them to take comfort in the simple peacefulness of finally being reunited again. Nathaniel and Nellie had finally returned home, and neither of them wanted to leave anytime soon. Their visit had been exactly what Virgil and Angel needed. Seeing their children happy, in the middle of making something out of themselves, reminded them of what the world had to offer instead of what it could take. If they could have it their way, the kids would stay at the Holliday Ranch and build their lives on the acreage that'd been their family's home for so long. That wasn't how things worked anymore, though.

The ranch was humming with life, a stark contrast to what it had become in the middle of their fight against the man named Joe Clanton. A dozen cowboys were out sorting bull calves and heifers, breaking in new colts and mares in the process. Craters in the pasture had been filled, bullet casings had been plucked from the yard, and all of their financial problems were washed away with a single swing of a shovel. It had been restored to its former glory, and when the money started rolling in, it was like a faucet that couldn't be turned off.

The family home was even more alive. The kitchen table was crowded with disbelief, shock, and even the sweet sound of laughter that had been missing for too long. The bullet holes and broken glass were gone, and with them, the worries and anxiety and fear that what they had built might not last. They had secured their future by fighting until there was nothing and no one left to fight. All they had to do now was enjoy the fruits of their labor.

Everything was as it should be, at long last.

A single gold coin sat in the middle of the kitchen table, the same one that Virgil had found alone before the gunfight in the front yard would change their lives forever. It gleamed bright, like it couldn't stop smiling at what it alone had begotten.

Nathaniel and Nellie eyed it carefully, but it was Angel who decided to break the silence when she turned to Virgil to ask him a question so serious, so urgent, she couldn't wait any longer.

"How did it feel bein' a damsel in distress?"

As the laughter erupted once more from the table at Angel's dark joke, Virgil's phone began to ring in his pocket, giving him just the distraction he needed to avoid giving an answer he may never be able to live down again. "Gonna have to rain check that one," he said, pulling the vibrating phone from his jeans while flashing a quick smirk. "Be right back, y'all."

He made it a few paces away before he touched the screen to answer the call from an unknown number and pushed the phone to his cheek. "Hello?"

"Virgil!" a familiar voice came through the other end.

"Davy!" Virgil exclaimed before slipping out of the front door to stand alone on the porch.

"Haven't heard from ya in a bit, was startin' to get worried. How's the wife and kids?"

"Better than we've been in a long time," said Virgil, as he watched the cowboys in the distance roping calves and kicking up dirt.

"I can't tell you how good that is to hear," said Davy. "I caught wind that those men I was tellin' you about were on the move, somethin' about a claim they found, and I figured that must've been you. Figured I'd give you a heads up they were on their way, is all."

"They already showed up," Virgil said, leaning against a post and taking in the fresh air. "They evened out those scales of justice pretty damn good, too. I won't ever be able to pay you back for puttin' me onto them, truly."

"Did they really? Well, that's news to me," Davy admitted.

"I'm still not sold they are really the Wild West heroes they claimed to be, but we wouldn't be where we are without 'em. They walked through a wall of bullets for my wife and I."

"I ain't learned too much in my years, and what I have learned pretty much all came from my own wife, but there is one thing I do know for a fact," Davy explained. "Legends sure are hard to kill."

The brief call came to an end as soon as it had started. Virgil jammed the phone back into his pocket, took one more deep breath—savoring everything the ranch had to give him in that moment—and turned to walk back inside to be with his wife and kids. Before he could open the front door, he looked down at the newly painted floorboards and stared at the faint traces of what remained of the Clanton family brand that had been burned into their home. The fight may have come to an end, but the scars would always linger.

He swung the door open to a chorus of chants from his family, each one hollering for him to recount the story one more time of what had been notoriously named—against his best wishes—*the shootout at the Holliday Ranch.*

A Look at Book Three
SURE SHOT

ONE SHOT TO MAKE IT RIGHT.

Phoebe Ann was born with a steady hand and a dead aim. Her Winchester 1873 was her pride, a gift from her father—the only one he ever gave her. But after he's wrongfully imprisoned, and that rifle ends up in the hands of a man named Butler—a man she once trusted—Phoebe's world begins to unravel.

Years pass. Butler builds an empire. Phoebe is left behind, scraping by in the same rundown cabin she grew up in, hunting to keep her and her mother fed. Then one day, Butler's voice echoes from the radio, announcing a grand event to celebrate Texas's new governor: rodeos, wild crowds, and the first-ever *Texas Sure Shot*—a shooting competition with a prize no one can ignore. The winner gets an executive order from the governor himself. *The kind that could set a man free.*

To save her father, Phoebe enters the fight. But to win, she'll have to step into a spotlight built by the man who betrayed her—and face every ghost she's tried to outrun. Locked, loaded, and burning for justice, Phoebe Ann has only one shot to rewrite her story. And if she's not afraid to love a man… she'd better not be afraid to shoot one.

AVAILABLE APRIL 2026

About the Author

Nicholas Osborn is a second-generation ranch owner and storyteller from the heart of deep East Texas. With a career encompassing everything from entertainment marketing to news journalism over the last decade, he has studied the craft of authentic storytelling and honed his writing throughout the years.

Nicholas's debut series aims to mythologize the pineywoods he grew up in and welcome readers to a new chapter of modern Westerns, born of the tall tales that helped shape the genre. His writing is inspired by the history of the Lone Star State, the greater United States, and the larger-than-life heroes, gunslingers, and "black hats" that gave us the myth of the west we know and love today.

Nicholas is an owner at his family's limousin cattle ranch and first-time father with his wife of over ten years. As one of multiple generations of his family working on the Red Rock Limousin Ranch, Nicholas has put his experience into words as an author with a passion to keep timeless Western culture alive and thriving for today's readers.

www.ingramcontent.com/pod-product-compliance
Lightning Source LLC
La Vergne TN
LVHW040217110826
845146LV00005B/1321

* 9 7 9 8 8 9 5 6 7 4 2 3 9 *